FINAL PROPOSAL

S.I.N. SERIES
book three

NEW YORK TIMES BESTSELLING AUTHOR
K. BROMBERG

PRAISE FOR K. BROMBERG

"K. Bromberg always delivers intelligently written, emotionally intense, sensual romance . . ."

—*USA Today*

"K. Bromberg makes you believe in the power of true love."
—#1 *New York Times* bestselling author Audrey Carlan

"A poignant and hauntingly beautiful story of survival, second chances, and the healing power of love. An absolute must-read."
—*New York Times* bestselling author Helena Hunting

"An irresistibly hot romance that stays with you long after you finish the book."
—#1 *New York Times* bestselling author Jennifer L. Armentrout

"Bromberg is a master at turning up the heat!"
—*New York Times* bestselling author Katy Evans

"Supercharged heat and full of heart. Bromberg aces it from the first page to the last."
—*New York Times* bestselling author Kylie Scott

Published by JKB Publishing, LLC

Cover design by Indie Sage, LLC
Editing by Marion Making Manuscripts
Formatting by Champagne Designs and Formatting
Printed in the United States of America

FINAL PROPOSAL

CHAPTER ONE

Ford

WIND WHIPS THROUGH THE TREES, AND THE SKY FLASHES bright as the lightning strikes in the distance beyond. For the briefest of moments, I get a glimpse of the angry ocean beyond the wall of windows before me.

And then darkness hits again.

The drive here did little to abate my rage.

The half-drunk glass of whiskey in my hand even less so.

I was certain that with every mile I put between myself and my brothers, their placating tones, and bullshit explanations, the fury would dispel . . . *but I was* wrong.

The time has only served for my thoughts to run wilder, and the gut punch of hurt to intensify.

I can still see it. The newly printed hardcover on the table. The words on its pages edited for consumer resale. For the public with its voracious appetite for one of three things: scandalous backstories, a how-to guide to make billions out of nothing, or tidbits to tarnish a reputation.

Shock and awe have always sold well.

Who knew the benign biography of Maxton Sharpe, my father, would leave me feeling this way?

What was in the book shouldn't have bugged me. *Or rather, what wasn't in the book.* It shouldn't still bug me.

But it does.

I take another sip, welcoming the burn and warmth of the alcohol, and mutter, "Just Ford."

Fuck that.

Noises filter into my thoughts. The low hum of chatter from the bar patrons who are stuck here like I am. The howl of the wind outside. The vibration of my cell on the bar top beside me alerting text after fucking text. *My brothers.* Little too late on their part.

Dramatic.

Sensitive.

Ridiculous.

Aren't those the words they used to describe me? To invalidate everything?

It's only what the people you love say that matters.

My mom's words echo in my head.

My phone vibrates with another text. What? Has the jet landed back in New York, and they're suddenly worried about me driving into this storm? Where was their concern earlier?

Like I said, *fuck that.*

I'll sulk through this drink.

And the next one.

And the one after that.

It's not like I can go anywhere else right now.

I glance around the small bar. I'm more than certain the crowd in here isn't usual, and they're not here because of the ambiance. We're just the only dumbasses who chose to drive through a tropical depression, waiting for an uprooted tree to be cleared off the road a mile or so from here.

The bar is attached to a rather nondescript, non-spectacular, non-everything inn nestled on a strip of beach just outside of the Hamptons. A town halfway between here and nowhere. A middle ground that the well-to-do ignore on the way to their Hamptons playground and the lower middle class notice, wishing they could afford to stay at one day.

This place . . . hell, I don't even remember the name of it—it's that plain and unexciting its name escapes me—is dated and generic. Burgundy leather and dark wood seem to be the theme. Cheap fixtures and generic, mass-replicated pictures are the décor that no place ever needs.

It has potential.

But it seems that whoever owns this place doesn't choose to invest the money in it to allow it to reach it.

Not that I fucking care.

There might not be any vacancies for the night, but it's dry, and for now, seems secure against the raging storm outside. Oh, and it has alcohol. That's a definite plus.

Something thumps rather loudly on the floor to the right of me, followed by a woman's frustrated sigh. "They closed the roads. Fucking closed 'em. Can you believe that?"

If I can't be at the Sag Harbor house—where I was heading—I should be able to drink in peace.

And a Chatty Cathy choosing to sit next to me is not exactly peaceful.

Nor what I'm in the mood for.

"Nice mouth," the man on the other side of me mutters.

"Hello? Did you hear me?" she repeats, drawing a heavy sigh from me. "Closed. We're stuck."

She didn't get the hint from my silence—or his comment—that I really don't fucking care.

"Brilliant observation," I say into my drink. "There's a reason we're all sitting in here, and it's not because of the ambiance."

"I don't believe I was speaking to you."

"Good. Great." Thrilled to not have to speak with anyone, I lift my finger for another drink to the bartender when something she said soundly hits my ears. "Wait. They closed the roads?"

CHAPTER TWO

Ford

I TURN TO LOOK AT THE STRANGER STANDING BESIDE ME WITH THE raspy voice and intriguing perfume. A pair of large, sapphire eyes meet mine, narrowed but full of curiosity. Her lips are full and currently pursed, her cheeks pink from what I can assume is the cold outside. Her dirty-blonde hair is swept up in some kind of messy bun but currently is more damp than dry, as is her jacket.

To say she's pretty is an understatement. In fact, she's really quite gorgeous in her own way.

But it's the kind of gorgeous that is equal parts cute and beautiful all rolled into one. She's more girl next door than sophisticated sexy, and the quirk of one of her eyebrows tells me she knows I'm looking and assessing.

And she's not exactly thrilled about it.

Tough shit.

"Chandler?" she says into the cell phone I didn't notice she's holding to her ear. "Yeah. I have to go. Don't ask. I'll figure it out. I always do." She drops her cell with a clatter onto the counter and turns to me with a sigh even heavier than mine. "Yes. That's what I said. As in the road*s*." She emphasizes the S. "As in more than one. You've got a stretch of about a mile going either way and that's about as far as you're going to get tonight."

"Christ."

"Sorry to be the one to break the bad news to you." She shrugs unapologetically.

I wave my hand in indifference. "What happened?"

"Um . . . the torrential downpour outside? Storm Watch 2022? The same reason I'm assuming you're sitting here in this less-than-appealing bar like I am?"

"What the actual fuck?" I mutter.

"Oh. So it's okay when you say *fuck*, but when I say it, you mutter under your breath like that's not how a lady should talk?"

I chuckle to ignore the *she's crazy* alarm bells going off in my head. I've learned from experience to heed them. "I didn't say a word or give a look or anything over your fucks." I shake my head and scrub a hand over my jaw. "I just . . . I thought the road closure was temporary until they cleared the tree from the road."

"Well apparently, another one fell past that one and then the other way." She hooks a thumb over her shoulder. "The ocean water is breaching the sea wall and flooding the road, so it's been deemed too dangerous to pass."

"I would laugh, but it's par for the course tonight." I scrub a hand through my hair. "Thanks for being the bearer of bad news."

"It could be worse. This place could be closed. They could be out of alcohol. I mean—"

"I get the picture. Thanks."

"C'mon," she coaxes and then nudges me as if we haven't just met. "It can't be that bad."

I give her a smile that's anything but amused. "Aren't we Miss Rainbows and Sunshine?"

"Says the man trying to be a grumpy asshole to ensure I don't talk to him or disturb his"—she makes a show of looking at my glass—"whiskey, is it?"

"Sunshine, rainbows, and a mind reader?" I raise my eyebrows and give a low whistle. "More than impressed."

She mock curtsies and gives me a smile that lights up her face. Jesus, I was wrong. There's a whole lot of sexy there too.

"Thank you. It's one of my many party tricks."

"One of your many?" I ask.

"Oh, he *does* know how to smile," she murmurs just above the fray, her eyes meeting mine again. "It's a good look on you. You should try it more often."

I slide a bemused look her way. "Noted."

"Oh, see, a glimpse of cute and then right back to grumpy." She takes a seat and swivels on her stool to face me. A hint of her perfume hits me with the motion. The irony that it smells like bottled sunshine isn't lost on me.

"Exactly." I give a curt nod as if I'm annoyed by her and her interruption—which I was and still should be—and yet I engage when I could easily excuse myself from the bar. "See? It's fruitless to waste your time trying to make me smile."

"Noted." She repeats my word back to me and smirks. "I have much better things to do than try and make you smile anyway."

It's my turn to swivel and face her, my knees bumping against hers. "Is that so?"

"It is." She orders a glass of Cabernet sauvignon and looks back at me expectantly.

"What exactly do you have that's better to do?" I point around the bar and as if on cue, thunder rumbles again to emphasize that we're stuck here and she can't leave.

She angles her head to the side and works her tongue in her cheeks. "Stuff."

"Stuff? How descriptive."

"How about, stuff I don't want to do? Stuff I'm avoiding doing? Stuff I'm simply trying to make sense of? Is that descriptive enough for you, Mr. Grumpy?"

Something flickers in her eyes that tells me she's glossing over whatever it is. "Sure. Fine. Whatever floats your boat."

"Apparently, I'm going to need that boat to find my way out of here if the water keeps rising."

"And she has jokes too."

"Always. Why is it that you're grumpy? Is this an everyday occurrence?" She narrows her eyes and studies me, her teeth sinking into her bottom lip as she does. "Hmm. I don't peg you as the type though. Moody possibly. A brooder perhaps but simply for effect. But not perpetually grumpy."

"Thanks for the psych eval." I slide my empty glass toward the bartender, signaling for another. "I didn't ask for one."

"And yet that comment just confirmed my diagnosis."

"Aren't you the jack-of-all-trades," I say.

Her smile just grows wider and damn it. It's hard not to smile in return. Doesn't she know my plan was to come here and brood? To self-medicate with this whiskey and tell myself how I have every right to be hurt and pissed and everything in between?

"So what is it? Girlfriend problems? Dog got run over? Car out of gas?"

My only response is a blank stare.

"Oh my God." She brings a hand over her heart. "It's your dog, isn't it?" Tears well in her eyes—something I totally don't expect—as her voice lowers. "I'm so sorry." She reaches out and squeezes my knee.

Here's my out.

I can let the lie stand as it is and use it to pull sympathy and get her to leave me alone. Nod my head and abandon my seat for one of the chairs over by the opposing window.

All alone.

But when I open my mouth to do just that, nothing comes out. I mean ... there's worse company to keep than a gorgeous woman who seems—so far—to have a great personality.

"Sorry to burst your bubble, but I don't have a dog who died."

Lightning strikes again and there are a few gasps around us. The woman beside me nods, almost as if she's disappointed in me and I'm not sure why.

"I never claimed to have one either," I continue. "You're the one who jumped to conclusions."

"You do have a dog, though, right?" she asks, as if it's a very important question.

"And that matters why?"

"Because it says something about you if you have a dog."

"Like what?" I ask, even though I'm of the same mind.

She shrugs. "That you think about more than just yourself. That you're willing to share time and space. That you're not afraid to get your hands dirty—I mean, picking up poop is a necessity."

"What?" I all but spit my drink out.

"No one likes a person who isn't willing to pick up their own dog's poop."

"You surprise me at every turn," I mutter and stare into my glass before looking back to her.

"Good. Surprises are a good thing." She flashes a megawatt smile.

Who is this woman and why do I suddenly want her to not stop talking? "So? Dog? No dog? What?"

"No dog." I hold up my hands. "But don't judge. I love dogs. Big dogs. But that's the downside to living in the city." *And why do I care that she'll think differently of me because of my answer?*

"The city?"

"Manhattan."

She raises her eyebrows but doesn't disclose whatever supposition her expression reflects. "And why is it the city's fault?"

"Because dogs deserve a yard to run around in, and my place in a high-rise doesn't exactly allow for that."

"There are such things as dog walkers."

"True, but taking a walk and having a yard to roam around in are two different things. So, is the dog inquisition over now?"

She purses her lips and gives me that look again but doesn't elaborate on whatever she's thinking. "Yes. Sure. But still . . . oh, I get it. I'm interrupting a pity party," she murmurs with a soft nod, and then she redirects this random conversation once again. "Couldn't pick a more apropos night to have one in my opinion. I mean, they don't accomplish anything, but they're definitely needed every now and again."

"Yes. Sure. Something like that."

I know the next thing she's going to ask is, *what's wrong?* She's a woman. A woman with a vivid imagination no less.

But rather than doing the expected, she shoves out of her seat and looks around before heading to the other side of the bar. I watch her grab something before coming back and setting a wooden bowl—that looks like it's from the 1970s—between us on the bar.

Engagement ring alert.

How did I not notice the rather large diamond ring on her left hand? And why does seeing it surprise me?

"Is there a problem?" she asks.

I shake my head and realize I'm staring at the bowl she just brought over while wondering what her fiancé or husband—*the prick*—is like. "What's this?"

"Chex Mix. Please tell me you've had this childhood staple."

A roll of my eyes is my only response.

9

"Every pity party needs to have some food." She takes a mouthful of the snack mix. "And alcohol." And then a sip of her wine. "And . . . someone to commiserate with and tell you you're one hundred percent in the right even if that person thinks you're in the wrong." She raises her hand. "So I'm contributing as best as I can with this poor offering since this place doesn't seem to have much of anything." She takes her seat again. "You should feel honored."

"I am." I genuinely smile for the first time. I don't think I've ever worked as hard as she has at making a stranger feel comfortable. "Truly."

"I mean, this place can't offer you a vacant room or much of anything else besides this bowl that's probably had ten different hands in it so far tonight, but I can offer you my great personality and my indiscernible ear." She smiles cheesily.

"And you just ate a piece of the germ mix," I point out.

"And then I drank some wine so the alcohol killed off those germs. Simple as that." She takes a gulp of wine to emphasize her point. "An added bonus is this roof seems sturdy and we're currently dry."

"*Currently* being the operative word."

She taps her glass against mine. "So, cheers." When all I do is simply stare at her, she continues, "What? I'm a glass-half-full kind of girl."

"Clearly."

She reaches her hand out. "Elle. Ellery, really. Nice to meet you."

"Ellery? That's unique."

She chuckles. "Ha. That's the way to say it's an interesting, weird, fill-in-the-blank name." She shrugs as if she's heard it all before. "It's a family name. Celery Ellery," she singsongs like a kid teasing and then laughs. "God, how I hated it when I was younger, but I don't mind it so much now."

"Ford. Fordham, actually." I shake her hand. "And I'm named after a university—or a car company—so I have no room to talk, *Celery Ellery*."

"Then I guess we're even in the name department."

"We are," I murmur.

We both glance down and realize we're still holding hands and quickly pull them apart before looking toward the window to break the sudden awkwardness settling between us.

Awkwardness laced with attraction.

Shit. I didn't expect that.

I scrub a hand through my hair and slide a glance her way. She smiles softly as she watches the show Mother Nature is putting on outside— snapshots of destruction highlighted by flashes of light—and for the first time, I notice the slightest dimple.

Of course, she has to have one. Funny. Forward. Gorgeous. And has a dimple. *I'm such a sucker for dimples.*

"So where were you headed when Fred deterred you?" she asks me when the lightning lulls.

"Fred?" I ask, averting my gaze from her.

"The tropical depression we're currently sidelined by."

"Yes. Sorry. *That* Fred." I glance around. Some people have dozed off. Others are occupied with their cell phones. Very few are talking with the strangers beside them. But when I bring my eyes back to her, apparently, it's her turn to study me. My hands. My forearms where the sleeves of my dress shirt are folded up. My chest and the top two undone buttons on my shirt. She jolts when her eyes meet mine and knows she's been caught.

Now we're even.

"Thanks for nothing, Fred."

"Amen to that," she murmurs, suddenly busying her hands by using a cocktail napkin to wipe away the condensation our glasses have left.

I make her nervous. That's interesting. Or is it the fact I caught her checking me out while she has a ring on her finger that has her unsettled?

"So . . . where were you headed, Ford-named-after-a-university? Does it have anything to do with the pity party we're throwing?"

"Sag Harbor," I say gruffly.

"Nice." She raises her eyebrows but then narrows them when she notices I'm not sharing the same enthusiasm. "Not nice then?" When I don't respond, she continues, "You have to pick one or the other. Indifference isn't an option when you're throwing a pity party. But Sag Harbor. Huh. You're close but oh-so-far from it with this weather."

"I am." I nod but don't say anything else as Ellery sips her wine and makes small talk with the bartender.

I observe their interaction. She's definitely sexy. Indisputably gorgeous. And that easy smile of hers that lights up her face when she offers it.

She's taken, Ford.

11

And by the size of the rock on her finger, her man wants everyone to know that she is. *Understandably so.*

It's late. The whiskey is starting to hit me. And I'm no closer to figuring out why tonight and everything that happened earlier hit me so hard. I take another sip of my drink before closing my eyes for a beat.

I could buy her a bigger diamond.

Jesus. Where the hell did that thought come from?

I shake my head and chuckle. It's the alcohol talking. Hands down.

But when I look over at Ellery, those blue eyes sparkle with curiosity and her brow furrows as if to ask me what I laughed about.

"I was contemplating whether I should switch to beer," I say as if that will explain my random laugh.

"Beer?"

"Yes. It's going to be a long night, and I'm thinking I should pace myself."

"It all depends on what you're pacing yourself for." Her laugh is rich as she shrugs, while my mind ventures to a few places and all of them have to do with her. She crosses her arms over her chest. "So lay it on me. The story. The culprit of the pity party. Tell me who I'm supposed to hate on because they upset you."

I walked in here not wanting to talk to anyone and now, for some reason, she's made it so I don't mind so much. My initial hesitancy is gone.

"It's stupid really—"

"Clearly it upset you, so I wouldn't say it's stupid."

"I had a fight with my brothers," I finally say.

"Okay. So family stuff. That's always a tough one. What was the fight about?"

"It's a long story."

She looks around the room and takes in the scene before shrugging as she meets my eyes. "It's not like we don't have time for one since we're basically stranded for the time being. Does it have anything to do with that?"

"With what?" I ask, looking down to where she's pointing.

"To the bow tie hanging around your neck. I mean, I'm very curious what idiot would follow through with a black-tie event in weather this dreadful." She mock shivers but her smile is playful.

I snort. "Me. My brothers. We're the idiots."

"Oh. *Whoops.* I guess now would be a good time to insert my foot in my mouth."

"Being called an idiot is definitely the nicest of all the insults I've been called today . . . so I'll take it."

"That bad, huh?"

I nod. "Something like that."

Someone laughs loudly across the room as she takes another handful of the germ mix. I eye her as she proceeds to pick all the pretzels out and place them on the counter beside the bowl. Bizarre.

She meets my gaze and winks. "I'm living dangerously."

I laugh. "A tropical depression and germs all in one night."

"You forgot to mention engaging a mysterious and grumpy man too."

"Yes. That too." For some reason, the tension in my shoulders eases with each comment exchanged between us.

"Black tie . . ." She twists her lips as she contemplates. "Too early for a Christmas party."

"Considering it's April, that would be a safe bet."

"So my guess is either an awards banquet for the higher-ups—which if you and your brothers put it on, that would mean *you*—or a fundraiser for something or other. Oh. I know. It was a movie premiere." She cocks her head to the side. "Don't tell me you're a famous actor who's hiding out here in this sleepy seaside town and is buying this inn to breathe new life into it? You plan on making it a destination—an elite bed and breakfast, if you will—because you and all your friends are sick of not being able to go on vacation and have privacy."

"Anyone tell you that you have an overactive imagination?"

Her grin widens. "Another one of my many party tricks."

"Clearly."

"Is your lack of an answer confirmation that you are in fact Chris Hemsworth in disguise?"

"Shh. Don't blow my cover."

"Your secret's safe with me," she whispers. "Your American accent is perfect. So . . ."

"A charity fundraiser."

"Yes," she says and pumps her fist.

"It's an annual black-tie event we host," I say, thinking of the

Alzheimer's charity gala we throw in our late father's honor. "And yes, we went on with it despite the impending storm because it's tradition and . . . who the fuck knows why."

"Because you're men and no one, not even Mother Nature, tells you what to do."

"Now, when you put it like that, it sounds rather ridiculous. But, yes. Something like that."

She nods and eyes me above the rim of her glass. "And so, your fight was about what? They didn't have the right canapes at the event, or one of your brothers hit on your girlfriend and it pissed you off? Or . . ." She shakes her head as if to ask the question. "Something even more scandalous than that? Give me all the juicy details."

"Nothing juicy or scandalous. Sorry to disappoint you." I smile. Imagining my brothers taking their eyes off their wives long enough to look at anyone else is comical. If there were ever a visual of what falling hook, line, and sinker looked like, it would be them.

Besides, we may be triplets, but our taste in women is completely different. I'm . . . *Just Ford.*

I bristle at the thought and my anger fires anew.

How do I tell her that what I'm upset about has more to do with feeling invisible without sounding like a pussy? That my last name defines who I am, and how people perceive me—it always has—but I didn't realize how it also obscured me too?

"We just . . . we had a difference of opinion. Something unexpected came up, and I had a different perception of it than they did. Words were exchanged, and I was less than thrilled with what was said."

"That means you guys are close."

"Aren't all siblings?"

She snorts and there's definite derision to it that piques my curiosity. "Of course," she says but doesn't sound convincing.

"So yes, we are close." And isn't that partially why it bugged me so much? That they didn't see where I was coming from? That most days we can finish each other's sentences, thoughts even, but this time they didn't understand why I was hurt not by what *was* said, but by what *wasn't* said?

She nods as if she understands. "Okay, so your brothers are who we don't like right now then? Who we're so pissed at that we're going to order another round over?"

I nod. "Sounds good to me."

"How many brothers do you have? What are their names?" she asks. "I mean, it's hard to stick pins in homemade voodoo dolls if we don't have specifics."

She's made me so comfortable that I almost answer her without hesitation.

But I'm a Sharpe, and I've learned over the years that people knowing that I am one isn't always a positive. Especially with the publicity that's about to hit my family with the release of the biography. The last thing I need is to give her my brothers' names so she can put two and two together at some point and cash in with a story about the bereaved brother sulking at a roadside inn.

"There are two of them," I say with a wave of my hand, neglecting to tell her we're more than just brothers, but that we're identical triplets. "Their names are irrelevant. It's just . . . have you ever realized how other people look at you or perceive you, and it knocks you back some?"

She picks more pretzels out of the germ mix and sets them on the table with the pile of others. "In a way, yes. It's unnerving. Sometimes it's sobering. And more often than not, it's not exactly flattering."

Especially when it's your father's observation.

I clear my throat from the sudden emotion clogging it. "You hit that nail on the head."

"I'm sorry."

The purity in her simple response gives me pause. A sincerity I seldom hear these days—especially when coming from an absolute stranger.

The look in her eyes is just as genuine.

And it must be a mixture of the late hour, the third glass of whiskey, and the fucking events of the night, but Jesus . . . I hate the sudden pressure in my chest and need to move about.

I rise abruptly from my stool and Ellery's eyes widen in surprise at my sudden movement. "What's wro—"

"Excuse me, everyone," a woman near the entrance of the bar shouts. The opening is a cased doorway that leads to a foyer. People shuffle but fall silent as they turn to face the woman's kind smile and guarded eyes.

"Listen up," our bartender bellows to get the attention of the last remaining patrons too preoccupied to pay attention.

"Hi. My name is Amy. As some of you know," she says when the room falls silent, "the authorities have just informed us that they've closed the road for the night in both directions. For those who didn't know that yet, *oops*, sorry to be the bearer of bad news. So yes, that means you're stuck here for the night if you haven't already secured a room at one of the other hotels down the way. As for us, we're also completely booked." A collective groan rumbles through the room.

"The good news," Amy continues, "is that you're welcome to stay and make yourself comfortable in here. It's not the Ritz, but it's dry, has comfortable chairs, and the light show outside is spectacular." She smiles as she motions to the windows. "The other bad news? By state law, we were required to stop serving alcohol about forty minutes ago. So we're going to have to close down the bar—"

"Seriously?" a man slurs from the far side of the room with numerous empties on the table beside him. The bartender slides a glance over to Amy as if to say, he'll handle him if need be.

"Seriously," she repeats with an understanding smile. She holds her finger up. "But that doesn't mean we can't sell you a bottle of your favorite poison *now* . . . or what's left of a bottle so you can drink at your own leisure throughout the night." A few whoops sound off across the room. "I thought that might make some of you happy."

Clapping breaks out in a show of our sad state of desperation, and Amy curtsies.

Ellery leans over, that sunshine scent present again mixed with her shampoo, and murmurs, "I guess it's time to make a decision, Ford."

"About?"

"Whiskey or beer?"

CHAPTER THREE

Ford

Four Hours Earlier

I T'S EATEN AT ME ALL NIGHT.

That's a lie.

It's eaten at me ever since I read chapter twenty-two. The one titled *Fatherhood*. The chapter where my father talked about his three boys. His greatest accomplishments. He detailed his struggles with Callahan and how proud he was of him, and then how Ledger was the epitome of him, clearly born to step into his professional shoes when he chose to vacate them.

Paragraphs upon paragraphs devoted to my brothers and their place in the Sharpe family. The Sharpe universe, really.

"What's your deal tonight?" Callahan asks as he walks into the penthouse. Shit's everywhere—clothes, food, luggage, their wives' makeup cases—from all of us flying in and getting ready here for the event. He doesn't care. He picks up a piece of candy and pops it in his mouth as he sinks down onto the couch. "Did you take that stick Ledger removed from his ass and insert it into yours?"

"Callahan. He was the one who challenged me the most," Maxton says with a laugh. But beyond the laugh is a sense of pride. A sense of love. A feeling that the only thing that could bring this hard man to his knees was his boys. "Callahan's stubborn streak is a mile long, but damn does he continue to surprise me. He hides his intuitive nature and knack for knowing just what to do behind his reckless behavior. Almost as if he's uncomfortable being as good as he is at whatever it is he sets his mind to. He was just like his mom in that respect. And having him around is like having her near me still."

"Back off, Callahan."

Wrong thing to say.

That's like throwing chum to a shark when it comes to my little brother. I can practically see his ears perk up at that.

And maybe I want them to. Maybe I want him to push me on this so I can have the fight I've been itching for all night long.

"Ooooh," he says with a whistle.

"What's that sound for?" Ledger asks as he enters the room, looking from Callahan to me and then back to Callahan.

And this is why being a triplet is a pain in the ass. It's always a plus that we can intuitively sense what's going on with each other . . . except for when you don't want anyone to know.

And right now . . . shit, right now I don't know what the fuck I want.

"Your stick? It's up his ass now," Callahan fills in.

"Fuck off," I mutter.

And now Ledger's intrigued.

"My oldest. Ledger Maxton Sharpe." The namesake's said with the softest of smiles and admiration adorning his eyes. "When I look at him, I see a younger version of myself—only ten times better. If there is an obstacle, he faces it head-on. If there is a challenge, he can't wait to prove he's better than it. He's a formidable opponent in all things business."

"Is that how you think people perceive you?" I ask and get what I've learned to expect from the man across from me. A slow crawl of a smile deepens the lines etched in his face. Lines I'd love to know the history behind but have a feeling that would equate to book after book filled with his stories.

"I don't care how people perceive me. Never have. I think Ledger is similar in that respect. He's more dogged than I was if you can believe that, but he shows more of his heart than I do. He's more in touch whereas I was so busy trying not to be Maxton Sharpe of the Bronx that I didn't care who I stepped on to get where I needed to get."

"And what of that?"

"It makes him a better man than I was. Than I am. With that comes higher expectations, but I doubt the man that Ledger grew into will have any problems exceeding them."

"First you didn't drink tonight and now the attitude," Ledger, ever the diplomat, says as he perches himself on the edge of the couch, catty-corner to me. "What's going on?" I hear his question, but all I see is page after fricking page of praise leveled in his direction. Top of his class at Wharton. Young Entrepreneur's Award. Story after story of how he's exactly like the man he idolized.

The man I idolized too, but now feel like I was invisible to.

"Ford?" he asks again.

And as if on cue, Callahan shifts on the couch, and a thud sounds as something hits the floor. He leans over and chuckles.

"It looks like Dad wants in on this conversation too," he teases as he picks up the advanced copy off the floor and sets it on the table. "You know how much he hated when we fought."

Silence falls over the room as we stare at the book's cover. A close-up, black and white photo of our father. You can't tell the color of his eyes, but the clarity in them—in both the quality of the picture and the striations of his irises—is mesmerizing. His expression is stoic, and his lips, identical to ours, are in a straight line.

It's a stunning snapshot of the man we all loved. One that somehow reflects the intensity of the man we grew up with juxtaposed by the softening heart of a man nearing the end of his life.

A lump forms in my throat as I try to process the emotions that book cover, and those three hundred thirteen pages after it, represent.

An exposé on his life. The moments of his childhood that were life-defining. Poverty. A father who ran off. A mother who struggled and worked nonstop. His desire to never be in the same position when he grew up. How he scraped his way through college only to never graduate because funds ran short.

How he started his empire by being a busboy who befriended the right guests who later believed in him and backed him, only to be rewarded handsomely when he'd reached a level of success only most dream of.

The biography talks about the love of his life, our mom. His first thoughts when he met her. His last thoughts as he buried her at such a young age. And the heartache he still felt to that day.

There are chapters on underhanded deals and people who tried to sabotage him. On his antics and superstitions. On his philosophies in business and in life.

Most of it I knew. Some of it I learned for the first time and will be forever grateful to have more to hold on to of the man who was our whole world for most of our lives.

And who now is gone.

What I didn't expect was to feel curious—hopeful even—to get insight into how he looked at me as a man. And when I read his take on Callahan and then his thoughts on Ledger, I held my breath when I turned the page.

"So you have Callahan the rebel and Ledger the Type A, tell us about your middle son, Fordham."

Maxton's eyes grow wistful, and a smile ghosts his lips. "My wife went to Fordham University. That's where I met her actually. I had a side job delivering flowers, and I accidentally ran into her. I plucked the card out of the bouquet right then and there and gave them to her instead." His smile widens. "That's where Ford got his name from. A nod to the day I knew I would marry Carly."

The imposing man sits back in his chair and looks out the window of his tower in the sky. The city moves at breakneck speed beneath him, and I wonder if he misses the pace or if he enjoys his unhurried life now.

I wait for him to gather his thoughts. Moments pass. Memories are silently relived, and the emotions from them fleet through his expression.

"Ford is . . . the peacekeeper of our family. The even keel in our sometimes-stormy life. He's . . . just Ford."

Just Ford.

Not Fordham Rhys Sharpe, second in his class at Wharton by a very small percentage. Not Fordy, son of Maxton and Carly, who kept the family together after his mother's death. Not Ford, the man who streamlined some of S.I.N.'s chain-of-command issues to make the company more efficient and more successful. Not *my son*, the one who called every night to make sure I was okay.

Fucking Just Ford.

And that's all I could think about tonight as my brothers and their wives, Sutton and Asher, stood before a whole host of people with wide smiles and welcoming hugs.

How do they look at me? Am I invisible to them too? Am I *Just Ford*, the middle son they often forget—*and surprisingly*—don't really know much about?

"It's the book, isn't it?" Ledger asks, pulling me from my thoughts. "Reading through it has reminded us of everything we're missing with him gone. Was it as hard for you to read as it was for me?"

"For that." I give a measured nod. "And for other reasons."

The drink I've rejected all night long is calling my name right now. But I don't move toward the refrigerator stocked with beer. I think once I start, I won't stop. Rather, I hold Callahan's stare.

"It doesn't mean anything," he finally murmurs quietly, almost as if in a warning.

What the fuck?

"What doesn't?" Ledger asks while I wonder if Callahan's comment means when he read the book, he noticed it too. Or more to the point, my absence in it.

Surprising if that's the case. My brother, who used to only think of himself, noticed while the one who typically knows every "T" that needs to be crossed and "I" that needs to be dotted, didn't.

But why the warning?

"God forbid, *Just Ford* rocks the boat, right, Cal?" I ask.

"Does someone want to clue me in why the two of you are staring at each other while I'm over here standing in the fucking dark?"

"Just Ford," I repeat.

"What about it? Did you forget your name? What am I missing?" Ledger asks, but I know the minute it registers because his hand falters bringing his drink to his mouth.

"Like I said, it doesn't mean anything. Like all books, not everything is included in a final product. Things are edited out. Winword probably had a lot left on the cutting-room floor that he just couldn't use," Callahan says, referring to the author.

"Edited out? You mean the boring parts that aren't interesting, right? Because why would he use anything Dad said about me when he has the bad-boy Callahan and protégé Ledger to talk about?"

Because he didn't have anything to say about me that was worthy of being in his book.

And there it is.

Most things roll off my back. Little affects me emotionally. Rarely anything. But to think that my dad thought so little of me is upsetting. I'm confused by this pressure in my chest. I'm confounded by this need to prove I'm more than *Just Fucking Ford*.

"That's bullshit," Ledger says.

"Bullshit?" I bellow.

"You're goddamn right, *bullshit*," Ledger says stepping into my space. "I paid prices you don't have a clue about, so fuck you and your bullshit comments."

The muscle in his jaw pulses as fury I rarely see from him sparks in his eyes. Well good, because I'm furious too.

"Ford," Callahan says, trying to break the tension when typically, he incites it. "We've grown up with cameras in our faces and false rumors being the norm. We all know how they twist words and sensationalize shit to sell an extra copy. It's the same with that." He points to the book.

"But these were Dad's words," I shout. "Those weren't made up."

"You're being ridiculous." Ledger rolls his eyes. "Dad was proud of all of us. Even you—"

"What if the roles were reversed? What if—"

"I wouldn't fucking care. Neither should you," Callahan says. "Quit being so goddamn sensitive."

But I do care.

I care more than I want to admit.

"Fuck this. And fuck the both of you." I head to the door and ignore their shouts of my name.

There is no point in continuing this dead-end conversation.

None.

I'm so much more than *Just Ford*. Fuck them if they think otherwise.

I will not settle for being a mention.

For being the disregarded Sharpe.

For being *just* anything.

CHAPTER FOUR

Ellery

I LOOK AROUND THE DARKENED ROOM. SOME STRANDED CUSTOMERS have selected chairs and curled up in balls to settle in for the long haul. Others have purchased their bottle of alcohol and are finding a place to get comfortable. Some have stupidly opted to leave and try their luck at getting around the roadblocks.

I, on the other hand, am standing with my bottle of cabernet tucked under one arm, the bowl of germ mix in one hand, and my wine glass in the other, scanning the room while completely ignoring the constant buzzing of texts from my phone inside my purse.

There was a reason I took this road trip, and the person most likely texting is it.

I scan the room and find myself rather disappointed that I don't see Ford.

Did he leave too?

Did he buy his bottle of whiskey and then escape to a room he had reserved but didn't say anything about?

Why do I even care?

Because I do. Isn't that me? To care about everyone and everything at the expense of myself?

But it was more than that. It was . . . *him.*

Without knowing the exact details of whatever happened to him tonight, I know that I can commiserate. A battle with your brothers. Seeing how they perceive you and being knocked back a bit.

And it didn't hurt that the man hits every check mark on what I find attractive. Jesus, did he. The dark hair with a slight wave to it. The amber eyes with flecks of gold. The strong jaw and straight nose. The broad shoulders and seriously sexy forearms. The hands . . . oh, he has good hands.

The whole unbuttoned shirt and bow tie hanging around his neck only adds to the sex appeal.

But for every part of him that tried to be grumpy, a glimpse of something else came through. He came across as kind when he wanted to be gruff. As welcoming when he wanted to be left alone. As interested even when he tried to be aloof.

And maybe that last part hit me a little harder than it should have. Especially when it's been forever since I noticed someone looking at me with that kind of heat in their eyes.

Or maybe it's just the first time as of late that I've cared to notice. *Or wanted someone to notice.*

Is it ridiculous that my breath catches in my throat when Ford walks back into the lounge area? That I'm excited by the prospect of getting to know him better? That I'm relieved he didn't leave?

And by how his white dress shirt is soaked and clinging to his chest, one could assume he went out to his car for something.

But I'm not thinking about why he went to his car or the wine in my hand or anything else for that matter, because I'm too busy being captivated by him. How he walks over to a settee on the far side of the room where I now see his bottle of whiskey and glass on the table beside him. How he unceremoniously and nonchalantly unbuttons said wet dress shirt that's clinging to him, strips his arms out one by one so that every damn muscle contracting is on display.

His defined abs.

His broad chest with a slight smattering of dark hair.

The bronzed tone of his skin that reflects hours spent outdoors and shirtless.

For the love of all things holy . . .

I'm certain the thud I hear is my jaw dropping to the ground.

He bends over and messes with something in the bag he brought in, giving me an equally appealing look at the definition of his shoulders before pulling out a sweatshirt.

It's faded and looks worn when he pulls it over his head to end the Magic Mike portion of the program, but I do a double take when I see the

Wharton Business logo emblazoned across its front. *Small world.* A man doesn't wear a sweatshirt that well-loved if he didn't attend the school.

It seems Ford is well-educated too.

But it's when I look up from the letters now sprawled across his chest, that I meet those amber eyes again. *Whew.* Funny things happen to my insides that aren't supposed to happen when our eyes lock. His smile is lopsided, and the lift of his whiskey glass in my direction is a welcome invitation to take the empty seat beside his.

Against my better judgment, my feet move toward him.

What are you doing, Elle?

The angel on one shoulder pretends it doesn't hear the devil on the other. Good thing the text alert knocks both off as I approach him.

"Contemplation over?" I ask as I set the bowl of germ mix down on the table and smile at him.

He looks at me above the rim of his glass, drops of water shaking loose as he nods. "I've always been a sucker for a good whiskey, and surprisingly, this place has some."

"I've never been a fan of the hard stuff myself." I make a sour face and wince as his smile widens. It's then that I realize the innuendo of my statement and shrug unapologetically.

"It's an acquired taste. With time, I'm certain I could get you to like it," he murmurs as his eyes dart to my lips and then back up.

I guess when he shed that dress shirt, he left the grumpiness behind with it.

"What is it that you have against pretzels?" he asks with a lift of his chin to the bowl and the two pretzels I just picked out.

"I'm salty enough when I want to be. I don't need to add to it."

He bursts out laughing. "Seriously?"

"No. Maybe." I lean over and pick another one out of the bowl. "Perhaps I just like being quirky."

He gives me a disbelieving look, our eyes holding for longer than they should, before he breaks the stare and shakes his head. "I like that you are too."

Hot and gives heartfelt compliments.

Can the man stop climbing the perfect meter?

With a look around and a rock back on my heels, I say, "I guess this is our bed for the night."

"Seems that way. At least it's not the floor. The bonus is it has a killer view of the light show going on outside."

The couch is the same deep burgundy as the barstools, but despite its stiff appearance, when I sink down onto it, I'm surprised by how comfortable it is. I wiggle my butt to make a show of approval before stopping, leaning over, and whispering, "I'm wondering what's wrong with this couch?"

"What do you mean?" he asks, a sigh falling from his lips as he sits. But the sigh falters when our hips touch due to the limited space of the settee's cushion.

I have a flustered second where I wonder why I'm even flustered. He's a man. I'm a woman. We have a place to sit for the night. Our hips touching shouldn't be a big deal.

And yet . . . I'm suddenly a little flushed and desperately thinking about anything other than the heat of his hip against mine.

It's hot in here.

Is it hot in here?

I work a swallow down my throat. It's definitely hot in here.

Movement. I need to . . . move so I don't also think about this man's firm, muscular thigh against mine. I shift so my back is against the arm of the couch, my knee is bent and touching his thigh so that I'm facing him.

Shin-to-thigh contact is way better than hip-to-hip contact.

Of course, that gets me thinking that there are way better contacts than just hip to hip—pelvis to pelvis, chest to chest, mouth to mouth. *Stop it, Elle.*

I roll my eyes and when I look up, I'm met by a bemused lift of his eyebrow as if to say he sees I'm flushed and knows exactly what I'm thinking.

To say the image of his bare chest and abdomen doesn't flash through my mind would be a gross understatement.

So I ramble.

"What were we talking about?" I ask, busying my hands.

"Our bed for the night."

"Yes. The seat. The settee. This spot right here." I pat the back of it with my hand. "The question is, why had no one taken this spot yet? It's prime real estate. The windows. A table to prop our feet on. No drunk, snoring men like over on the other side of the room. I mean"—I place my hand on his forearm out of habit. *Skin. Touching. Again.* And all but yelp as I pull it back just as quickly as I touched him—"clearly there's a sign somewhere that says it's been reserved for Chris Hemsworth."

He levels me with a droll look, but the corners of his mouth turn up. He may have left his grumpiness aside, but he's still quiet. Still troubled.

"Oh, is that what that sign said that I crumpled up when I came over here but didn't read?"

"Of course, it is." I pretend to huff. "I'm sure your people reached out to their people and set this all up."

He smiles again, and it's worth the silliness just to see it. As a reward, I pick up his bottle of whiskey and pour more into his glass without asking. He nods and takes a sip, his gaze settling on his hands wrapped around his glass.

Despite his discarded grumpy shirt and the smile he gave me, it's clear his fight is weighing heavily on him.

"I'm sorry about your brothers. I'm sure whatever you fought about was valid and real and, at some point, will work itself out."

He nods, but it's not convincing. "Perhaps."

"For what it's worth, I work with my brothers too."

"The start of that sentence tells me there is a story to tell."

"Meh." I shrug. "It's partially my company, but I don't feel like it is. You see, I own twenty-five percent of the business like my two stepbrothers and stepfather do, but because I have a vagina—" He coughs over his drink, and I just look at him with a face of innocence. "*What?*"

"Well, it's a good thing you have one. A vagi . . . whatever. I'd hate to think I'd be this attracted to someone if they didn't . . ." He laughs and his cheeks turn pink. It's adorable and more than flattering to think he finds me attractive. "I just . . . let's just say it's my turn to stick my foot in my mouth."

"We're even then."

"Yes. Sure. It's the whiskey talking." He takes a sip and lifts his eyebrows. "Where were we?"

"Talking about vaginas," I say purposely to watch his reaction.

"Yes. How could I forget? Clearly, it's of the utmost importance," he teases. "Tell me about them."

"Them?" I tease. "I assure you I have only one."

31

"No. Not your vag—" He stops, that boyish grin back. "Brothers. Family. Those people."

"Those people. Got it." I chuckle. "There's not much to tell. I took over my mother's ownership of the company when she died."

"I'm sorry."

"It's okay. It was a long time ago." I shrug subtly. But it's not okay. I miss her dreadfully. Every minute of every day. But for anyone who mentions it, *it's okay.*

"I know it is, but I'm also part of the Moms Who Have Passed Club so unfortunately, I know that *it's okay* doesn't always mean it's really okay."

I'm not used to such blatant honesty from a man. It's welcome and foreign and makes the ring on my finger feel even heavier.

"I'm sorry for you too."

"It's okay." His echo of my answer makes me smile.

"So much easier to talk about vaginas than this, right?"

His smile tells me he welcomes the levity. "So, Ellery, tell me all about the wicked stepfather and evil stepbrothers."

I laugh this time and decide to explain it as best I can, when normally I'm known to just suck it up and hold it in.

"My real father died when I was nine. My mom remarried a very business-driven man with two sons of his own from a previous marriage. They started a company together doing remodeling, found moderate success, and when she passed away, her percentage of ownership was passed on to me."

"I sense a *but* coming."

"Nothing gets past you," I say. "*But* they're both assholes, vying for Daddy's attention and approval."

"Stepdaddy, right?"

"Yes, but it makes my life easier to just drop the step and not remind them that I'm not blood related."

"And therefore, you are equal."

"Exactly. Besides, they spend all their time hoping to be the one selected to take over dear old Dad's ownership when he retires. Hell, everything I achieve they try and take credit for. Every idea I float out there is shot down only for them to say the same thing the next day, and it's deemed the best thing in the world."

"In other words, they're misogynist pricks, and you're living your own personal, modified Cinderella story."

"Pretty much to the first and unfortunately, I am to the second part. In their eyes, I should just sit there, look pretty, and stay out of the way except to answer phones and get them coffee."

"But that's not what your mom did."

"No. But they knew she trumped them in their dad's eyes, and their shit would never fly. Now that she's gone though . . ."

He snorts. "I may not know you well yet, but I can't exactly see you accepting a subservient role."

"Right?" I sigh. "It's frustrating. Being a part of the company is my right. My mom helped build it. I want to help make it succeed . . . maybe it's a way for me to remain close to something of hers. Just because I'm a woman—"

"With a vagina."

"Yes, so we've established." I chuckle, appreciating his attempt to lighten the conversation that somehow turned more intense than I expected.

"What is it about being a woman? I'm sorry. Please finish what you were saying before I cut you off."

"No. It's okay." Why does his apology for having manners fluster me? *Because you're not used to men treating you with respect, perhaps?* "But it's not so much being a woman per se. It's constantly being undervalued that's the problem. Is it so wrong to have the desire, the want, to build something that's truly my own? To have the chance to fail? To maybe succeed?" I blow out a breath in frustration, and when I look back toward Ford, there's clarity in his eyes, an understanding that makes me feel heard in a way I haven't felt in forever. "In a family business, much like you alluded to with your brothers and whatever happened tonight, it's easy to get lost in the grand scheme of it all. The company's day-to-day and overall success. My brothers' needs to impress my stepfather so they get the biggest prize or pat on the head or whatever it is they need from him. I'm sick of being part of the noise. I want to be the one who's making it."

"Then make it," he says matter-of-factly.

"It's not as easy as you think it is."

"Nothing worth wanting ever is, Ellery."

There's something about the way he says my name in his deep, hushed tenor that has me pausing for a beat to quietly sink into the sound of it.

"Take your chance. Shoot your shot." He taps his glass against mine. "You might never know what could be if you don't put yourself out there."

I worry my bottom lip through my teeth as I pour more wine into my glass. He's right. I know he's right. And yet . . . the question is how?

There was the overhaul of the Carlton Hotel that I spent hours grinding out the details only to have the project handed to one of my brothers because I was needed elsewhere. And that elsewhere was reorganizing our job files.

There were jobs I'd negotiated and won to later be told the owners preferred a man to be the one in charge. A preference I knew was bullshit and resulted from a boys' night out where my brothers wined and dined the project lead with his weaknesses—strippers and Wagyu steaks. No amount of fighting would change his mind after they were chummy together.

Not to mention the underhanded crap my brothers pulled. Telling me the wrong location or time for a meeting so I'd look flustered and unprofessional when I showed up thirty minutes late. Deleted emails that they somehow handled for me. Screwing up a construction schedule to prove I didn't know what I was doing when I did.

And on and on . . .

So how do I step outside of my world to prove my worth, while staying in it? How do I, and I alone, bring a unique opportunity to the table of Haywood Redesigns to prove my value that my brothers can't?

Leaning back on the couch, I put my feet up on the table and stare at the ceiling as a comfortable silence falls between us.

"Why did you brave Frank?" he asks. Alcohol is the culprit of the giggle I emit.

"Fred?"

"Whatever. Fred. Frank. Phil." He waves a hand. "Why were you out here?"

"A road trip."

"Just because?"

"I needed to clear my head. Make some decisions. Like I said before, *stuff.*"

"Ah, yes. The elusive *stuff.*" He holds his glass out for me to tap mine against. "Here's to dealing with the hard stuff. Cheers."

"Cheers," I murmur and watch him above the rim of my glass as I take a sip. He follows suit and then rests his head on the back of the settee and closes his eyes.

"I'd kill for a real meal right now," he murmurs.

"A cheeseburger and French fries sound like heaven right now."

He groans at the thought. "Way better than the germ mix."

"You're right. It's infinitely better." I look around the room and notice since we've been talking, more people have nodded off. "This place is interesting."

"How so?"

"It has serious potential, but it just seems like someone gave up on it."

"People give up on a lot of things too easily, Celery Ellery."

I roll my eyes but secretly like when he calls me that. "True. But think about it. This place has a great location. On the beach with what appears to be some privacy. If someone gave it some TLC, updated it a bit—"

"Gave it a restaurant. My God, you're brilliant. Can you imagine how much money they could make tonight from all of us if they had one?" He pats his stomach. "I'm starving."

"Agreed. I'd ditch the bar here and add a—"

"Nope. Keep the bar. The markup on alcohol is ridiculous and can help turn a profit when a restaurant is slow."

"Good point," I say.

He turns his head still on the back of the couch and opens his eyes to meet mine. They're sleepy and his lids are heavy, but there's an earnest intensity to them.

"What?" I ask.

"We've sat here and talked for hours, and yet you've never mentioned him."

"Him?"

Ford's eyes dart down to my hand where the diamond sparkles even in the dim light. "*Him.* I'm assuming the reason your phone has been going off all night."

I glance at my ring, trying to figure out how to respond. "Maybe that's why I took a road trip. Maybe . . ."

"Maybe it's all part of the *stuff*?" he asks, and I meet his discerning gaze again. I expect to see judgment, even though I've done nothing wrong in befriending him, but there is the exact opposite. A quiet understanding laced with an unspoken curiosity.

I nod. "*Lots of stuff.*"

"Your secret's safe with me, Elle." He reaches out and pats my knee.

I blink back tears that shouldn't be there in the first place and when I look back up, Ford's eyes are closed once again. His hand is heavy on my leg as his chest begins to rise and fall in an even cadence. He's drifted off.

I probably should do the same.

But sleep eludes me. I'm restless. My mind won't stop.

"*Your whole reasoning behind this road trip is asinine, Ellery. For God's sake, when are you going to take this life, our relationship, seriously and end this wait? Let's set a date already.*"

I rest my head on the couch and watch the world rage on the outside while trying to calm the anger within. And while I try to figure out how to settle the discord Ford's statement causes within.

Your secret's safe with me, Elle.

CHAPTER FIVE

Ford

I THROW A FOREARM OVER MY EYES TO SHIELD ME FROM THE SUNLIGHT.

Christ, it's bright outside.

Why does my back ache?

Why are the trash trucks so fucking loud this morning?

Then it hits me. Where I am. Last night. The storm.

Ellery.

Why she's my first thought when I open my eyes is beyond me, but when I look beside me, she's not there.

Nor is her bag.

Or any goddamn trace of her other than a pile of pretzels beside a half-empty bowl.

And I don't know why it bugs me so fucking much that she isn't here.

I twist in my seat to look around the room. Most people are still in the same positions they were in last night when I dozed off. Curled into balls. Leaned against walls with legs kicked out and crossed at the ankles. Lying on the floor, using their spread-out rain jackets as a barrier between them and the old carpet.

The sun is out. *Clearly*. Which means the storm's passed on. And if the room is emptier than it was last night, then that means maybe the road has been cleared.

"Christ," I murmur and scrub a hand over my face, the scrape of my stubble a reminder of just how rough I must look.

It's then that I see the napkin with the scribble on it under my half-finished whiskey bottle on the table in front of me.

I lean forward to pick it up and smile when the pretzels on its corner fall to the floor.

Fordham the University—

It was a pleasure meeting you. I had to hit the road early and deal with "stuff."

Thank you for the company, the advice, and the ear. I'm sure everything will work itself out with your brothers. Maybe our paths will cross again someday. Until then . . .

—Celery Ellery

I hold the napkin in my hand and lean back again on the couch, staring at her handwriting.

She didn't leave me her phone number.

Then again, she *is* engaged.

So why do I have the distinct memory of waking up last night and she was tucked under my arm with her head on my chest? And why do I remember liking it?

I scrub my hand through my hair.

My phone's dead. I'm in desperate need of a toothbrush, a shower, and a shave. And by the looks of the clear sky and Ellery's absence, the road appears to be open.

Let's just hope it's open in the direction I need it to be.

I'm in the parking lot within minutes, bag in my hand and eyes darting around. The sun may be out, but there's still a chill in the air from the breeze from the ocean.

Debris from the storm is everywhere. Tree branches. Trash strewn about. Sand blown around by the wind.

It's when I look back toward the inn that I notice it as a whole for the first time. In the past, the gray clapboard building was something off in the distance of the road when I drove past. Last night, the hotel was something I ran into to escape the storm.

But this morning with the sun out, the sound of seagulls in the distance, and my current stance in the middle of its parking lot, I take a closer look.

White Sands Inn.

It's what the faded sign says. There's a lighthouse for a logo on said sign despite there not being a single one in sight.

I guess they took some creative license.

The place has curb appeal. Its overall size doesn't overpower its back-drop of blue skies and what I can assume is the boardwalk and beach on the other side. Too many places make that mistake. They think the size of the structure and the capacity it can hold is what's most important because more rooms equal more revenue.

What they don't understand is that if the hotel isn't in an appealing location—in this case the beach on one side and the lush foliage of the New England trees surrounding the other—people don't want to stay at the actual hotel to do more than sleep.

And it's the guests staying at the hotel—to order room service, to drink at the bar and watch the surf crash on the beach, to eat at the hypo-thetical boardwalk café—that earns the added profit.

Potential.

That's what Ellery said it had last night. She's right. That's what I see when I look at the weathered façade that's worn and needs some atten-tion. The immediate landscaping could be improved, the entry to the fa-cility made more attractive, and the retaining wall to the west redone so it fits the inn's overall style.

My thoughts are reflexive. Curb appeal. How to draw people in. How to make a lasting impression so customers come back. It's what I've been taught to assess and correct and refine. It's what we, my brothers and I, all have actually. It becomes second nature when you grow up with a father who's a hospitality mogul and who would quiz you at random.

What's wrong with this place?

What would you change to attract more customers?

How would you increase their revenue?

What do you think they're doing well?

I can hear my father's voice asking the questions, and it's a bittersweet, hollow feeling I don't expect to have.

Just Ford.

Did he see me as that when I answered those questions of his? Did he hear the thought I put into my responses to prove to him that I knew my shit? That I had made certain I was worthy of the last name I was du-ally blessed and cursed to be given?

Lost in thought and brought back to last night and that goddamn bi-ography, I wander to the rear of the property. There's a meandering path

41

that like everything else, could use a lot of attention. Add some flowers to the beds on either side and throw in a few benches for the social media crowd to take pictures and tag the resort. You can never go wrong with built-in marketing opportunities like that from guests.

But thoughts—of my dad, of the biography, of the shitshow that was last night—fade to the background when I look up to find a gorgeous beach.

If you've seen one beach, you've seen them all is a bullshit misnomer.

Some are littered with garbage. Some have shitty sand. Some have rocks and kelp and everything in between.

But this beach, shit, *this beach* lives up to the inn's name even after a violent storm. In fact, maybe the wind and the rain added to its beauty. The sand has been windswept into waves of white, not a footprint to be found on its perfect surface. The water is a deep blue that laps at the shoreline.

I can picture what summer could look like here. Umbrellas and cabanas set up for guests. Servers carrying rum punches and daquiris across the boardwalk and into the sand to keep them happy. Add a horseshoe pit and a volleyball net for those who can't keep idle. Team up with a bike rental or electric scooter company to supply guests at a discounted rate.

Out of habit when I'm looking at sites, I lift my phone to take pictures. "Shit." *It's dead.*

You're not supposed to be working, Ford.

But the instinct to observe and assess and improve has been ingrained in me my whole life, so it's easy to slip back into that mode without thinking about it.

On that note, get the fuck out of here. Go to Sag. Figure out . . . whatever you need to figure out.

And eventually, deal with the endless texts from Callahan and Ledger.

I shove my hands in my pockets, and my fingers hit the napkin Ellery left me. The one I kept for some reason. The one that reminds me *it will all work itself out.*

That remains to be seen.

With one last look at the unexpected view, I turn on my heel and head toward my rental car.

It's then that I see the sign posted in the window of the inn. For Sale. Huh. Guess that makes more sense why things haven't been kept up here. But you'd think you'd make it look its best to get a higher sale price.

Then again, maybe it has been dressed up and it was worse before.

Not your problem, Sharpe.

And it's not. S.I.N. deals in sophisticated, luxurious resorts that are massive in scale, not mom-and-pop hotels on postage stamps of land like this. It's not our brand. Not our expertise.

But it doesn't stop me from taking one long, last look before I climb behind the wheel and start the engine.

Potential.

CHAPTER SIX

Ellery

I STUDY HIM.

Just like I did this morning as he slept. I contemplate why it felt so hard to walk out of the bar earlier this morning.

Those thick lashes on tanned cheeks.

The wave of his hair over his forehead.

A faded white scar above his right eyebrow I didn't notice in the dim light last night.

The inexplicable pull he somehow has on me when I'm usually immune to second glances and electric touches.

There's a reason I chose to leave without saying goodbye.

I could tell myself it was because I had things to do and a schedule to keep, but that's total bullshit. I have no schedule or set place to be. Truthfully, the reason I stood in front of the settee for a good five minutes, debating whether to wake Ford up before I left, has a lot more to do with the object that with the sun's help is creating prisms all over the inside of my car.

Or rather everything that's tied to it.

My engagement ring.

Chandler Holcomb.

And the duty that comes with being a Sinclair-Haywood.

But I don't think about any of those things as Ford stands with his back to me, shoulders broad, ass tight, and studies the inn with a hand shielding his eyes from the sun.

And it sure as hell didn't cross my mind when I woke up last night with my head on his chest and his hand absently and possessively spread over my thigh.

I know he was asleep.

I know he didn't mean it.

Yet . . . it seems so vivid in my mind when normally I don't remember a thing when or if I wake up at night.

I push the ignition button and my engine jumps to life.

Get going, Elle. Move on. It's not like any of last night mattered.

With one last look at Ford, I shift my car into drive and turn out of the parking lot.

I think of opportunities missed.

Of *what ifs*.

And how I need to push a little harder on the gas before I do or say something I might regret.

CHAPTER SEVEN

Ford

Four Weeks Later

"WHAT'S THIS?" LEDGER ASKS FROM THE DOOR OF MY office, holding up a file folder that I can't exactly differentiate from the hundreds of others we have in our office.

"What's what?" I ask. "Pretty sure that's what we call a folder. It opens and you put papers inside of the two flaps to protect and keep them all together. You can even put a label on it for quick reference of its contents."

"A regular, fucking comedian," Ledger says drolly as he walks into my office and drops it on my desk.

The file's label, White Sands Property, written in my block-style handwriting, looks up at me. I knew this would be coming. No time like the present to get down to brass tacks.

I lean back in my chair and simply stare at my brother. "Since when do you take shit off my desk?"

"Since when do you make moves on your own regarding properties without consulting Callahan or me first?" he counters, crossing his arms over his chest and sitting in the chair in front of my desk.

"I wasn't aware you were the king of all things around here." I pick up the folder and toss it back onto the other side of my desk. "Last I checked, my last name is on the sign out there in the lobby too."

"True, but it's my name too. And considering all your correspondence is on company letterhead, that would seemingly make it my business as well." He shrugs, but his eyes narrow. "Funny though how I've never heard of this place before and here you are about to bid a shit ton of fucking money to buy something that doesn't even fit in our portfolio."

"The amount is a blip on our financial radar."

"That doesn't mean it's okay."

"No. It doesn't. It doesn't make it wrong either." I point to the folder that our real estate team has composed for me. Comps for similar properties. Preapproval papers from our lenders. Notes on other buyers who might be competition for its purchase. "It's going up for auction, and I plan on being there to buy it."

"This motel, inn, whatever the fuck it is, is beneath S.I.N. and you know it. Let's end the charade. Move on."

"Jesus, Ledger." I push up out of my chair and pace to the window, hands shoved in my pockets, and look at the city below. I don't really see it through my anger, though. "Can you just stop being . . . *so Ledger?*"

It's been four weeks since our fight. Four weeks where in typical Sharpe fashion, we've brushed it all under the rug and acted like it never happened.

Things have smoothed out between us—we don't bring it up so we don't have to talk about it—but it's not the same.

I'm still hurt, and they still think I'm being a pussy.

The kicker was I thought my brothers and I'd gotten better at this. That we'd learned how to talk or communicate or whatever the hell you call it. We've worked through a lot in the past four years since our father's death. How to cope with his loss, how to be a family when there are no parents left to parent, and how to be who the other one needs when they need it.

Or maybe it only matters when the issues pertain to Callahan or Ledger. After all, I'm *Just Ford.*

Yeah.

It still fucking bugs me.

And I think what fucking pisses me off more is that they still don't understand why I'm hurt. Or moreover, haven't even addressed it with me again other than to ask, "*We good?*" when I came back from Sag Harbor that next week.

It's not like the book or the fanfare around it is going away any time soon. With its release day coming up, and a sizeable advance having been paid to the biographer, the publishing house will do everything they can to recoup their money and then some. Press junkets. Radio ads. An hour-long special in prime time. My father would love all the attention. Too bad the mere mention of it feels like a knife twisting in my back.

"What's going on, Ford? What are you not telling me?" His voice sounds sincere, and I hate that.

Because this is what I wanted. For him to ask and for me to answer but now I don't want to. It's suddenly easier to be angry at him and Callahan rather than to talk.

I rock back on my heels and sigh. "Do you ever just get a feeling sometimes . . . one that . . . you know what, never mind." *It's not worth it.*

"Do I ever what?"

His words hang in the air as I turn to face the man who is the spitting image of me, save for a few scars and a slight difference in height, and wonder how we can be so close yet feel so far apart.

I glance down to the file folder, its label, and then back at him.

"I'm buying the property."

"For what? To tear it down and restore the beach's integrity by getting rid of that eyesore?"

"Don't look, Ledger, but your privilege is showing."

"So is yours when you assume you can take millions without asking and throw it away on a pet project."

"Fine, I'll use my own money. Not a problem." Our glares hold as the silence stretches. I pace from one side of my office to the other before scrubbing a hand through my hair and groaning. I've been working nonstop for over a decade. Nonstop to build this company and its name. The constant pressure. The relentless pace. My brothers have found love, taken breaks, and created families, while I've stayed put and held down the fort through it all. God for-fucking-bid I want something that I can call my own. Sure, it'd still be under the Sharpe name, but it'd be *mine*. My vision. My success. My failure. "I need a break."

"Okay. Take one. You've been working nonstop and deserve some time off. You know you don't have to ask. Just fucking take it. Hell, it's not like we don't have over twenty resorts worldwide to pick from. Ocean. Desert. Mountains. What's your pick and what woman are you taking?"

"Not *that* kind of break."

"Then what? What are you saying? Do we need to wait for Callahan for this kumbaya? I can call him in here after his meetings and we can—"

"No." I hold my hand out in front of me to get him to stop. "You can fill him in later."

"Fill him in on what?" he asks and, for the first time, I sense he comprehends that I'm struggling here.

"I have an idea I want to go with, and you two are going to back me on it."

Ledger leans back in his chair, his eyebrows raised, an indifferent, bordering on surprised look on his face. "Go on."

"The Sharpe Signature Collection."

His brow furrows, but ever the businessman, ever curious, he nods. "Keep talking."

"What if we create a new series, and a new select branch of our hallmark? A signature collection that we market to the elite or famous. A smaller venue with a private concierge, security, or added rooms for the security teams guests like that usually travel with? The elegance and luxury that S.I.N. is known for . . . but at the same time, making them feel *normal* again. A seaside inn per se."

"You mean as in the White Sands type of seaside inn?"

I bite back my smart-ass remark when his distaste for the outdated hotel rings through his tone. And knowing by-the-book Ledger, he's already looked up and scrutinized pictures of the inn. But pictures won't do it justice, even with our trained eyes for potential. I would have never believed it either if I hadn't seen the place firsthand.

"Yes, I mean as in the White Sands, *A Sharpe Signature Collection* type of inn."

Ledger is the one of us who needs to think before he reacts, and he doesn't disappoint me right now by being any different. I study him with his pursed lips and furrowed brow as he ponders the idea, knowing he's weighing the pros and cons like I did when the idea first came to me.

It was on the back patio of the family Sag Harbor house. I was sitting there, and the sun was warming my skin as I nodded off. In that state of in-between sleep and awake, I could picture it perfectly. The inn remodeled with luxury suites where we combined three or four standard rooms into one great, big one. Balconies that looked out toward the sea and let the ocean breeze in. Private Jacuzzis with each suite. On-site chefs to cater to the clientele's tastes. A private beach.

Potential.

Isn't that the word that kept drifting through my head as I flipped channels earlier that night? One channel had a story about the press hounding a pop star who just wanted privacy on her vacation. Another story featured a software magnate who couldn't escape his everyday life and just feel normal. Memories of our own family trips when we had to skip activities because the paparazzi were trying to get a shot of us to earn a paycheck.

Who else could build what is needed better than someone who has experienced it firsthand?

I stare at my brother as he considers what I've said. He knows what it feels like to have your privacy invaded. He knows what it's like to want to make memories with your family but not have the space or place to be able to do that.

"The rich like to be treated like they're rich. They also like to be made to feel normal. We know that better than anyone. Why do you think Dad took us to Montana every summer as teens? To let us feel like everyone else in America." I sigh and pause for a beat, thinking of the summer months spent away from New York. It was a shift from the time we'd normally spend at the Sag Harbor house, but after our Mom had passed, it was too painful to stay there. "It's a tricky balance, but one we could pull off in a venue that's a smaller magnitude than our normal ones."

"Everyone says they want to be treated normally until they are, and then they bitch they aren't being stroked enough."

"Know from firsthand experience?" I taunt and receive a middle finger in the air and a roll of the eyes in response.

"Look, in theory it's a good idea, but we'd never recoup the money we'd sink into a place like that. It would take years to come close to the type of overhaul you're talking about."

"And you think we made back the fortune we spent at Ocean's Edge or The Retreat in a day?" I ask, pointing out the two most recent property purchases and resort overhauls.

"It's not the same and you know it. It's a moot point. As I said, it's not on-brand for us."

"Fuck the branding. Step outside of it. Redefine it. Add to it."

"This isn't an exercise at Wharton. This is our company. Good idea. Bad business decision for us."

"Tough shit. It's my business decision and as I said, you're going to go along with it." I don't believe the words coming out of my mouth. By the look on Ledger's face, I don't think he does either. "You make decisions every day about S.I.N. and the directions we take. Decisions we all follow. Now it's time for you to do the same for me."

Ledger's forehead creases as he huffs out a breath. *I've ruffled his perfect feathers. Good.*

He crosses his legs. He looks around the room. There is no hurrying Ledger when he's in this mode. But it's when his eyes meet mine that I see the concern deepening in them. "Where's all this coming from, Ford?"

"Sometimes it's about more than the money. And yes, it's so very easy for me to say that considering we're drowning in it. I won't deny that. But it's about needing to do something more. Different. To stretch and challenge myself. It's not an unreasonable ask."

His nod is slow and measured. So is the sigh that falls from his lips. "It is about the book then." When I don't respond other than to stare at him, he continues, his tone softening, ever the big brother. "Dad loved each of us in his own way. Just because some author and publisher decided to edit the biography in whatever way they decided, doesn't mean he loved you less. The people who matter to you, know the truth, Ford. And buying some dilapidated seaside something or other isn't going to fix what it is that did upset you."

I clear the emotion clogging my throat. "I've never asked you guys for anything like this. I'm asking now."

Ledger rises from his seat and heads to the door but stops before heading out. He waits for a beat before looking over his shoulder and meeting my eyes. It's a simple nod. It's all he gives. But it's enough to know I've been heard and while he might not understand the why, he definitely understands that it's important to me.

CHAPTER EIGHT

Ellery

"E LLE . . . I DON'T UNDERSTAND."

"Of course, you don't." My smile is tight, and my need to keep this uneventful even more so. "You and my brothers, or my dad, and whoever decided it was a good idea for you and me to get married. It was simply a merger of sorts to tie our families together personally and professionally."

"That's not—"

"It is." I reach out and grab Chandler's hand, the diamond ring on my left finger sparkling. A symbol of love that we don't really feel.

Or at least I don't.

"It was easy to get caught up in everything. You. Me. The promises that were made behind my back to bring you into my family business and cement the future of our families simultaneously."

"How did you . . ."

I didn't know. I assumed. But his response just confirmed my hunch. That makes my need to do this even more urgent. Our chance meeting that wasn't by chance. My brothers' encouragement to go out with the man they deemed to be a great guy. Good stock. All the right boxes ticked. The whirlwind romance and the over-the-top proposal.

Everything you'd think a girl could want. Textbook romance but with a clinical feel to it.

It was all manufactured for a desired result. A successful business merger disguised as a picture-perfect relationship.

And I went along with it. Until I didn't want to.

The question is, what made me have a change of heart?

Maybe waking up one day after a storm to realize that I wanted more than a contract to decide my happiness.

"Elle. Sure, it—us meeting, us dating, how beneficial us being together would be for both of our families—was an idea floated by your brothers, but then we actually fell for each other."

"You realize how that sounds, right?" My nervous chuckle fills the room.

"I'm aware. Just as I'm sure you're well aware of how the things you've said in the past sound."

"As in?" I cross my arms over my chest and prepare for Chandler of the Hurt Ego to begin his degradation of me.

"As in the fact that you don't even believe in love. That romance is a ridiculous notion. That a relationship needs to be mutually beneficial for everyone involved."

"You're right. I did say that. I do believe that," I reply, hoping those same words will be what lets him off easy. "But don't you want more than that? Just because I don't believe in it, doesn't mean you don't deserve better."

Kill him with kindness. Make it all about him. Flatter his ego.

"Elle . . . look at you. You're intelligent and successful and beautiful. What man wouldn't want you at his side?"

"One who deserves love? Who wants a family? Who . . . I don't know."

"But our sex life is good, is it not?"

A tight smile paints my lips. "Of course, it is."

But good sex isn't enough.

Isn't that what this is all about? It has to be. Because for a woman who's only ever been left by the ones she truly loved—first my father when I was nine and then my mother when I was eighteen—I don't exactly subscribe to the notion of love.

It only leads you into a false sense of security before it devastates you and leaves you to fend for yourself.

So yes, this arrangement of sorts would have professionally benefited us. It might have given me a leg up in my family business dynamic.

Chandler is a great guy. He's polite and successful and yes, he's a decent lover. I was willing to go along with it. There are worse things than being stuck with a good man when the notion of love doesn't exist.

But I realized it also made me a pawn in a game I had no control over.

And this entire epiphany came from one damn, unexpected night.

The same night I fell asleep on a stranger's chest after talking for hours. The same night I dreamt for the first time in forever. Dreams filled with faded memories of my parents and scenes from their unique and unmatched love for one another.

The same night someone told me nothing worth wanting is ever easy. Ford.

Ford, named after the college and the car. Ford of no last name, which in a sense makes everything that much more profound. The man with the grumpy scowls and beautiful smiles. Sure, he was attractive and sexy and all of the above, which had my stomach twisting every time he leveled me with those amber eyes of his, but it was more.

It was the words he said and the conviction with which he said them. It was watching him struggle with some unknown demon and realizing that even though we were on different paths, we were in a sense going through something very similar.

One night talking to a man I never met proved to be the catalyst for change within me. A refusal to settle. A refusal to let my brothers and father take what is rightfully mine. A refusal to be stifled. And the need to prove I can have everything I want.

I remove the ring from my finger as gracefully as possible and meet Chandler's brown eyes while holding it out for him. "This belongs to you."

He squeezes his eyes shut almost as if to say if he doesn't see it, he doesn't believe this is happening. "Can we postpone this conversation?"

"What?" I laugh the word out, my hand still extended.

His shoulders sag. "I said can we postpone this conversation? The breaking up with me part?"

"Chandler—"

"Please, Ellery." He reaches out and closes my fingers around the ring so that it sits in the palm of my hand. "I feel like an idiot asking you, but . . ."

"The reception," I murmur, thinking about the event next month where he's being honored for all his work. Architect of the Year.

"Yeah. I know it's a lot to ask—"

"It's the least I can do." I sigh and pull my hand back, the ring weighing heavily in it. So much for leaving here with a clean break.

"You sure?"

Why does he have to be so nice? So understanding? It would make this ten times easier if he were a dick.

"I'm sure, but after . . . I'm giving this back to you," I say, holding the ring up.

The smile he gives doesn't reach his eyes but is genuine nonetheless. "No. I want you to keep it. Maybe you'll change your mind." The hope lacing the edge of his tone feels like acid in my stomach.

"Chan—"

"Please. I insist." He takes a step back and shrugs. "Give it a few months. Maybe you'll reconsider. Maybe you'll realize you can learn to love me as I have you." When I start to shake my head, he continues. "Please. For my ego's sake."

"Yes. Yeah. Okay." I nod when I already know I won't change my mind. I gave it twelve months. And now I know we're done.

Today is my day for starting new.

First breaking things off with Chandler.

Then, fingers crossed, everything else I've been working on over the past couple of weeks will fall into place at my next stop on today's schedule.

That's a big *if*, but it's a chance I'm willing—*no, I need*—to take.

Funny how you can meet someone in the oddest of times to find out they gave you the advice, the hope, and the will to change something that you haven't had the strength to change before.

One night stranded in a thunderstorm and my perspective changed. My wants have changed. I take that back. My wants have always been there; it's more the drive to secure them for myself that has been strengthened.

I'm a win at any cost kind of girl.

As I walk out of Chandler's apartment, past bits and pieces of me that have migrated here over the past year and into this new me, I just hope I have enough currency to make it all work in my favor.

Because falling flat on my face and proving everyone right isn't an option I'm willing to accept.

CHAPTER NINE

Ford

I BUMP SHOULDERS AS I MOVE THROUGH THE SMALL SPACE, surprised at the number of people here. The last time I was at a property auction was . . . *never.* Hell, I can't even remember how long it's been since I was involved in a project at the grassroots level.

I'm excited.

"By the size of the turnout, I think we're already outbid," a woman murmurs to her companion as I push past people and move toward the front of the room.

When I glance around, I don't recognize any faces in the crowd, nor do I expect to. The general sale price I think the inn will go for is less than a tenth of what we pay for our typical S.I.N. properties.

"Let her bid," a guy on the left of me says as I get stuck behind a woman oblivious to her surroundings. "It's her money. And if she's actually able to turn it around, then we quitclaim deed it into the company. Her risk. Our reward."

Underhanded fuck.

"She'll go broke," his counterpart replies.

"And that's a bad thing why? More proof that she can't handle shit. Besides, if she fails then it'll be ours even quicker."

Correction. They're both assholes.

I glance at the strangers—sure I know one of them from somewhere—and offer a subtle nod in polite greeting to the one facing me before the oblivious woman realizes there is a line of people waiting on her and steps out of the aisle.

"Can we get this damn show on the road?" a woman grumbles as I take a seat in the only available one beside her.

The smile I offer is unreturned. Perfect. That means I don't have to make small talk. And luckily it remains that way as the auctioneer takes her spot at the dais and begins to go through several of the properties on the block today.

Some are single-family homes. Others are commercial buildings. One is an apartment complex. Each one is an empty shell representing a dream shattered for whoever owned it before the bank took possession of it.

The crowd has dwindled with each successful auction and then re-filled with the start of each new one.

Right now is no different.

"Next up," the auctioneer says, adjusting the red frames of her reading glasses on her nose as she looks down at the paper, "is the White Sands Inn. Property located at 13212 White Sands Drive. This is a unique opportunity to create a world-class, income-producing luxury destination in East Coast's most desirable beach enclave a little more than two hours from New York City. Located on a sprawling five and a half acre waterfront parcel, this noteworthy compound offers sweeping views of the water and western exposure for spectacular sunsets." She goes into the details of the property at length. The existing number of cottages. The bulkhead waterfront. The private beach. Other possible ideas for the location such as razing it and creating a condominium complex or a sprawling high-rise hotel.

All details and possibilities my team has already vetted and verified while many of us wait for her to open the bidding.

And where I plan to step in with a price on the first bid that will knock everyone out.

"Bidding opens at ten million. Do I have any takers?" At a quick glance of the room, about a dozen people call out and lift their paddles. "How about at eleven million?" Paddles raise again with voices saying *aye.*

"Fifteen million," I state loudly with a raise of my paddle so that many people in the room look my way with eyes wide, including the auctioneer.

"Fifteen, sir? Did I hear you correctly?" she asks as her assistant next to her takes down my paddle number and scribbles furiously.

"Yes. Fifteen."

"Do I hear anyone at—"

"Fifteen-five," a female voice I can't see calls out from the far end of the room.

"Fifteen-five for the lady in red. Do I have—"

"Sixteen," I say.

"Sixteen-five," the female voice counters, which has me rising to my feet to look at my competitor. I can't see her. She's obscured by the two men earlier talking about letting her bid. I take in their smug smiles and knowing glances.

"Seventeen," I respond before the auctioneer even prompts, causing her to emit a slight chuckle as the audience swings their heads back over expectantly in the direction of my competitor.

"Seventeen-five," the woman says, and I can finally see her paddle raised above the heads of people seated around her. It's then that the two men shift, and I see her.

I do a double take about the same time she looks over at me. I know those blue eyes and that startled smile.

"Ellery?" I mouth her name as I stare at her in absolute shock, my head shaking, my jaw lax.

She stares at me and the men beside her—the one I know but can't place—stare at her in a way that tells me they know her. That . . . *it's her stepbrothers.*

The thought dawns on me as the comments I overheard earlier and her explanation of things a month ago take root in my mind.

"Sir, would you like to counter?" The auctioneer's voice finally breaks through the surprise that's shocking my thoughts.

Yes.

No.

They spend all their time hoping to be the one selected to take over dear old Dad's ownership when he retires. Hell, everything I achieve they try and take credit for. Every idea I float out there is shot down only for them to say the same thing the next day and it's deemed the best thing in the world.

I open my mouth then close it.

"Going once," she states. My eyes dart over to Ellery and the silent plea she's asking of me. "Going twice." I go to raise my paddle but don't.

"Last call for any bids." Ellery's eyes hold steadfast to mine. "Sold to the woman in red for seventeen million five hundred."

Applause ripples through the crowd as I stand there stunned, staring at her and realizing everything I pleaded with my brother for yesterday, she possibly needs more.

The question is, why did I give it to her? And where the hell did she go?

CHAPTER TEN

Ellery

I'M GOING TO THROW UP.

That's a normal thing to feel when you've just spent a large chunk of your life savings—including some of the trust fund you haven't received yet—and funds from a loan you are the personal guarantor on . . . for a property that needs a shit ton of money put into it to have any chance at thriving.

I'm seriously going to throw up.

My hands shake from the adrenaline—of the auction, of what I did, of seeing Ford there bidding against me.

Ford.

What the hell is he doing here?

I glance over my shoulder to see if I can find him, but my brothers usher me through the crowd, their hands on my back as they lead me to the cashier's office.

"Stop. Just give me a minute," I say, shrugging their hands off me as I take in deep breaths to prevent myself from hyperventilating.

"You okay, Elle? Get caught up in bidding to prove your point? Did you just realize how much money you spent?"

I level my youngest stepbrother, Gregory, a look. "Go away. Go gloat somewhere else."

"Me, gloating?" He chuckles. "You should be the one gloating after buying a dump for a cool seventeen-point-five mil just because you couldn't let the kings of hospitality outbid you."

"Kings of hospitality?" I ask as I put my hands on my knees and focus on breathing.

Almost eighteen million.

Oh my God.

"Fordham Sharpe? Sharpe International?" Gregory asks as if I'm a dumbass. And yes, my head spins at the name. At the conglomerate that is S.I.N. That's who he *was*? *Is*? Jesus. "We've stayed in their resorts before. We've discussed how we'd beg, borrow, or steal to get on their preferred contractors' list. We'd be set with work for life. Are you really that dense that you don't know who they are?"

I don't react to Gregory's condescending bullshit because I'm focused on two simple words: Fordham Sharpe.

Not just Fordham the University, grumpy guy whom I threw the word vagina around to numerous times because it made him blush.

But Fordham, the uberwealthy, wheeling, dealing, empire running, everybody knows his family, Sharpe.

"I went to Wharton with those fuckers too," Joshua says, and I look at him. "Triplets who think they're perfect in every goddamn way."

"Why thank you, Joshua. I didn't recognize you with the beard. I'd love to return the compliment, but I don't believe you were giving one." I look up to see Ford standing there, a smug smile on his lips, and his eyes on my brother briefly before they meet mine.

Whew.

He's still got it. Has it. Whatever. Because even now with my insides a mess and my head all over the place, one look from Fordham Sharpe reconfirms he definitely still has *it*.

And I still definitely want *it*.

And by *it*, I mean every single thing that makes everyone stand up and take notice.

Even me. Even now.

Fordham Sharpe.

Jesus. How did I not put that together?

"Sharpe." Joshua holds his hand out in greeting to Ford, trying to cover his ass. "You know I was just joking, man."

Ford looks at Joshua's hand and then back up to his eyes, his expression stoic. "Of course, you were. If you'll excuse me, I need to speak to Ellery alone for a minute." His smile is patronizing and if I weren't still reeling, I might find more amusement in Joshua being dismissed so easily.

In a show of awkwardness I'm almost certain I've never seen from my brother, he pulls back his un-shaken hand and shoves it in his pocket as if he never extended it.

When neither Joshua nor Gregory move away because they're too busy trying to figure out how to right their wrong and gratify Ford, Ford places his hand on my back and says, "Shall we go outside for a moment?"

"Sure," I murmur, but he's already leading us out the doors, and I attempt to process that he's here. That he bid against me. That his hand is the one currently heating my back and sending shock waves through my system.

We don't speak as we move through the random people milling around outside and take a seat on a bench under a shady oak tree. Ford sits so that he's angled toward me, leaning forward with his forearms on his knees and his face close to mine.

"Fancy meeting you here," he says, his eyes kind but curious. Cautious.

"Well, that certainly was unexpected," I say to give myself a minute to find words and thoughts that sound coherent, because the ones in my head are a jumbled mess.

"It most definitely was." He gives a measured nod. "What do you think you were doing?" he asks and instantly my back goes up because one, that wasn't what I expected him to say. And two, he sounds like my brothers, like he doesn't believe I can handle a project like this. I immediately have a sour taste in my mouth.

Don't ruin the man I thought you were, Ford. Please, don't.

I straighten my shoulders, prepared to defend myself. "What do I think I was doing? Seems to me I was doing the exact same thing you were. Bidding on a project that has a lot of possibilities. A lot of potential."

"You were bidding against me."

"I wanted it. Of course, I was going to bid against you and everyone else in there. How was I supposed to know that Fordham Sharpe of Sharpe International Network was going to march in there and try to steal the show?" I ask with a healthy dose of sarcasm. "It's not like I even knew your last name when we met."

"A conversation in a bar doesn't warrant a requirement for you to know everything about me. For the record, I talked to you way more than I normally talk to anyone, so . . . take it for what it's worth."

And the grumpiness makes its appearance.

But he's right. He didn't owe me shit, just as I didn't owe him anything.

I reach my hand out to him. "Ellery Sinclair. Of Haywood Redesigns."

"I assumed the Haywood part if those were your brothers. I didn't know the Sinclair part." He leans back on the bench and scrubs a hand through his hair. He smells of cedar and ocean and everything desirable. "Jesus. What a small fucking world."

"You know my brothers?"

"Joshua. I know him from Wharton and beyond. Not exactly a fan."

"Neither am I, as you know," I say as I study him.

"Then why did you let them urge you on?" He throws his hands up. "Why were you bidding? Why did you bump up the bid?"

"Me?" I shriek. "You were the one who wouldn't concede. And my brothers have nothing to do with this. This is all me. I wanted this project. And I just spent a hell of a lot of money to get it. So if anyone should be mad, it should be me for how you walked in there like you owned the place to inflate the price and screw everyone over. *Meaning me.*"

"Screwing you over? Maybe you should be talking to your brothers about that? They're the ones hoping you fall flat on your face so they can rush in and save the—"

"You think I don't know that?" I laugh. "There's a reason I just used my own damn money to qualify. To bid with. My trust fund. My name on the loan." There is a tinge of hysteria in my voice as reality hits me. I now have five and a half acres and a hotel that I could afford to purchase, but that price was driven above my comfort zone by the man currently questioning me. Do I still have money for the needed improvements? Yes, but with the inflated price from our bidding war, I don't have as much as I budgeted for.

And that's without accounting for unforeseen problems and expenses that always happen on a project.

Tears well in my eyes that I blink away because I refuse to give him any iota of the vulnerability I'm suddenly awash with.

"Then why did you keep going?" he asks, his tone softening as if he hears the panic in my voice.

"Because I wanted it. Because I needed it. Christ," I mutter as I pull my hair back and twist it into a knot on top of my head. "Clearly you did too." I glance over at him and hold his gaze, suddenly needing to know the answer to a question I haven't had time to think to ask. "Why did you stop?"

He lifts his chin toward the door of the auction house where my brothers stand, pretending not to be staring our way. "Because of them. What I overheard. And what you told me."

I do a double take. "So you gave up the property for me?"

His nod is slow and measured, his lips twisting for a beat as he thinks about his answer. "I think you need it more than I do."

The gesture hits me squarely in the gut and makes the panic flutter anew. "Thanks. Thank you." I shove up from my seat and pace back and forth in front of him. *What have I done? How did I think I could handle this project on my own? I could remodel it with my eyes closed. I have plans and projections and spreadsheets coming out my ass, but there is so much more to it than that.* And the *so much more* is hitting me now. Overwhelming me now. "It's yours. You can have it."

He snorts. "What the hell are you talking about?"

"Sorry. Never mind." I chuckle nervously and pinch the bridge of my nose. "Forgive the mini-panic attack, but it's one thing to dream it and want it. It's another thing to act on it and have the chance to. It's hitting me now. That I do have the chance. That it's mine. All at once. *Oh my God.*"

"Okay." He draws the word out, his eyes studying me. "I think panic might be a normal reaction. So would elation. Pride. Excitement. Anticipation."

I move back and forth in front of him again, my hands trembling from the adrenaline again. "Was I a fool for thinking I could pull this off? For getting caught up in the auction and going over what I had told myself I'd pay for it? I was, wasn't I? I was—"

Ford is in front of me in an instant, my hands in his, and his head stooped low so our eyes are level. "You're not a fool. Knock that shit off, Ellery. You know you can handle this. You know you're capable. *I know you're capable.* You know this is *exactly* what you want and what you deserve."

I shake my head back and forth as if it will prevent me from hearing what he's saying. "Being capable is one thing. Handling a project of this magnitude is . . ." Projects always overrun on costs. Manpower and rising costs on building materials. Labor shortages. My head spins with things I've already factored in but are still panic-inducing in this moment.

This is my own money.

Not Haywood Redesigns.

Mine.

I knew the risks. I was more than willing to take them. I'm aware you have to spend money to make money. But you can be the fiercest person in the world and still get overwhelmed when you take a chance on yourself.

"Ellery."

"Just give me a minute." I hold my hands up and force my feet to stop and my breath to slow down.

I can do this.

I know I can do this.

"Ellery. Look at me," Ford says in that implacable tone of his.

"What?"

"Have you filed the paperwork yet?" His question throws me.

"*Paperwork?*"

"For the purchase. The auction."

I stare at him, blinking, clearly not following him. "No. I mean, I was going to, but I needed some fresh air. Then you were here . . . and, no, I haven't."

"Okay. Then let's go fill out our paperwork."

My head snaps up to meet his. "What do you mean by *our* paperwork?"

"Ours. As in yours and mine. Co-owners split fifty-fifty. That's my proposal."

"*What?*"

"You heard me. *Ours.*"

"You can't just—"

"Yes, I can," he says nonchalantly as if he's used to people agreeing to whatever he tells them. He is a Sharpe, after all, and they have a reputation for getting exactly what they want. "We'd make a good team. You're stressing about capital, and I have capital I was already willing to spend. You're worried about risks, while my forte is the market and what the property needs to be competitive. The remodel part is your baby since that's your specialty. And then when you're done, I have the connections to market and sell its uniqueness to the clientele I have in mind. Add to that, us going in fifty-fifty lessens our financial exposure and risk."

"But it also splits the profits," I counter, more to sound like I'm being reasonable.

"Beggars can't be choosers," he teases as I stare at him dumbfounded. Here's a man I've met a whole of two times, asking to partner with me, telling me we'd be a good team, and the levelheaded, look-before-I-leap me is considering it.

What is wrong with me?

"What if our visions for the property are different?"

"We'll compromise."

I snort. "A Sharpe compromising?"

"Are you judging me, Ellery?" he asks, that playful grin of his owning my attention.

"No. Yes. I mean, you are probably used to—"

"Having partners and having to compromise? Yes. In fact, I am. What else are you going to throw at me?"

"But what about the division of duties? I'll be living on-site. If I'm there one hundred percent of the time while you're here in the city, then it shouldn't be a fifty-fifty split. I think we should revise your proposal to a forty-sixty split."

"Ohhh, she's already playing hardball. That means you'll negotiate well with subs. I'm impressed. *And I like it.*" He rocks his head from side to side as he contemplates my comment. "Well, if you're going to be on-site, then I will be too."

"You'll what?"

"You heard me. Hell, I'd welcome the change of scenery. I can work from anywhere, and if I'm needed in the offices, I can always have the chopper come get me."

The Sinclair/Haywood family is successful by almost anyone's standards. If we never wanted to work another day in our lives, we'd still be fine.

But we've got nothing on the Sharpes. They are at a whole other level of ridiculousness.

And Ford casually mentioning their private helicopter is a stark reminder of the disparity between our lifestyles when I live a damn good one without complaints.

"You're out of your mind, you know that?"

"But you're considering it, aren't you?" He flashes a boyish grin that has a smile tugging at the corners of my mouth.

I am, aren't I?

"Just like that?" I ask. "I mean . . . you don't even know me."

"I do too."

I cross my arms over my chest. "You do? What do you know about me?"

"I know you hate pretzels in Chex Mix, aren't shy about germs, and that you prefer red wine—a good cab to be exact—over whiskey. What else? Hmm. That you deserve more credit than you're given when it comes to your dickhead stepbrothers. That you rub your feet together like a cricket when you sleep." His shrug complements his chuckle. "Oh, and you have a vagina."

A woman walking past us gasps at that last part as I crudely burst out laughing. "Jesus." I cough the word out.

"You were the one who let it be known, not me."

I take a step closer to him. "You're serious, aren't you?"

"I thought we already established that."

"Don't you have to consult with your brothers or something? I mean . . . your fight that night. Are things better? Will they want approval? I mean—"

"Everything is status quo. Not the same but not any different. And, no. No approval needed. This is my decision. My choice."

"Ford . . ." I look around at the people walking through the courtyard as if they're going to give me an answer I'm pretty sure I already know. "I can't let you do this. I don't even understand why you'd want to—"

"Give me one good reason why you can't."

Because this is ridiculous.

Because I barely know you and we might end up hating each other.

Because this is supposed to be mine.

"All those reasons flashing through your eyes aren't good enough. Okay. You wore me down," he teases and holds his hand up in surrender. "Fifty-fifty split, we both live on the premises, and I'll make sure you have an endless supply of Chex Mix without pretzels in it."

"Hmm. I'm not sure if that's enough for me," I say, my grin telling him my words are just that. *Words.*

"Okay. Fifty-fifty split. We both live on the premises, *and* you get first pick on where you want to sleep. *Final proposal.*"

"Final proposal?" I belt out a low whistle. "You drive a hard bargain, Ford. That must be why you Sharpes rule the world."

How did I go from feeling like I had the weight of the world on my shoulders when I walked out here to suddenly feeling like this could be feasible?

"C'mon, Celery Ellery. Take a chance on me. Take a chance with me." He holds his hand out—the one he withheld from my brother's handshake. "Deal, *partner?*"

"I can't believe I'm agreeing to this," I groan as a thrill of excitement shoots through me.

"Is that a yes?"

I meet his eyes, take in his smile, and reach out to shake his hand. *What the hell am I doing?* "Yes."

CHAPTER ELEVEN

Ford

SHE DIDN'T HAVE A RING ON HER FINGER.

I just signed on the dotted line to co-own a property with a woman I don't particularly know, and as I slide into the back seat and my driver heads back to the office, that's the one constant that keeps going through my head. That big, sparkly diamond engagement ring was nowhere in sight.

And believe me, I looked.

My cell rings, and I know who it is before I even look at the screen.

"It took you long enough," I say as a means of greeting.

"Dude. If you only knew the hell I've just endured. A bazillion-hour Zoom call. Trying to figure shit out through broken English and my non-existent Portuguese. I deserve a goddamn medal," Callahan says.

"Oh. Poor baby. You actually had to put in some hours today where you couldn't fuck off in between calls?"

"Says the man trying to buy . . . cottages? A motel?" He snorts. "What the fuck, Ford?"

"So you're calling to read me the riot act because I ignored the one that Ledger gave me earlier?"

"Nope."

I let silence sit on the connection as I wait for the *but* to come. However, nothing comes. "What do you mean, *nope*?"

"You have an MBA. I'm pretty sure you know the meaning of the word."

"Fuck off."

"Gladly." He chuckles. "Honestly though, I think it's an interesting idea that has decent potential."

"Wait? You're serious?" Callahan is agreeing with me? Is hell freezing over?

"I am. Sutton thinks it's a good idea too," he says, referring to his wife.

"Well, that's an unexpected turn of events."

"See? I'm not always an asshole."

"Just most of the time," I say.

"Pretty much. So you really bought an *inn*?"

"You could say that."

"Aren't you full of surprises."

"Always," I say as my driver honks his horn when a cyclist cuts in front of him.

"So, the usual? Hillary on the transition team? Stanley on the off-sites?" he asks, referring to our project managers.

"No. I'm taking lead on this."

Callahan's laugh rumbles through the line. "Funny."

"I'm dead serious."

If disbelief had a sound, the silence stretching between us would be it. In our dynamic at S.I.N., I'm the big-picture guy. I look at our properties, old and new, and assess what they need, what's trending that we need to follow, ensuring that our overall brand is consistently strong. Callahan is the hands-on one. When resorts are making the changes that I suggest, he's the one who oversees the transition. And then there's Ledger who oversees the entire company as well as being the point person for all acquisitions.

So for me to tell Callahan I'm going to be hands-on, doing what is typically his realm, is understandably comical to him.

"So you're going to be staying there? On-site? Boots on the ground?"

"Yes. I'm going to live there for a bit. Work remotely. Fly into the office when I'm needed."

His chuckle is disbelieving. "Who's the woman?"

I startle. "What do you mean, *who's the woman?*" How does he know about Ellery?

"I mean, this isn't like you, and when a guy starts changing shit this drastically, there's usually pussy involved somehow."

"Jesus Christ, Callahan."

"Tell me I'm wrong."

"You're wrong."

"Not buying it. Who is she? Does she live near the property? Nothing like being able to roll business and pleasure into one, right?"

"Yeah. Sure. That's it. I just blew millions so I can be close to a woman. That's a move out of your playbook. Not mine." I chuckle. "Did it ever occur to you that maybe I need a change of pace for a bit, and this presented itself so I took it?"

"Mm-hmm."

"Believe me. Don't believe me. I don't fucking care."

"Testy. Jesus. You *do* need a change of scenery."

"I'll be at the office soon. I need to meet with you and Ledge on this. We want to get started ASAP on this project."

"*We?*"

"Yeah. We." I'm not sure why I grin at the thought. "It's a long story, but I partnered with someone on the purchase, and we went in fifty-fifty on the project."

"Partnered? I thought we were your partners?"

"You are. This just . . . just go with it. Everything will be fine."

"Everything will be fine? Jesus. I'm already worried when you say shit like that. That begs me to ask, who's the partner? What's his name?"

"Her name is Ellery Sinclair."

Callahan's laughter echoes through the connection. "Told you a woman was involved," he says. "Next thing you're going to tell me is that she's ugly."

"Horribly. A snaggletooth. Disgusting breath. Warts all over her body," I say in jest, while my mind is filled with the exact opposite. Blonde hair. Blue eyes. A great smile. And a killer body with curves I never noticed that first night because they were hidden by her baggy clothes.

"So there's no need to worry about you sleeping with her and fucking up your partnership since she's repulsive, right?"

"Never even crossed my mind," I lie. "I've gotta take this call coming in."

And just as I'm about to push the button to switch over to my incoming call, I hear him mutter, "Change of scenery, my ass."

CHAPTER TWELVE

Ellery

"Y OU *WHAT?*" JOSHUA STARES AT ME WITH EYES WIDE AND expression horrified.

But my focus is on my stepfather, Garland Haywood. He sits before me with his shock of gray hair going every which way as per usual and his dark brown eyes locked on mine. There's the slightest lift to one of his eyebrows as his lips purse.

"Starting when?" he asks in that gravelly baritone of his that used to strike fear in me as a teenager. Now it just sounds pathetic.

"A few weeks. We're finalizing the details and schedules now. I'll know more in the next week or so."

He nods as a muscle pulses in his jaw. "And you've been using company time to do this? To meet with them and plan things?"

"No. Not at all," I lie. It's amazing. They don't want me around "in their way" most days, but when I'm possibly doing something other than fetching coffee, taking calls, and filing, suddenly, where I am and what I'm doing matters. "It's been in my free time at night."

"And you didn't use any company funds for the purchase of this whatever it is?"

"None." Like he wouldn't know if I took millions from the company. Give me a break.

"Ballsy," he murmurs but doesn't say anything else. His words have me standing a little taller. Garland Haywood's words of praise are few and far between. *Ballsy* is the most I've gotten in years.

I'll take it.

I remain standing, refusing to sit and be at eye level with them. I've rehearsed this entire scenario in my head over and over. What I'd say. How

I'd say it. What might be said to me. And the trump card I know I'll have to pull at some point to secure my position here at Haywood while I'm away doing my own thing at the White Sands Inn.

I'm just curious how long it will take before I have to show my hand.

"She can't do this," Joshua says. "She can't leave for months on end for this project that has nothing to do with Haywood. It's dereliction of duty, Dad. It's grounds for her to forfeit her stake in—"

That didn't take long.

"Beg, borrow, or steal to get on Sharpe's preferred contractors' list? How Haywood would be set with work for life? Those were your words, right, Joshua?" He blanches at my question, clearly still pissed about Ford's snub. "Or is it only okay if *you* secure work with S.I.N.? Because from my perspective, my partnership with them could be a win-win for all of us."

I play my card and hold my breath as Joshua sits there looking like a guppy, his eyes flitting back and forth between Garland and me.

Asking for a leave of absence was always going to be an issue. I knew Joshua or Gregory would attempt to use it as validation as to why I should no longer be a part of Haywood. With me gone and with Garland soon retiring, it would allow each of them to have a fifty-fifty stake in the company versus one of them holding a greater majority.

I wouldn't put it past them to undercut each other either.

When I wondered how to play it, Joshua's words kept coming back to me. His desire to be on S.I.N.'s elite and exclusive contractors' list. I have absolutely no intention of propositioning Ford or his brothers to give Haywood Redesigns work. None whatsoever. But that doesn't mean I won't use the suggestion of it to my advantage.

That I get to leave and remodel the inn while keeping my place here at Haywood.

It gives me options should this project crash and burn, and every good businessperson likes to make sure they have a Plan B.

"Those were your words, right?" I repeat. "What does it hurt to let me show the Sharpes the kind of work we can do? To sell them on Haywood while I do it? Dad?" I turn the conversation to him. He's the one who makes the final decision, we all know that.

"I'm not happy about this, Ellery. You're valued here at the company."

I snort. *To do what?* Get coffee? Have my ideas and work ripped off by your sons?

But I don't voice my thoughts nor do I back down from his scrutinous stare.

"I trust your judgment on this, Ellery." Ford points to the proposal I suggested with the schematic I think will best fit the inn. A vibe that is completely opposite of the one he prefers. "If you think this is the way to go, then this is the way we go."

"Just like that?" I glance around, expecting to see someone else in the conference room he's putting on a show for. I typically have to fight for my opinions to be valued. But when I look back at him, there is no hint of uncertainty in his expression.

"Yeah. Just like that. Quit feeling the need to prove yourself to me." His grin disarms me. "I mean, you said Chex Mix was better without the pretzels. Guess what? I tried it and you're right. It is."

"And that's your basis for trusting me?" I laugh. Pretzels?

"It was a good start." He taps his finger on the proposal. "But this is why I trust you. You have a good eye for what will work. You have an understated knowledge of why it will work. Why should I question you when you clearly know what you're doing?"

I just stand there with my hands on my hips and my head shaking, not used to someone having such unequivocal confidence in me.

"But that trust goes both ways, Sinclair." He winks. "When it comes to things I specialize in, you're going to have to trust me too."

"Like what?"

"Like what type of pizza we're ordering for our working dinner, because I'm frickin' starving."

I'm valued at Haywood? That's the last thing I feel. And that exchange with Ford last night proved what real professional confidence feels like.

It was such a little show by Ford, but it meant so very much to me.

And to hear Garland say I'm valued here at the company without ever giving me one ounce of respect Ford gave me last night only reinforces why I need the freedom and blessing to take time off for this project.

"It's nice to hear you value my input here," I lie, and the smile that strains on my lips says as much, "but—"

"But I think you might have a point." He pauses and jots something down on his pad of paper in front of him while I slowly exhale the breath I'm holding. "I can move one of the boys onto your Revlon project to take it off your hands."

Ha. Case in fucking point.

"You already did that. After I did all the legwork and scheduling, you told me it was better suited for Gregory," I say, my smile lacking amusement. "Remember?"

"Oh. Yes." He nods and waves his hand back and forth. "It's neither here nor there now, is it? Since you'll be leaving now anyway."

"So that's a yes?"

"Yes."

I fight the urge to do a fist pump when I leave the conference room, but that doesn't mean I'm not doing one in my head.

CHAPTER THIRTEEN

Ellery

Seventeen Years Ago

"WHAT ARE YOU DOING, SWEETIE?" My mother's eyes meet mine from her reflection in the mirror.

"Just thinking."

"About?" She turns to face me, her long, elegant neck exposed as she pulls her hair to one shoulder and continues to brush it. I watch the continuous motion of her hand, mesmerized by all things that are my mother. Her delicate skin. Her bright blue eyes that my eyes mimic. Her signature scent—rose and ivy. The hint of the South in her voice.

"Things. Stuff. You know." I shrug from where I lie on the bed, face in my hands, feet kicking back and forth in the air over my butt.

My eyes veer past the brush to a picture on her vanity. It's tiny and faded, and I know what it looks like from memory even though I'm across the room.

It's of my mom, dad, and me. We were at the beach. I'm in one of his arms and his other is around my mom. She's looking at him like he's the entire world, while he's looking at me with the same, adoring look.

It's the expression I always think of when I think of him.

I don't remember the moment because I was so young, but I savor the image and the feeling it gives me.

"What's wrong, Elle? You've got that look on your face," she asks, her head angling to the side to study me.

"Does it bug him that you have that picture?"

"What?" She looks over her shoulder and her entire body relaxes. "That's my absolute favorite."

"Mine too."

Her expression softens. "He loved you with everything he had, you know that, right?"

I nod, the funny feeling in my chest returning just like it always does when I think of him and miss him. "Why did he . . . never mind."

Why did he not love himself enough then? Why did he do it? Why did he rob me of a life with him?

Questions. They're always there. Always haunting me.

Because I know I loved him enough to make up for all the love he didn't have for himself. Wasn't that enough? Weren't *we* enough?

"Daddy had an accident, Elle."

I don't understand why tears are streaming down Mom's face. Why her hiccupped breaths can barely come out.

"He smashed the new car?" My eyes grow big. We just got it, and he loved that car so much. Oh, he's going to be so mad when he gets home.

"No. Not that kind of accident."

Why does she keep shaking her head back and forth as if she doesn't believe what she's saying?

"Then what? Did he accidentally cut himself with that super sharp knife in the kitchen like I did?" Man, I got in so much trouble for trying to use that to cut an apple last month.

"Baby. You need to listen to me." My mom kneels in front of me and puts her hands on my face. Her mouth opens and closes as she blinks away more tears. It looks like she's already cried so many she's probably out of water inside to cry more.

"Okay."

"Daddy has gone away and . . . he won't be coming back."

It's hard to swallow and my tongue feels heavy. Thick. "Why? He's my dad. He loves me. He wouldn't leave me."

She makes the most horrendous sound as she pulls me against her and just holds on. Her chest heaves against mine and her fingers dig into my shoulders.

It's then I get it.

It's then I know.

Daddy's gone.

My perfect world inside my perfectly pink room on my perfectly lacy bed-spread with my perfectly perfect parents will never be the same.
And he's never going to be able to come back.

"Sometimes people's minds are sick. And they can't help it. I loved him and you loved him . . ."

I nod again because it's easier than speaking. We both study the photo. A picture of love . . . until it wasn't. "You have his smile and his laugh and his intuitive sense to make people who are nervous, comfortable."

It feels good to hear all those things, to feel like I'm like him some-how, some way . . . but it doesn't take away the sting of his absence.

"Do you still love him, Mom?"

Tears well in her eyes as do mine. "I do. Yes. I'll always love him."

"So will I."

"Of course you will. You're a part of him."

"But you married Garland, though," I say of my stepfather.

"I did." She gives a measured nod.

"So you love him too, then?"

Her smile falters. "He's a good man." Her eyes dart to the doorway as if to make sure no one is there and then back to mine. "But our mar-riage . . . it's different from the one your father and I had."

"How? Isn't being married the same thing?"

Her sigh is hesitant as she moves to the bed and sits beside me. "Garland is kind. He treats us well. He's a good provider. I mean, look at the company and everything it has allowed us to do and have. Who would have thought that this could happen to us? That I could build that with him." She smooths a hand over my hair and leans down to press a kiss on my forehead.

"But wasn't Dad kind and didn't he treat us well?"

"Yes, silly. He did and then some. What Garland and I have is just . . . how do I explain this? Sometimes two people meet and decide that they want a partnership in a sense. Meaning, we want the same things out of life, for our children, and in most respects, really." Her smile is tight, almost as if she's trying to convince herself of it, and I'm too young to understand why.

But I do know that when I look at my mom, when I see her talk about my dad and then Garland, her eyes go from being alive to hollow.

And I'm old enough to understand that's how I feel inside too with my dad being gone.

Love isn't enough.

Lesson learned the hard way. Love is glorious but fleeting. It hurts. It will cut you open and bleed you dry before emptying every other part of you.

I've only loved two people in my life. They were my whole world. One is gone. Little do I know that within years of losing Dad, I will have lost them both.

Seems the pain that comes with real, true love isn't worth it.

CHAPTER FOURTEEN

Ford

SHE STANDS WITH ONE HAND ON HER HIP AND HER LIPS PURSED as she studies the papers laid out on the conference room table in front of us. Structural prints for the changes we're making to the interior—combining rooms to make suites on each floor with individual exits and entrances to them for privacy. Then there are the elevation drawings to show what the new exterior will look like. Next to those are interior design choices on spec boards—colors, carpets, fabrics, tiles. Elegance and luxury mixed with comfort and decadence.

It's been five weeks since we partnered up and signed the papers. Five weeks of waiting for escrow to close while we prepared for every facet of the remodel. Our hope is to complete it at lightning speed because time spent is money lost. Five weeks of being surrounded constantly by people helping us plan and plot and everything in between or on Zoom calls scheduling and brainstorming from our individual offices across town as we get ready to move on-site.

Five weeks, and this is the first time we've been completely and utterly alone. My staff has gone home. Her assistant has left. It's just her, me, and the night sky outside of this skyscraper's windows.

The thoughts running through my head right now shouldn't be there as I study her while she's busy contemplating something trivial on the table before her.

I welcome them, though. Oh, how I welcome them. What my fingers would feel like digging into her hips. What her lips would taste like as I delved my tongue between them. What her pussy would feel like as it pulsed around me.

Oh, how I've thought about them. About her.

And way too fucking much.

My eyes are bleary from staring at prints and my mind is exhausted, but I can still imagine and want and then tell myself I can't want. Can't have.

She's off limits.

The best way to fuck up a partnership is to fuck your partner.

End of story.

But another look at those pursed lips has my *dry spell* feeling like a goddamn drought.

The big question though is why is there still a tan line where her engagement ring was? Five weeks is a long time for a tan to fade and yet it's still there. Still a blaring symbol that she belongs to another.

So is she just not wearing it in my presence? Did it drop down the sink drain? Did she chuck it at her fiancé as she told him she wanted me instead? And if she's not wearing it because of me . . . what in the hell does that mean?

"What?"

When I snap from my thoughts, I realize that I've been staring at Ellery with narrowed eyes. "I'm sorry. What did you say?" I ask, trying to run that last fantasy of bending her over the conference room table from my head.

Yeah. It's bad. And no matter how often I tell myself it's going to be a long, torturous few months living on-site with her if these are my thoughts now, I can't stop them.

"I asked what that look you're giving me is for because it's really intense. Did I miss something?" She glances to the table and then back to me. "If I did, please let me know. The last thing we need is for one of us to not be in sync with each other on everything."

"And if we're not, we'll figure it out," I say as I move to her side of the table.

"Spoken like a man used to having such huge decisions on his shoulders." She sighs as if she doesn't exactly trust herself. She should though. She's brilliant.

And her brilliance, input, and keen eye for detail has made me wonder why we never contracted with Haywood Redesigns before. Oh, that's right. Joshua Haywood. Prick extraordinaire.

"I believe you were the one who wanted to step out from beneath your brothers' shadows and prove that you could handle the types of projects they handle. That being the coffee girl wasn't enough for you." I lean my ass on the table and look at her. "Are you chickening out on me, Elle?"

"Of course not. It's just—"

"It's just this is a lot of money and a lot of pressure and what the hell happens if it doesn't work or if you don't know what you're doing and, and, and . . . right?"

"It sounds ridiculous. I'm sorry." She emits a nervous laugh and starts to fidget with her hands. "You must be wondering why the hell you agreed to this. I'm a rookie. You're an experienced professional. I mean—"

"Stop." I step forward and close my hands over hers. The hitch in her breath is audible. So is the visceral reaction my body has from touching her. For someone so brilliant, she lacks confidence now and again. Most likely from years of her brothers disregarding her. Well, not anymore. Not with me. "Quit stressing. In case you haven't figured out by now, I'm pretty low-key. If a problem arises, we'll figure it out. If we disagree, we'll . . . I don't know, we'll yell at each other and you'll tell me I'm being an ass and I'll tell you you're being stubborn, and then we'll shake hands or something and move on."

"Why is everything so effortless for you?" she asks with disbelief woven into her tone. "Don't you ever doubt yourself? Don't you ever question things?"

Her words hit me squarely in the solar plexus. Isn't that why I took on this project? Because I doubt the man I am? Because I wonder if I'm more to everyone than the man who sits between his notable brothers? Because I want to know the eyes through which my father saw me?

"All the time," I murmur without giving more of an explanation. Doesn't she remember the bar that night? The turmoil I was in? I offer a smile. "This project. Our partnership. We'll figure it out."

She inhales a shaky breath and gives a definitive nod as she takes a step away and breaks our connection. After a moment, she turns back around with a more fortified smile. "Okay. I apologize again. I'm normally not one who needs a pep talk, so forgive me for sounding so . . . weak."

"Not weak. More like strong. Determined. Admirable." I shrug as she emits a nervous chuckle. "Taking chances is a hard thing to do. I promise it'll all work out."

"Thank you." There is a softness to her tone that matches the look in her eyes. Both give me pause. Another more convincing smile as she takes a step back toward the conference room table. "Then it looks like we should be able to hit the ground running."

"It does." I turn to look at the plans, and then step up beside her. "You'll get there tomorrow and do the final walk-through. I'll be there Wednesday once I'm done with my meetings."

"Sounds like a plan." She tries to stifle a yawn but just gives in and lets it happen. "Sorry. It's been a long couple of weeks."

"Exciting weeks though," I murmur as I lean forward and flip a page of the elevation drawings. "With even more exciting ones to come."

"I know."

We both move to leave, but as if choreographed, we turn and bump into each other. She wobbles on her heels, and I grab her biceps to steady her.

We're face-to-face, chest to chest, and I'm reminded of the smell of her hair as she slept on my chest that night. The fullness of her lips as she murmured in her sleep. The warmth of her body against mine.

We both draw in ragged breaths as our eyes meet. We should step away from each other. We should let go.

But seconds pass.

Breaths are inhaled. Exhaled.

Goosebumps break out on her skin beneath my palms.

Every sense of mine is way too damn aware of her. Of everything about her.

My eyes dart down to her lips, to the pulse pounding in her neck, and then back up to her eyes as my body fights against reason. Against desire.

The ring of her cell phone has the two of us jolting apart as if we were doing something wrong.

Or perhaps about to.

I turn my back and pace a few steps from her as I run a hand through my hair and gain some distance.

"Chandler?" Her voice is soft, almost as if she doesn't want me to hear.

Chandler. The same man who was on the phone the first night we met. Clearly, he's still in the picture and the reason behind the tan line on her finger.

"I said I'll be there." Her sigh is one of frustration. "You know I won't let you down." She moves a few steps toward the window and looks out to the night beyond and murmurs something I can't hear.

I begin to collect the prints and the papers to look like I'm not doing exactly what I am doing, eavesdropping.

"I understand. Yes. I have meetings all day with . . . clients. I'll have to meet you there." Her voice is soft, soothing even, and my curiosity is piqued. "Agreed. Okay."

But no, *I love you*. No, *I'll see you later*.

"Everything okay?" I ask absently as I roll up a set of blueprints and rubber band the roll of paper.

"Yes. Fine."

"That doesn't sound convincing." I chuckle and spare a fleeting glance her way to find disquiet etched in her expression.

"It's a long story." She waves a hand my way as if to say it's irrelevant. "Let me help you with that."

"No, I've got it. Why don't you take off?"

"You sure?"

"Yes. I'll have Phillip give you a ride home," I say, mentioning my driver who's taken her home before.

"I couldn't impose. I'm sure you need him for—"

"I have an hour or two left here. Please. I insist."

She gives me a halfhearted smile and nods. "Okay. Thank you." She lifts her designer tote bag weighed down with her laptop onto her shoulder and looks around to make sure she hasn't missed anything. Her eyes meet mine one last time. "I appreciate the pep talk, Fordham."

I watch her walk out the conference room door, her heels clicking on the marble floors. The elevator dings. The door shuts. I take a seat and lean back in my chair, hands behind my head, feet propped up on the table, and exhale a long, low breath.

I know they're already there.

I know they've been waiting for her to leave to make a comment.

"Shouldn't you both be home with your families?" I crack one eye open and see Callahan standing, shoulder leaning against the doorway.

"Snaggletooth is looking absolutely horrid tonight." Callahan coughs out a laugh and raises his eyebrows in appreciation.

Ledger whistles. "And you're going to be living on-site with her for how long?"

I lift my middle finger at my brothers and then go back to closing my eyes and ignoring them.

"Beds everywhere," Callahan says.

"Long nights alone. Just you. Just her. Just sheets to get tangled up in," Ledger adds.

"If you looked close enough, she has a ring line on her finger," I say.

"But no ring on it." Ledger lifts his eyebrows and glances at Callahan. "So . . . she just broke up? She needs a good rebound screw?"

"Ha. That's what I thought and look where that landed me," Callahan teases, but I know he wouldn't change his life for the world. "Married with kids."

"Rebounds can be good. Great sex. No want for attachment."

"Hell, Ledge, I think we should give him the same speech you two gave me when I headed to Ocean's Edge to work with Sutton," Callahan says, referring to a conversation we had the week before he left to go to the Virgin Islands with his then consultant—now wife.

"I don't remember any conversation," I mutter, full-well knowing what's coming, and wishing for a beer to at least give me something to do while enduring this harassment.

"Selective amnesia. Convenient." Ledger snorts.

"Let me refresh your memory. Something like: don't sleep with her. Be professional. It's our name on this company too, not just yours." Callahan flashes a shit-eating grin at me. "Would you like me to keep going?"

"And you followed the rules so well." I lift my eyebrows and level him with a look.

He shrugs. "Yeah, but breaking rules is expected of me."

"And what exactly is expected of me?" I ask.

And isn't that the question of the day?

CHAPTER FIFTEEN

Ellery

THE SKY IS PAINTED IN COLORS, PINKS AND ORANGES AND EVERY color in between. I've waited almost five whole weeks from signing on the dotted line to standing here with the sunset as my backdrop, the crash of the waves as the soundtrack, while I dig my toes in the sand and stare in awe at what is now mine.

Technically, *ours*, but that's just semantics.

I've felt pride before. I've felt ownership. I've known fear. But I've never known how potent a combination of the three could feel as I stare at what was formerly called the White Sands Inn.

It's D-Day. Or technically, tomorrow is, so I'm going to soak up the silence and solitude of being here all by myself before the chaos ensues. We have an army of contractors ready to take this place by storm.

The sand is cool beneath my bare feet as I imagine our renditions coming to life. The seaside café we're adding on to the left will offer cuisine from a renowned chef that Ford's people are currently in talks with. The balcony to the right, which was an empty conference room, will be converted into a lounge. And then the rooms in between will become suites with top-of-the-line amenities.

Pipe dreams.

Isn't that what Chandler said to me last night after all the pomp and circumstance of his big night died down, and we were left with that awkward silence that only proved we would never have worked?

"He's only partnering with you because you won the bid."

My eyes whip up to Chandler's. "Ford?"

He nods. "Who did you think I was talking about? Think about it. Why would a man of his stature buy a little-known nothing on a beach with some-one he barely knows?"

Because we have the same vision. Because we both need this reprieve from our day-to-day. Because we want something of our own.

"I'm thinking that was meant as an insult. Jealousy doesn't look good on you, Chan."

"I'm not jealous. Not in the least. But don't be surprised if you get there and he pushes you aside and steamrolls you right out of the picture. The Sharpes don't take a back seat to anyone."

"God forbid a man thinks I'm competent, capable, and worthy of a partnership."

"You are. That's why this whole thing hits me weird."

There is no use arguing with him, so I simply smile and nod. "You're on the outside, though."

"When it all goes to shit, just remember I warned you."

"Good. Great. Thanks for the vote of confidence." Sarcasm drips from my voice.

"Look, Elle. I get your need to fulfill this pipe dream of yours. Maybe it'll work. Maybe Sharpe won't railroad you and take over. And if he doesn't and you accomplish your goal, maybe you'll be satisfied and be ready to settle down. Be ready to marry me."

It is the first time I've ever looked at Chandler Holcomb and not liked him. Hence why the engagement ring he refused to take back is tucked away in my Tribeca apartment, safe until this project is completed.

How weird is it to have one man essentially mock me and the other unconditionally support me? Ford barely knows me and he believes in me while Chandler, regardless of how much of a good guy he is, clearly thinks I'm in need of a hobby to knock some sense into me.

The weird thing though is I honestly don't care what Chandler thinks anymore. I'm so over and done with men who think less of me because I want more for myself.

And I was going to marry him. Jesus Christ. If I thought being the cof-fee girl at Haywood was bad, I can only imagine what being married to someone who expects the same at home would be like.

No fucking thank you.

I should be angry.

I should be disgusted.

What I really feel is relief. Pure, unadulterated relief that I escaped this fate I had willingly subjected myself to.

Chandler the misogynist in disguise who I'm grateful to be rid of.

And Ford . . . *whew*. Ford, the man who knows how to get to a woman without even trying. He's been in my dreams in ways that are definitely not safe for work. He's constantly on my mind because of the project and the many things I need to tell him or want to discuss with him.

And now we're going to be living under the same roof. In close quarters. Day after deliciously torturous day.

There is definitely chemistry there. Hell, it was there that first night we met. But we're partners. It's never a good idea to sleep with your equal. Because you mix things like feelings and emotions and that makes things not so equal anymore.

But then again, it's me we're talking about. The woman who only does the physical. Who only likes lust and refuses anything remotely close to love.

Emotions are irrelevant. Always.

Concentrate, Elle. On the project. On making this work.

And so, I do. I leave the sand behind for the worn brick of the inn's back patio. The terrace and balconies will offer incredible views when they're modernized.

When I enter the hotel through the back door, the stillness hits me again, just as it did when I was handed the keys an hour ago and everyone left.

I found solace in the silence then and now. What I didn't expect is the sudden eeriness I feel in being the only person in an otherwise empty hotel. Not creepy as in *The Shining*, but rather desolate with every creak of its structure compounding the next.

Maybe that's why I turn on every light as I walk through the old building. Perhaps that's why I put my earbuds in and crank up the music as I tread over worn floors with an extra bounce in my step to the beat. What I can't hear, I can't be freaked out by.

I run my fingers up the dated oak banister that will soon be replaced with a more modern cable railing, and wonder what laughter and secrets have been shared in these hallways. And what new ones will happen when we're done?

I make notes on a pad of paper and add things to my checklist that I need to address with either Ford or the contractors. Things we possibly need to alter or things we didn't know needed to be addressed since it's hard to figure out a remodel when you haven't been given complete access to the property. Headlights light up the road outside. Some pull into the parking lot and turn around to go back the way they came, and I wonder how we'll make this the private haven for the elite when there's a public access road outside.

Another question to add to my list.

And call me crazy, but each item added makes me happy. I relish the excitement of this new venture.

You've got this, Sinclair.

CHAPTER SIXTEEN

Ellery

WHEN I LOOK AT MY WATCH, I'M SHOCKED TO SEE THAT hours have passed. I guess my excitement to get started has trumped my rationality of having one last night of nothing before the real work starts. So much for settling in the room I've picked, eating the sandwich I grabbed on the way in, drinking a glass of wine, and finishing the last few chapters on my romance novel before falling asleep for the night.

The book may still be an option. Then again, I still have a slight bruise on my forehead from last week when I fell asleep and dropped my Kindle on it.

I'll read on my stomach this time. At least that will help prevent any droppage injuries.

Deciding that I'll take my shower first, before the eating, reading, and sleeping portion of what's left of the night, I make my way back downstairs to the room I've picked as my short-term residence.

A room with a door that I've debated closing and locking behind me when I go to bed. Or is it better to leave it propped open so I know what's going on in the rest of the hotel? Which should be nothing.

I double-check the entry doors on the bottom floor to make sure they're locked as one of my favorite songs comes on. I have no shame as I dance down the hallway. With each shimmy and shake, I discard an item of clothing, before closing the door behind me and dumping clothes un-ceremoniously on the bed. The room is dim, save for a muted desk lamp and the bathroom light I left on earlier.

I give another little shimmy and a hard shake of my hips before twirl-ing around and running smack dab into something.

Or rather into someone.

A whole lot of wet, naked someone.

The screech I emit is on a whole other level as I jolt back—earbuds falling out, phone clattering to the ground. I have a brief glimpse of the man in front of me. Chiseled and tanned and perfect and . . . cock. *Oh my God*. I've just seen Fordham Sharpe's impressive cock.

The thought registers at the same time I step in a puddle of water and my feet slip out from under me.

I fall backward in all my own naked glory—boobs bouncing, arms flailing, and hips jiggling. Graceful isn't exactly the word I'd use to describe me. Instinct has me reaching out to Ford, and he tries to catch me.

But then he slips in the same water that I do.

His curse echoes off the tile walls, followed by the *oomph* as I hit the chaise lounge behind me, seconds before Ford lands smack dab on top of me.

I'd like to think my first thought is thank God these old, oversized bathrooms have a soft chaise lounge in them I could fall on instead of the hard edge of the bathtub. That should be what's first and foremost on my mind. My safety.

But it's kind of hard to think rationally when the only thing that's hard is about six foot three inches and planking my entire body right now.

And whose hands are grabbing my wrists beside my head and whose grinning mouth is inches from mine.

I've never been more aware of every nerve ending in my body than I am at this moment.

We stare at each other for a beat. I'm not sure if our minds are catching up with what just happened to our bodies, but our eyes lock and our bodies tense.

Which of course presses that rather impressive cock against my thighs.

"I'm sorry," we say in unison.

Kiss me.

It's not the first time I've thought it.

It most likely won't be the last either.

How can any normal woman not think something like that when she's skin-to-skin, body to body, with a man as gorgeous as Ford?

I part my lips to say something, anything, as the agonizing and embarrassing seconds tick by.

"You're in my bathroom. What are you doing here? What in the hell do we do?"

He chuckles. "You're in my bathroom. I texted you that I was coming." He quirks an eyebrow at his word of choice, his grin widening, and his voice suddenly lowering. "And as far as what we do now . . ."

His eyes shift to his right seconds before I catch a glimpse of something glance through his eyes. A warning? Fear? I don't exactly know what, but he pushes up off of me in a hurry. Before I can comprehend what's happening, yet again, Ford throws a bath towel my way, giving me nothing but a perfect view of his bare ass as he walks away.

I look.

Of course, I look as I scramble to wrap the towel around me and rise from my more than awkward position on the chaise—because it's hard not to.

"What in the hell are you doing here? Why?" I ask as he keeps his back to me and yanks another towel off the towel rack next to the shower door.

"Taking a shower. *Clearly.*" Annoyance tinges the edges of his tone when moments ago he was lying on top of me, smirking.

"But my bags were in the room. I was here first. You weren't supposed to be here until tomorrow." I sputter each sentence out.

"And I texted you I was coming early. I called out when I came in the front door. It's not my fault you had earphones in or didn't check your phone," he says, and I'm confused by his sudden wintry tone.

When he turns to face me, he's holding the towel over his crotch so that every maddening gorgeous inch of him is on display. The hip dents. The happy trail. The firmness of his thighs. The definition in his chest.

Lord, have mercy.

I make a concerted effort to look up at his eyes, and when I do, there's indifference in his expression, almost anger, that matches the tone of his voice. That throws me.

Talk about fueling a woman's insecurities in herself when she's at her most vulnerable.

He's in my shower. In my bathroom. When I'm supposed to be alone. *And he's mad at me?*

"You shouldn't be here."

But don't be surprised if you get there and he pushes you aside and steamrolls you right out of the picture. The Sharpes don't take a back seat to anyone.

Chandler's words flood back to me and sow seeds of doubt that shouldn't be there. "*Come again?*"

He drops his head for a beat. "That's not what I meant."

"Then what exactly did you mean because last I checked, I own half of this building too."

"You *do*. We *both* do. Fifty-fifty." He chuckles and holds one hand up in front of him, the smile I've come to know breaking through the pained expression on his face.

Despite his smile, I'm already on the defensive. Already primed for a fight reserved for Chandler that Ford doesn't deserve.

"Then why are you being a dick? You were in *my* room. In *my* shower. Using *my* towel that I brought here." I point to the one he holds over his dick.

"Fine. Here's your towel back," he says, holding it out to me without flinching. My eyes meet his, hold, and as much as the woman in me wants to look, I refuse to back down from the dare sparking in his eyes. I meet him gaze for gaze and in a sudden moment of bravado, not to be upstaged by him—my partner—I drop my own towel.

He emits a hiss in restraint, a smile toying with the corner of his mouth as his eyes widen.

"*What?*" I ask innocently. It takes everything I have to stand there. I'm not modest by any means, but willingly standing in front of a man as gorgeous as him is a feat in and of itself. Talk about feeling insecure. "It's only fair since everything between us from here on out will be fifty-fifty."

"Even-steven." His ghost of a smile turns into a full-blown grin.

It's a game of chicken. Who will look first? Whose curiosity will make them break? Which one of us will swerve first?

"Good." I return the grin and the dare that paints its edges. "Now that that's settled, you can see your way out. I'm going to take my shower now."

"Don't forget your towels. I wouldn't want you to not have anything to dry off with," he says as he takes a step back, his eyes dipping down briefly.

He swerved.

And I promptly follow suit and do the same. Yep. Still gorgeous. Still hung. Still the definition of perfection.

Our eyes meet again. *Jesus.* The aloofness he just had? Completely gone. The man knows how to look at a woman and make her feel like she's the only one in the room.

Granted I am, but I'm talking figuratively.

There's an intensity in them. A desire that shouldn't be there but that I feel equally as strong.

He's off limits.

Every incredible inch of him.

"Thank you for your concern, but I can handle myself."

"Noted, but I already knew that." He takes a step back, his eyes dipping again, and his nostrils flaring in reaction. "Good night, Ellery."

"You're naked," I shout after him in warning as he opens the door. And I realize my stupidity only seconds after I say it. The hotel is empty. There's no one else out there. He's not walking into a crowded hallway.

When he turns around, all I see is the smirk on his face and the amusement in his eyes. "So are you."

CHAPTER SEVENTEEN

Ford

THE WHOLE THING LASTED SECONDS. RUNNING INTO ELLERY. Landing on top of her. Having proof of how goddamn perfectly our bodies fit together.

I groan.

It may have only been seconds, but it's all that's needed for a match to strike and flames to ignite.

And fuck did they ignite.

Desire. Need. Want. Greed. The four battled within me in those split seconds. Fuck decorum. Screw our partnership. The things that were going through my head were anything but partnership-amiable.

What I would have given to lean in and kiss her lips. To thread my fingers through her hair and knock her thighs apart with my knee and taste her there.

And I bet that taste would be as addictive as the feeling of sinking into her. Of hearing her moans as I did. As reveling in her slick heat as we drove each other to the brink.

Ellery naked.

Christ. I can't get the image of her out of my head. The peaches and cream of her skin only accentuated the pink of her nipples and the gorgeous curve of her hips.

Curves are my kryptonite and damn, does she have them.

I shift again, the sheets falling off me as my dick hardens and thoughts run crazy.

She's all I can think about.

A wall between us.

A bed away.

A closed door apart.

And I was tempted. God, how I was tempted with her body beneath mine—soft and warm and inviting—until I looked to the wrist my hand was pinning and was snapped back to reality.

To the tan line on her finger.

To the *Daily Transcript* article I read this morning and the picture accompanying it. One about Chandler Holcomb and his fiancée Ellery Sinclair as he accepted his award for Architect of the Year.

And that reminder was like a shock of cold water despite the heat between us.

CHAPTER EIGHTEEN

Ford

Twelve Years Ago

I KNOW HE'S STANDING THERE. EVEN IF I HADN'T HEARD THE CLICK of the front door or his even breathing, I would know he was there. My dad most definitely has a presence about him that owns any room he walks into.

Even my apartment.

"Who let you in?" I groan as I roll onto my back on the couch and cover my eyes with my arm.

"I own the building. Last thing I need to do is ask for access from anyone."

The thought has never bugged me until right now. Until this moment when I simply want to wallow in my own sorrow and drink myself into oblivion without him being *him*.

"Invading my privacy doesn't come with the landlord duties."

"Then answer your phone, and I won't have to show up here."

I hear the motorized blinds moving open and already hate him for doing that. Besides the extended hangover I've been wallowing in, I don't think I've seen sunlight for a few days.

"You can spare me the lecture. I already know what you're going to say." *Get up. Don't let a woman steal your worth. Fuck her if she doesn't see your value.*

Blah.

Blah.

Blah.

"I'm not here to give you a lecture, son."

"Ha. That's funny. Isn't *lecture* your middle name?"

"That's not exactly fair." I hear him move about the room. I feel the dip of the couch's cushion beneath his weight. "I like to think I offer more than that."

Huh. There is a tinge of *something* in his voice. Did I just insult the great Maxton Sharpe and it affected him?

His sigh hangs in the stagnant air of my place. "It's inevitable, you know."

"What is?"

"Heartbreak."

"Thanks for the brilliant observation. Can we skip to the good part where you leave?"

"Don't be disrespectful."

"Don't enter a man's apartment unannounced."

"Ford." He reaches his hand out to my shin and squeezes. "I'm sorry about Jennifer."

"Yeah, well, you just said heartbreak is inevitable so—"

"Son." He pauses for a beat. "You have this incredible ability to put yourself out there. For being you without holding back and not caring what anyone thinks. That's admirable."

What does that have to do with getting my heart broken? Is this another case of him just wanting to hear himself talk?

"It doesn't feel very admirable," I say and pull the pillow over my head.

Admirable is the last thing I feel. Hurt is first and foremost. Then disbelief followed by anger before returning right back to hurt again.

He's silent, but his hand remains.

"She cheated on me. Cheated. After two years together . . ." The images are burned in my brain. Opening the front door to hear the unmistakable sound of moans. Following said sounds to find Jennifer straddling one of my fellow MBA classmates. *Fuck.*

"So your brothers told me."

"With a classmate no less."

"And how does that make you feel?" I cock an eyebrow at him. *How does he think it made me feel?* I don't think I've ever heard those words come out of his mouth before. Since when is he a therapist? "I asked a question, Ford, and I expect an answer."

"Pissed. Angry. Wanting to fuck someone random to get back at her."

But there's no way in hell I'd do that. Even after that. *I'm not that guy.* I'm far too loyal to purposely have a revenge fuck. All she had to do was break up with me for fuck's sake. How hard would that have been?

Then again, she's a cheater, so she's probably too chickenshit to end things before moving on.

He purses his lips and nods. "Go ahead, but it's not going to make you feel any better."

"Then what will? Because it's been days and it still fucking hurts as much now as it did when I saw it for my own eyes."

"She doesn't deserve you."

"That's supposed to help?"

"No. But it's a fact."

"More brilliant wisdom from the one and only." I groan as I sit up, my head pounding and my eyes squinting. "Tell me something oh-know-er-of-all-things. How exactly do you know this?"

"First, this will be the one and only time you will ever get away with speaking to me with such utter disrespect. Hurting, heartbroken, I don't care. I taught you better than this so watch how far you push, Fordham."

Then leave me to my own fucking peace. I fist my hands and fight back the need to be more of an asshole and take my frustration out on him.

"Two, she wasn't the one. I could have told you that since day one."

I snort. "Lay it on me, Dad. How exactly did you know this?"

"Because she was a matter of convenience. She looked at you as a meal ticket, and you looked at her as someone who fit the role."

"That's bullshit." I say the words with more conviction than I feel.

"Is it? Because I never saw her as being the one you'd walk through fire for just to see for a minute."

I'm about to laugh but when I glance his way, amber eyes that match mine are looking back at me with an unrivaled intensity. "Are you missing Mom?" I ask him, suddenly feeling like an ass for not looking closer sooner.

A soft smile breaks on his lips. "I will always miss your mother. That's a given. But no, this isn't about Mom. This is about you."

"Would you have walked through fire for her?" I ask, my voice barely a whisper.

"Yes." His voice breaks on that single syllable.

With every passing day, passing year, her memory grows fainter and fainter regardless of how hard I try to hold tighter to it. The sound of her laugh. The scent of her perfume. The way she'd hug us as if her life depended on it. The love she gave. *God, she knew how to make you feel loved.*

"Yes, I would have." I wonder if they were just an anomaly—the love they shared and he seemingly still feels. "I did. I still do. I'd go to hell and back for her. Some days I feel like I have after living all this time without her. Seeing you guys grow up, enjoying every minute of it, and knowing she's missed every part of it."

"I'm sorry for what you've missed," I murmur.

"Don't be. At least I had the chance to have that kind of love." He clears his throat, making it clear the kumbaya session is now over. "And I want that for you. For your brothers."

"You actually think Callahan will settle down?" I snort.

"He'll find someone to tame that fire of his, whereas you need someone to help stoke yours."

"What's that supposed to mean?"

His half-hearted smile doesn't tell me much. "When you find her, you'll know."

"I'll know what?" Now he's just making shit up to feel fatherly when he's currently in over his head. "If you know the answer, please impart your wisdom."

"Son, when a woman's temper makes you love her even more, when her defiance makes you want to challenge her, and when her smile makes you want to earn each and every one, then you know she's worth the goddamn fire."

His words make me uncomfortable because I sure as hell didn't feel that way about Jennifer.

"Got it."

"At some point, you will get it. And when you do, I just hope I'm around to see it."

"Yeah, yeah." I wave a hand at him.

Can he just go and leave me in my wallowing?

"Hint taken. I'll be going now." *Thank God.* But as he reaches the door, he turns back to look at me. "Promise me something, Ford."

"What's that?"

"Don't ever stoop to that level. Stealing another man's woman shows who a man really is . . . or rather isn't. And any woman willing to do the same isn't worth the fire anyway."

CHAPTER NINETEEN

Ellery

THE PROPERTY IS ABUZZ.

Contractors and laborers are everywhere. In the halls. In the rooms. Outside. *Freaking everywhere.*

Noise fills the air from the demolition of interior walls of the suites, the backup alarms of the trucks hauling out the debris, and the jackhammers chipping up concrete to make way for the café.

It's complete and utter chaos, and I welcome every second of it.

Especially because it keeps both Ford and me busy—in different parts of the property—at almost all times.

Every time I walk into a room, it seems like he walks out of it.

And that's probably for the better seeing as every time I catch a glimpse of him, I'm brought back to a few nights ago. To the sight of him naked, to the arrogance in his smirk, and the taunt in his eyes.

Partners are off limits.

Isn't that the motto I settled on last night as I laid in bed fantasizing about my absurdly attractive *partner?*

Then why do I so desperately want to shove that motto where the sun doesn't shine?

But now that I need to talk to him, he's nowhere to be found. I walk through hallways lined with floor liners and past furniture being moved out to be resold. "Do you know where Ford is?" I ask several people along the way only to get random gestures in the direction of where the rooftop bar will be.

"There you are," I say when I see him. He has drywall dust in his hair, his shirt has a ring of sweat around the neck, and his jeans have a tear in the knee.

And my ovaries were just put on standby to explode.

Dress shirt and tie-Ford is handsome.

Wharton sweatshirt over soaking wet skin is tempting.

And yes, naked Ford is more than mouthwatering.

But contractor, average-joe-looking Ford is a whole other level of deliciousness.

Partners are off limits.

"I've been looking all over for you." I hold up my clipboard and the ever-growing list clipped to it. "I need to ask you a few—"

"No, you don't." He flashes a smile and averts his eyes. "Make the decision, Sinclair. I have complete confidence in any and all decisions you make." He looks around as if he's looking for someone. "Now if you'll excuse me, I'm needed downstairs."

"Wait." I reach out and grab his arm as he starts to walk away from me. "What's going on? It's day one and you're already avoiding me. I thought we had a good week or two at least before you got sick of me."

I don't get the laugh I was going for. Instead, I get a shrug of his arm from my grip while the muscle in his jaw pulses as he clenches and unclenches his teeth. I hate that he won't look at me. "More like trying to do the right thing."

"What's that supposed to mean?"

He lifts his gaze to meet mine, and I wish I knew what that look in his eyes means. Confusion? Discomfort? Why would either of those be there?

"Look. It's a busy day. I have a lot on my mind. And I truly do trust you to make the decisions that need to be made."

"Then why do I feel like I'm being avoided and blown off?"

He drops his head and sighs before looking back up to meet my eyes. "You know how you had *stuff*? Well, I have *stuff* too, and rather than take my frustration out on you, it's best if I just avoid you for the time being for your own sake." The smile he offers doesn't quite meet his eyes. "Yes, Grumpy Ford is back."

I narrow my brows, wanting to ask more, needing to understand, but force myself to bite my tongue. In my thirty years, I can count on one hand the times a man has verbally expressed to me that he needs space. The norm has been lashing out and irrational behavior to push me away.

So as much as it kills me, as much as I wonder if I'm at fault for whatever is bugging him, I simply nod and give him what he asked for. "Okay."

I watch as he walks away, my mind still curious, and my common sense telling me how arrogant I am assuming his problem was with me instead of *stuff*.

So we work as a team but apart, each of us tackling different facets of day one. Ford works with coordination and flow, while I do what I know best—dealing with the individual trades, one-on-one.

But even with the accelerated schedule and the agreed-upon extended work hours, at some point, the noise starts to abate. The crews start to stack their equipment in corners for the night. The rumble of engines can be heard in the parking lot as they start their cars and head home.

And we're left with a gutted hotel and a whole lot of silence.

I move through the first floor and the lounge Ford and I met in two months ago. It's the only place that hasn't been touched yet with a sledge-hammer or a Sawzall. Its burgundy chairs are stacked in one corner waiting for the consignment shop to pick them up tomorrow, and the bar remains still partially stocked with half-empty bottles lining the dark wooden shelves.

It looks exactly like it did the night of the storm.

Exhausted but still wired from the high of the day, I prop open the door to the boardwalk, unstack one of the chairs, and awkwardly move it out onto what's left of the old patio. Night has fallen, and the moonlight brightens the white of the sand and sparkles off the water on the horizon.

When I slink down into the seat, I wonder if I'll ever be getting up. I'm *that* exhausted. The hiss and crash of the waves hitting the shore is a lullaby all in itself.

"Here."

I jump at the sound of Ford's voice. I must have been so lost in thought and exhaustion that I didn't hear him walk up behind me.

When I turn, I find him holding out a glass of red wine to me while he carries a tumbler of something else in his other hand.

"Thank you," I murmur, taking the glass from him, uncertain where we stand at this point of the night.

He disappears momentarily and returns, setting a chair next to mine. His groan sounds exactly how I felt when I sat down minutes ago.

I wait for him to start the conversation and the longer it takes, the more I wonder if we're simply going to sit in silence under a canopy of stars. I'm fine with that too.

He lifts his drink and swirls it around in the glass before taking a sip. "It's a cool feeling, isn't it?"

I don't even have to ask what he's referring to because I've been reveling in it all day.

Ownership. Having something that's mine. Being able to create as I see fit.

"It is. I've never had something of my own that I get to be hands-on from start to finish."

He holds his glass out and taps it against mine. "To new beginnings," he says.

"To new beginnings." I chuckle, my head spinning with how much life has changed for me over the last two months.

I've bought this property, taken a hiatus from my job, broken off an engagement, gained a partner, secured my place at Haywood, and spent endless hours planning the transformation of the building behind us.

It's been a whirlwind to say the least.

And there's still so much left to do.

"What does that mean?" he asks.

"What does what mean? My chuckle?" I can see him nod in my periphery, and my thoughts veer to where I was supposed to be today versus where I am—sitting here, beside him. "Today was supposed to be the final fitting for my wedding dress."

He clears his throat. "I'm not exactly sure how I'm supposed to respond to that."

"No need to respond to anything."

"So you rescheduled the appointment so you could be here for demolition day? That's awfully generous of you."

"No. I didn't reschedule."

"No?"

"Uh-uh." How do I explain to him that I was going to marry for the sake of marriage? That doesn't exactly paint me in the greatest of lights.

"I can ask if you want to talk about it, if this is the *stuff* you were figuring out that night . . . but it's not my place to, so I'm going to sit here, enjoy a drink with you, and relax."

"Thank you." I slink down and lean my head back on the chair, my eyes focusing on the stars above.

The need to talk is there, to explain so he understands, but I'm not even sure that I understand the why behind my actions with Chandler.

"I can hear you thinking over there, Elle."

I smile. "I'll try to think quieter."

"For the record, you don't owe me any explanation."

"I know I don't."

Just like he didn't offer me one today either.

"Do you think there's any leftover Chex Mix behind the counter?"

I laugh. I don't know why the comment strikes me so funny, but it does. "It's probably stale."

"And full of pretzels."

"The horror." I mock shiver.

"There's that smile of yours," he says, pulling me to look directly at him for the first time since he sat down. "It's about time it showed up."

Our gazes hold as my heart begins to race. I'm grateful for the glass of wine so that my hands have something to do besides fidget, because that confession just cost me in ways I'm not even sure I understand yet.

"I'm just tired is all."

"Exhausted." He groans and runs a hand through his hair. "And they'll start bright and early at seven in the morning."

"Ten whole hours from now." My shoulders sag.

"You're the one who wanted an accelerated schedule."

"We. We are the ones who wanted that," I correct.

"I think we weren't comprehending how exhausting it would be." His groan turns into a chuckle.

"No rest for the weary, Sharpe. Even if it's us who are the weary."

CHAPTER TWENTY

Ford

"AND THINGS ARE GOING GOOD WITH THE SNAGGLETOOTH?" Ledger asks.

"Yes. Fine. We're feeling our way around each other."

"Does that mean there's trouble in paradise?"

"No. Not at all."

"That doesn't sound convincing."

"I don't need to convince anyone of anything."

"Huh."

"What the hell does that mean, Ledge? I'm tired and not in the mood for bullshit."

His chuckle reverberates through the connection. "It's been a long time since you've been on the ground level. It's a lot of work."

"It is. Is that why you're calling? To razz me, or is there something else?"

"You haven't R.S.V.P.'d yet."

"And you know this how?"

"The publisher called. They asked that we all be there."

"I might be busy here. I'm not sure yet since we've just started."

I already know the look on my brother's face right now, and the way he's chewing the inside of his cheek as he contemplates how to control a situation he has no control over. It has to be killing him. "You're really going to miss it?"

I shrug, not that he can see. The last thing I want is to go to the book launch party for the biography. As it is, I can't escape the hype of it. It's everywhere. Inquiries for interviews or requests, comments to use as a lead-in for an article.

Why do they need us to promote it? Isn't my father and his success enough cause for intrigue? *I mean, there is the whole incredibly handsome and successful triplets thing going for us of course.*

But no.

It's because people are obsessed with money. Nothing captures an audience more than a family dynasty, and the drama that comes with it.

And I refuse to contribute to the family picture I fear they want to paint.

"I said I don't know. If that's not good enough for you, I don't know what is."

"Don't be an asshole."

"You're one to talk." I chuckle.

"Look, I know you're still bothered by *Just Ford*. I can't change that. I wasn't going to tell you until I knew for sure, but I did reach out to the biographer and ask him if we could have copies of all of Dad's taped interviews."

"What for?"

"He has over fifty hours of tapes. I thought it would be cool to hear new things about Dad in his own voice. Things we might not have known. Have something to help keep him alive for our kids someday." When I don't say anything, he continues, "We don't have much of Mom so I didn't think it would hurt to ask."

"Smart." My throat feels like it's constricting. Will tapes only prove I was just a bystander in this family in my father's eyes? "Hey, I've got to go."

"So the launch party?"

"Ask me next week."

When I end the call, I'm antsy. Unsettled. Not used to the confines of this small hotel room, I need some fresh air.

But haven't I felt that way all day even when I have been in the fresh air?

Ellery.

Isn't that what prompted my restlessness? This . . . irritation?

There must be a simple answer to why she cancelled the dress fitting. Her lack of explanation only served to muddy the waters even more.

Desire is a son of a bitch when you can't act on it.

A run. Some exercise.

That's what I need to clear my head. The ocean. The moonlight. Some exertion. Distance from her and her perfume that I catch whiffs of every now and again.

It's been less than a week here, and I already feel like I'm going fucking crazy. I knew I wanted her. I knew it would be tempting with her so close. What I didn't know is that it was going to be absolute bedlam to my system every time she gets close to me.

Talk about torture.

I fling open the door to my room and head out into the hallway. I reach the corner and pull up when I come face-to-face with Ellery.

She's standing there, face scrubbed fresh from makeup and hair piled on top of her head. She has an oversized sweatshirt on that's lopsided, exposing one shoulder, and a pair of tiny shorts that display her killer legs.

Yeah, desire is definitely a son of a bitch.

"Hi," she says, her smile sheepish as she takes a bite of an ice cream bar.

"Hi."

Who knew the sight of one shoulder could be so sexy?

"I'm sneaking an ice cream bar. You caught me."

"Why do you have to sneak it?"

"Because that's what women do. If we eat it and no one sees us, then the calories don't count."

"So it's only if someone sees you that they count?"

She nods, her bun bobbing with it. "And now you've saved me the hassle of having to hide the wrapper in the trash."

"There's a whole routine to this, isn't there?"

The bun bobs again as she eyes me up and down. "Where are you going?"

"For a run."

"Like that makes me feel better." She snorts. "This is why you have muscles that have definition, and I have curves that are squishy."

"There's nothing squishy about your curves, Ellery." The comment is out without thought. Her cheeks flush, but her eyes never back down from my stare.

She nods. "Then maybe I should eat another ice cream bar while you jog. Since these calories count now, and those won't since you won't see them. And getting a few more milligrams of calcium is never a bad thing."

"I think you should."

"Never openly encourage a woman to eat more ice cream. It will cause an irrational and obsessive attachment to the person doing the encouraging." She flashes a grin that reminds me of the first night when I thought she was adorable before I saw her as sexy.

Right now, I'm trying to hold on to that picture of adorable because this woman does things to me that shouldn't be legal.

"I'll try to remember that."

"You should. It'll save you someday."

"I'm eternally grateful." I place a hand to my chest and mock bow.

"Go. Run. Before my irrationality sets in," she says as I simply stare at her and shake my head. "What? Why are you looking at me like that?"

Because the more I know you, the more you surprise me . . . and that's not a bad thing at all.

"No reason." I go to jog past her at the same time she moves to the right to let me. Too bad I went to her right too.

We collide against each other, the ice cream bar in between us. Its chill hits my skin, and at the same time she yelps and jumps back.

We both look down at the vanilla ice cream mark squarely in the middle of my bare chest.

"Oh my God. I'm so sorry. Let me—" She reaches out with her bare hand to wipe the ice cream away, but once her hand connects, she realizes her hand isn't going to do any good.

Thoughts of her tongue on my skin as she licks up the ice cream invade my thoughts. Own them. The heat of it. The feel of it. *Christ.*

I force a swallow down my throat as her hand stills and her blue eyes flutter up to meet mine.

Time stands still for the briefest of moments as I realize my hand is on her wrist and her face is inches from mine.

She's off limits, Ford.

Fucking off limits.

I draw in a ragged breath. Lips part, but words aren't voiced as the tension practically snaps between us.

Does she have any clue how bad I fucking want her? Since that first night stranded here. Since seeing her again at the auction. Every minute of every goddamn day I think about her in some way, shape, or form . . . and the notion of her tongue on my chest isn't helping matters any.

"Oops," she finally says, her smile widening but her eyes steadfast on mine.

"Don't worry about it," I murmur as I consciously try to remove my fingers from her wrist and take a step back. "Next time I know to go to your left." She nods, her eyes looking at my chest and then back to my eyes. "And now you really need another one since I just ruined that one."

"Yes. Sure. Okay." Her words come out in a stilted staccato.

I need to get out of here before I do something I'm going to regret. Like pin her up against the wall and kiss her until that ice cream bar is a melted puddle on the floor.

I take another step back, the smile on my lips strained. "I'm going to go. Take my run."

She nods and runs her tongue over her thumb where ice cream has dripped. I grit my teeth. "I'm going to get another ice cream."

"Save one for me, will you?"

She takes a bite of the mess that's left of her bar, her lips closing around the chocolate innocently as I wipe the ice cream off with the shirt in my hand, but my imagination has already been fired. "So you're one of *those.*"

"That doesn't exactly sound like a positive statement."

"Most people don't go for a run and then eat ice cream." Her eyes scrape down my torso. "Do abs just appear out of nowhere as you sleep too? There's an ab. Oops, and another one. I mean, how do you ever get any sleep with all these abs forming left and right?"

I throw my head back and laugh, grateful for the levity to interrupt my thoughts. "It's a hard job—"

"But somebody's got to do it," she murmurs.

I give her one last look before turning and pushing open the door.

Run.

Distance.

I need to keep my distance from her and from fucking things up.

And if taking a run every minute of every damn night while I'm here will help achieve that, then I guess I'm going to be the fittest damn guy on the planet. *With self-growing abs apparently.* Can't say I mind that she noticed.

Seems fair given I stare at her hot-as-sin body every chance that I get. Squishy curves, my ass.

CHAPTER TWENTY-ONE

Ellery

"Y OU'RE KIDDING ME, RIGHT?"

"I wish I were, Ms. Sinclair—"

"Ellery." I correct our demolition crew foreman for what feels like the hundredth time. If there is one thing I know about being a woman in construction, it's don't let anyone call you Miss or Ms. or ma'am. And sure as hell, not sweetie or honey. Any chance you give a man to reassert that you're a woman is a chance for you to be handled with kid gloves when all you want is to be treated like just one of the guys.

"Ellery," he says as I nod. "I wish I were."

I roll my shoulders and stare at him while feeling like my head is going to explode. "So let me get this straight. Your crew all came down with the stomach flu at the same time?"

He nods but doesn't meet my eyes. The question is why? "Yes, ma'am."

"And you have no other crew you can replace them with?"

His sigh is heavy. "I don't. No. You knew we were doing you a favor and traveling outside of our normal coverage area. They were all staying together in the hotel in town. The bug cycled through them."

"Well, fuck."

"I know it puts you in a tough position. I can make calls to some of the firms I know around here, but with the local union here on strike, I'm not sure how much help I can be."

I twist my lips and place my hands on my hips as I turn and take in the drywall-dusted debris disaster before me.

"I have plumbing and framing coming tomorrow for that wing, and they don't have any wiggle room on the schedule," I say more to myself than to James. This is the problem with an expedited schedule. Trades aren't moving in, finishing their work, and then moving out once the whole site is complete. We have them coming and going at all times for each of the varying renovations in various locations. It allows us to get one thing done and finish it in totality while other rooms are in partial stages.

It's perfect in theory.

Until it's not.

And right now . . . it's not.

"I know you don't. Believe me, I know." His sigh sounds like the stress that was just heaped on my shoulders. "But I'm here. I've found two day laborers who can help with some of the less technical tasks. Between them and me . . . and maybe anyone else you can spare, we can try to get as much done as possible."

"Thanks. Let me see what I can do." I take a few steps away, already frazzled when it's only seven a.m.

I lean my back against some rough framing and sigh as I fire off a text.

Me: My demo crew?

Joshua: What about it?

Me: A whole crew out sick. One you often use.

Joshua: Maybe they don't like working for you.

Me: Don't fuck with me, D.

Joshua: I don't need to. You'll fuck this up enough by yourself.

Me: Asshole.

Joshua: True, but I didn't touch them.

I stare at my screen with pursed lips and debate if I believe him or not. Is he that stupid that he'd try to screw me over when he believes my success will ultimately benefit him?

No. I might not be his biggest fan, but he's too selfish to do anything to jeopardize something he could gain from.

And now I'm left with the bare bones of a crew, a schedule I can't budge much with, and only hours to figure out how to fix the issue.

The worst part?

Now I need to hunt down Ford to heap bad on top of worse with the news reporting this morning that a summer storm is going to hit us in a few days. It won't exactly hinder our progress inside the inn, but it will slow things down on the café, kitchen, and rooftop bar.

Sure, our first week started off with a bang. It was productive. We further finessed our construction schedule as well as agreed upon interior choices so our designer could get everything ordered. Furniture, light sconces, fixtures, and everything in between had been selected. We have little room for errors or not being on the same page with our turnaround time to get this place back up and running so quickly.

And yes, Ford and I sat side by side or across the table while making these decisions, but every other waking moment has held a healthy distance between us. No more bumping into each other in the hallway while he goes out for a run, and I eat my ice cream. No more drinks on the boardwalk. Just grunts in response and him conveniently busy on a call whenever I need to talk to him.

Grumpy Ford has returned with a vengeance.

His father's biography is the only thing I can pinpoint as being the external source of annoyance. The few times the book and its impending release have been mentioned on the television in the old bar—kept for our entertainment's sake—he's promptly turned it off. Even his phone calls to his brothers—or at least the ones I've been within earshot of—seem clipped.

Either that or the honeymoon phase between us is over, the newness has worn off, and he's realizing he just doesn't like me.

It happens.

But it's worrisome when we have so much further to go and a contract—and this property—binding us together.

"Ford," I state as he walks by, head down, answering a text.

He stops and looks up. "Yeah?"

"Bad news," I say and then explain the situation with the help of James.

"I can help. Put me to work," Ford states when we're both done. "No offense, James, but putting a sledgehammer through some drywall doesn't seem like rocket science."

"No offense taken, but you really want to?" James asks, clearly shocked that a Sharpe is willing to get dirty.

"Yes." Ford flashes a smile. "I could use something to smash to hell to take my frustration out on."

"Follow me, then," James says.

The work may look easy, but it's exhausting. It's not just the weight of the sledgehammer that tires your muscles, but it's pulling the tool out once it's stuck in the drywall. It's the Sawzall vibrating as you cut the non-load-bearing walls and then hitting the beams with a hammer to knock them out of place.

And of course, since it's all hands on deck, I decide to help too. Ford shouldn't be the only one who has to switch gears.

"For like the hundredth time, Ellery, I can do this on my own," Ford groans when I grunt as I try to kick a cut two-by-four free.

My arms ache and my eyes burn despite the safety goggles, but I refuse to show any sign of it. "I know you can, but why should you get all the fun?"

"Fun?" He snorts.

This is anything but fun. However, I feel the need to prove I'm pulling my weight, especially given this strange weirdness between us. And if this shows that, then I'm here for it.

"Sinclair."

I wave the dust that's floating in the air away from my face and look toward one of our plumbers who is working upstairs. "Yeah?"

"Just walked past the lobby. Someone's looking for you."

"For me?"

"Guy in a suit. He's not too thrilled about the dust." He chuckles.

"Thanks." I set my sledgehammer against the wall and wipe the dust off the front of my jeans out of habit, despite how futile it is. When I glance up, Ford is standing across the room staring at me, and I just shrug as I walk out of the soon-to-be luxury suite.

As I turn the corner, I come to a halt when I see Chandler, stiff and definitely out of place, at the entrance to the inn.

He's picking something off the shoulder of his perfectly tailored suit, and no doubt his Bruno Magli shoes are gathering drywall dust simply because he's standing there.

Fish out of water.

"Chandler? What are you doing here?" I ask as I move toward him at a hurried pace. Almost as if I need to get to him before someone else does because he doesn't belong here.

Which is a totally irrational thought, but one I feel nonetheless.

The last place I want my past mixing with my future.

"Surprise." He holds his hands out to his sides. "I wanted to come and see how things were going."

"Why? Last we talked, you told me you hoped I'd be railroaded so I'd come running back to you with my tail tucked between my legs."

"Come on, now," he says as I stop before him. "Don't exaggerate." His expression sours as he takes a long look at me from head to toe. "Forgive me for not giving you a hug, but you're filthy."

When did he become such a prima donna?

I grin in response. "I know."

He studies me with an intensity and disbelief that is almost comical. "Is the charade over? I mean"—he gestures to me as a whole—"this really isn't you."

But it is. And that's on me because I was willing to marry a man who never took the time to see it.

My smile is placating. Condescending. "We're awful busy today."

"You can make time for me."

My smile is frozen in place as our foreman, Roddy, walks by and takes in the two of us standing there. I can already feel his judgment without him even uttering a word. Three months ago, I wouldn't have thought twice about standing next to Chandler, but I already feel like such a different person than the one who agreed to marry him.

It's crazy how perspective can do that to you.

"Clearly you're making progress," Chandler says to fill the awkward silence.

"Hmm."

"Sharpe has made a good choice on changing the front elevation of the building. It'll have cleaner lines and a more timeless esthetic. He really knows his—"

"Those were my choices."

Chandler's eyes snap over to mine, his condescending chuckle telling me he doesn't believe me. He doesn't believe either I'm capable of making educated decisions such as this or that Fordham Sharpe would ever let a woman make decisions for him.

Neither can be further from the truth.

And both piss me off.

"Like I said. We're swamped today. A whole crew has called in sick and we have a serious deadline to meet. Thanks for stopping by, but—"

"C'mon, Ellery." He reaches out and tries to lace his fingers through mine. I stiffen in response, repulsion the only thing I feel. "I made the effort to come all this way, the least you can do is show me around."

CHAPTER TWENTY-TWO

Ford

FUCKING PRICK.

I smash the sledgehammer into the drywall.

Fiancée, my ass.

The thud of it hitting the gypsum does nothing to abate the jealousy that streaked through me when he put his hand on her back.

Chandler Holcomb with his pretentious smile and condescending tone. He probably practices that smug smile in the mirror every morning. Little does he know it makes him look like an asshole.

How can she like him?

How can she want a man who looks at her as *less than* instead of as an equal?

Because he sure as fuck does. It was in the stupid questions he asked her. In the patronizing comments he made that clearly questioned her and her abilities. In the way he made it known to every person he talked to that she was his.

He made my blood boil.

And the fact that she is with him and looked so miserable being beside him, does even more so.

She deserves so much better.

She deserves . . . *me.*

I grunt as I lift the hammer up again, trying to work through the anger seeing him here created. *Why did she invite him here?*

Thunder rumbles outside as the storm moves in. Fitting for my mood. Fitting for an excuse as to why I need to keep going despite everyone already having left the site.

Lift. Smash. Yank.

I create a rhythm of destruction. A soundtrack to accompany my racing thoughts.

The plan is to do this until I collapse from exhaustion. Until I can no longer think. Until I can no longer want.

In theory anyway.

There is contentment in putting in the labor that I never expected. In tearing something down to build it back up. To having my hands dirty and my shirt sweaty.

I know the minute she's there.

I can faintly smell her perfume, even with the dust suffocating the room, before I hear her footsteps.

But I don't turn. I don't look. I keep working.

Lift. Smash. Yank.

Everything is pent-up—desire, rage, confusion, need—and it's best if I leave it all the fuck alone.

"Are you enjoying the show or are you going to say something?" I snip at her.

Lift.

"We have a problem."

Smash.

"Of course, we have a problem." *His name is Chandler Holcomb.*

Yank.

"The helpers today? The day laborers we were able to get to help?"

"What about them?" I don't even stop to look at her.

"They, uh . . . they took down the wall of your room."

"Great. Perfect. Par for the fucking course. I can sleep on the beach for all I care."

"You do that."

"Better than being in here with you," I mutter.

"What's your fucking problem, Sharpe?" she asks, stepping into my periphery.

Don't look, Ford. "My problem?" Do. Not. Look. "I don't have a problem."

"Could've fooled the fuck out of me."

"Wouldn't be hard now, would it?" I grunt as I hit the last large piece of drywall still intact.

"Will you stop for a second?" she yells.

"I've got to get this done. Got to stay on schedule. Got to—" She yanks on my bicep as my arm is in mid-swing. I drop the sledgehammer with a thud and turn on her, a ball of fury in my gut. "Are you fucking crazy?" I shout.

"Clearly I am for agreeing to do this project with you, a moody, asshole-ish fucker."

"Sorry if that was meant to be an insult . . . but it wasn't."

"I don't care." She puts her hands on her hips and huffs.

"Yes, you do."

She steps into me, her finger hitting my chest with each word. "No. I. Don't." I snort and shake my head at her. It seems that's more than enough to set her off. "You are the most pigheaded, frustrating person I have ever met."

"Me?" I kick a piece of wood. "Everything has to be your goddamn way. On your time frame. And God forbid I value your opinions and input—"

"What are you—"

"I don't take orders from anybody, Sinclair, least of all you."

"Tough shit. You're stuck with me."

Therein lies the problem.

"Tough shit?" I counter.

"You heard me. You can take all of your I'm-A-Sharpe-I-Rule-The-World bullshit and shove it where the sun don't shine."

I laugh. Head back, body shaking. She's like a ball of fire in a pixie's body and God, how I want that body.

So why is she like that with me and not her prick of a fiancé?

"You're a real piece of work, Elle."

Her smile drips with sarcasm much like her words do when she speaks. "Yep. Sure am. I'll gladly take this piece of work and *actually work* instead of purposefully avoiding you at all costs like you do me."

"Perfect. Please do. But your feet have to be moving in order to do that so . . . run along."

"Excuse me?"

"You heard me."

"You know what? Never mind. I'm going to stay right here just to piss you off. Since you don't like me—"

"Don't like you?" I bellow as I drag a hand through my hair and take a few steps away from her. *"Don't like you?* Jesus fucking Christ, Ellery, all I can think about every day, every goddamn moment, is how bad I fucking like you." I turn to meet her eyes. *"How bad I fucking want you.* But I'm trying to respect you. Respect our partnership. And the fact that you're engaged to that pretentious prick who was here earlier. So excuse me for staying the fuck away from you, for avoiding you, but Jesus, a man can only take so much."

She stands before me, a disaster of a mess. Hair sticking out of her ponytail, drywall dust on her cheek, a scratch with dried blood on her arm, and just blinks at me like I'm fucking crazy.

Well, it feels that way.

"What did you just say?" she whispers.

"You heard me." My voice is ten times louder.

"No, actually I didn't."

"I called your fiancé a pretentious prick who came to mark his territory for all to see while walking around here like he owns the place when in fact, it's you who does. Me who does. That's what I fucking said."

"He's not my fiancé."

My laugh is loud and mocking. "Yeah. Sure. That's not what the newspaper said at the I'm-an-Asshole-Architect-of-the-Year award ceremony the last week."

Ellery looks at me with a clarity I haven't seen before. "He's not my fiancé. I went with him so he could save face." To save face? *Pretentious and a fucking pathetic excuse for a man.* She takes a few steps toward me. "But that's not what I meant when I asked you what you just said. Say it again."

"What? That he's a pretentious prick?"

"No, you stubborn ass. The other part."

She's close. Too close. I reach out to pick a piece of drywall from her hair as I rack my brain to remember the word vomit I just spewed.

I squeeze my eyes shut, knowing damn well what I said. Desperate to repeat it. Terrified at the same time. "You mean the part about how bad I fucking want you?"

She nods and swallows forcibly as her eyes dart to my lips. "We're partners, Ford."

"I'm aware."

"It would be a mistake to . . ." Her voice cracks, and I nod.

"It would. But it would also be a travesty not to."

She runs a hand down my chest. "Is that so?"

"Mm-hmm," I murmur as I reach out and cup the side of her face with my hand.

She leans in, the warmth of her breath hitting my lips as she whispers, "But I prefer mistakes over travesties any day."

"Thank fuck for that." The groan I emit as I drag her against me is accented by the thunder that rumbles outside. My body coils tight as my lips find hers. As my mouth takes, my tongue delves, and my every sensation wants.

Jesus Christ. *I was right.*

This woman. Her taste. Fucking addictive.

And I can't get enough.

Drywall dust falls all around us as her hands fist in my hair and our mouths meet over and over and over in what feels like a free-for-all that both of us are lost in. That both of us never want to be found in.

We move backwards as our hands claim and our lips demand.

More.

Now.

I need more.

Of her.

Of this.

Of the moment.

Just fucking her.

"Ford," she groans as I lace open-mouthed kisses up the exposed line of her neck. "I don't want to want you, but I'm so tired of trying not to."

I fist my hand in her hair and pull her head back so I can meet her eyes. "Then stop trying."

And fuck do her lips tempt me. Do they own me. Do they call for me to have every goddamn ounce of restraint I can muster while shredding it simultaneously.

Then stop trying.

I heed my own advice and delve back in with my tongue and lips and hands as she pulls my shirt over my head, and I fumble with the clasp of her bra beneath hers.

We stumble through doorways as we push down our pants and trip over shoes as we try to toe them off.

I look for somewhere to lay her down. Somewhere that's not covered in dust or dangerous because time is of the essence, and I simply don't have the willpower to wait any longer.

As it is, I feel like I've been waiting a lifetime.

"Here," she murmurs as her hand that slides between my boxer briefs and my cock finds purchase.

My groan is guttural, but it's got nothing on the sensations overwhelming me right now.

The taste of her kiss.

The smell of her skin.

The demand in her touch.

The sound of her pleas.

Fuck this woman is going to drive me mad if I'm not inside her right fucking now.

"Ellery," I say as we bump against the door she's opening and push our way into her room.

We're a mess of fumbling hands and busy mouths as we kick off our pants and kiss each other without coming up for air.

Desperation like I've never known eats at me, claws at me, consumes me.

"Wait," she murmurs as she steps away and heads to the bathroom, giving me a damn fine view of her ass as she swings her hips.

I take the moment, brief as it is, to shake the drywall dust from my hair as best I can, and then stroke my cock as I wait for her.

When her feet pad back into the room, I look up to find Ellery Sinclair, little miss prepared, holding up a condom by her fingertips with a taunting smile on her lips.

"You brought condoms?" I ask as I take it from her and tear the foil with my teeth.

"*This* was inevitable. I knew. I prepared for it." She wraps a hand around my dick and squeezes. "And God, how I want it."

If I weren't already turned on, I'd be there in an instant with that comment and from her confidence.

She watches me as I roll the condom on, and the minute I'm done, her hands are on my ass, tugging me toward the bed as her lips tell me what she wants.

"I want you to fuck me, Ford. Long. Deep. Hard," she murmurs against my lips as my hands palm her breasts. Her breath hitches from the sensation. "We'll have time for foreplay another time, but right now . . . right now, I just want you. I want this."

She slides her hand over my jacketed cock and all restraint is lost.

"Get on the bed," I order. She sits her ass down and scoots back, her knees bent and her pussy on display.

Fuck.

That body I saw last week—the one I've dreamt of, fantasized over— is even better than I thought as she lies before me naked and wanting.

And fuck if I'm not going to enjoy every goddamn inch of it. The line of her thigh. The curve of her hip. The bow of her back. The hardened peak of her pink breast. The insatiable taste of her tongue.

"You're . . . stunning," I whisper as I crawl onto the bed, kiss the inside of one of her knees, and trail my fingertip over the other. "Gorgeous." Another kiss to the top of her mound. I breathe her in. Arousal and Ellery is an addictive combination. "Sexy." A kiss on her abdomen before I lick around her nipple and suck on it. Her back arches and a moaned sigh escapes her mouth—such a fucking turn-on. "Incredible," I say against her lips before slipping my tongue between them in a slow, languorous kiss that puts every one of my nerves on high alert.

She scratches her nails down my chest, making my cock jerk in anticipation and digs them into my thighs, begging to have me.

The woman doesn't have to ask again.

I sit up on my haunches and use my hand to run the tip of my cock up and down her slit. Her arousal glistens in the dim light as I push my way between her pink lips. I inch myself in ever so slowly, Ellery's moan of "So good" the only encouragement I need.

And when I'm fully seated inside her, after her breath hitches and her neck arches as she acclimates to the fullness, she looks back up and meets my eyes, almost as if to dare me to take her to the brink.

Her heat.

Her tightness.

Her wetness.

Fucking hell, yes, I will.

I begin to move, in soft, slow thrusts so I can pay attention to her every nerve. My hands grip the flesh on her hips as my eyes flicker between the pleasure blanketing her face and the indescribable turn-on of watching myself push into her and then slide all the way back out.

She feels . . . incredible. Like I want to go fast but am trying my hardest to go slow so that I can make this pleasure last. So that I can bring her with me to the edge.

"Ford. Yes," she whispers as her hands grip the sheets beside her, prompting me to pick up the pace some.

To bring my thumb to the top of her slit and add friction to her clit. Her gasp and panted breaths are all I need to know that I'm giving her what she needs while I take what I want.

I fuck harder and hold tighter to her hips as desperation takes over. The room is filled with the sounds of our bodies connecting. The slick withdrawal and push back into her. Our labored breaths.

Over and over.

In and out.

Yes. Now. Harder. Right there. *Oh my God.*

I squeeze my eyes shut to hold myself back, to wait my turn, but it's a fucking brutal struggle as I work her clit, faster, harder.

Her legs tense and her back bows seconds before her cry echoes around the walls of the room.

Her pussy tightens like a vise around me and fuck, I'm a goner. An absolute, fucking goner.

"Elle," I say when by the look on her—eyes closed, mouth lax, nipples hardened—I know she can't hear me. She's swamped in her own pleasure. "Elle." I draw the word out as every part of me that aches and burns in the best of ways ignites from my lower belly to my cock to my balls.

I jerk my hips, consciousness fading, as I absorb wave after wave of absolute bliss that burns white-hot as it courses through me.

Over and over.

Just like the pulsing of her muscles around me.

I drag a hand down the center of her chest and the goosebumps that chase over her skin.

Christ. *This woman.*

I knew she'd be incredible, that sex with her would be incredible, I just didn't know that the minute I had her, I was going to want her again.

I think this might be a problem.

But fuck if it's not one I'm willing to overcome by fucking her again and again.

CHAPTER TWENTY-THREE

Ellery

WHAT JUST HAPPENED?

I mean, I know *what* happened, but . . . holy shit *what now?*

A slow smile crawls over my lips as I stare at the ice cream bar I'm holding, knowing damn well that the satisfaction I once found in it has been replaced with a new craving. A new desire I want to enjoy in the darkness and keep to myself.

I close my eyes and smile, wanting to relive every delicious moment we just had together. And make no bones about it, it was incredible in every sense of the word.

But what now?

How do we go forward, be partners, when we just threw something neither of us expected into the mix?

I shift in my chair in the small alcove we've designated as a kitchen. It's nothing special—a table, a few chairs, a refrigerator—but it has a killer view of the beach, even now when I'm sitting in the dark.

"Having regrets already?" The deep tenor of his voice rumbles through the room, followed by the scent of soap from the shower he just had.

I don't speak. I'm not even sure what to say, so I continue to look out the windows in front of me and take another bite of my ice cream bar.

"Okay then," he murmurs when the silence stretches before stepping up beside me, turning a chair around, and sitting on it backwards. "I guess we'll sit here until you figure out what you want to say."

Why does he have to be so charming?

It's a huge problem because it makes him irresistible.

He's supposed to be my business partner. He's supposed to be learned and knowledgeable—*not* incredibly good at sex. He's not supposed to be charming and inviting and forgiving when I'm at a loss for words.

Without asking, he grabs my ice cream bar, takes a bite, and then hands it back to me as if it's no big deal.

Apparently, he doesn't have problems with sharing . . . unless it's with Chandler.

Chandler.

Is he who started all of this? Is he who I have to thank for some of the best sex of my life? I mean, sex for the first time with someone is usually a little awkward and not always that enjoyable. Sure, you both know what part fits where, but the rhythm is typically off. The coordination and the knowledge of what the other person needs isn't there.

Leave it to Fordham Sharpe to blow that notion to smithereens.

My thighs clench just thinking about it.

"I can't imagine what you must think of me," I finally say.

"Meaning?"

"Meaning Chandler was here one minute, and then we're . . . *you know*, the next."

"Sex, Elle. We were having sex. Pretty incredible sex I might add. Should I be worried that you're thinking of Chandler right now instead of me?"

"I'm not thinking of him." I sigh. "I'm thinking of you. Of what you probably think of—"

"For starters, I'm thinking you need to stop thinking." He chuckles. "And second, I'm starting to doubt myself and my skills if you're this depressed."

I laugh. "I'm not. It's just . . ."

"You're wondering if we fucked things up, right?" he asks as he rests a hand on my lower back. A charge jolts through me from his touch.

"Well . . . it's not exactly the smartest move we've made."

"You're regretting it already? Jesus. At least let the post-coital glow fade before you start to wish I didn't exist," he teases. "Talk about a blow to a man's ego. If the high doesn't last longer than a cringe of regret, I'm definitely not doing it right."

I glance his way and can't help the smile that slides onto my lips. "I'm not regretting it. No. And your ego should hold just fine. There are definitely no complaints here."

"Then why are you sitting in the dark like you're wallowing in every female emotion that I don't think I care to understand?"

"Because we both know we just made a huge mistake."

"Perhaps. Perhaps not. Only time will tell," he murmurs.

I turn to face him for the first time. His hair is wet and in waves. His jaw is unshaven, his eyes clear. How is it possible that a human being can be this attractive?

"Ford." My sigh is uncertain. "How exactly are we going to work together when we've seen each other naked?"

His smile is lopsided. "You forget that we'd already seen each other naked and have seemed to be able to work with each other just fine."

"That's not what I mean, and you know it."

"It's not?" He feigns naivety.

"No."

He shifts in his chair so that his knee bumps mine. "Then do you mean how are we supposed to look at each other, work side by side, and me not remember what it feels like to be inside you? Or remember what you taste like?" His eyes hold mine as every part of my body aches to remember and know all those things again *already*. "*Now that?* That might pose a little more of a problem, but I have a feeling we'll manage just fine."

The man sure talks a good game. Unfortunately for me, I know he can back it up too.

"You're not worried about what happens next?"

"You mean the part where we finish the ice cream and go to bed? Yeah, I don't have a room anymore since the wall was knocked in, so of course I'm worried about that. I don't exactly have anywhere to sleep."

"You're not funny."

He chuckles. "I am. You know I am." He squeezes my thigh, leaving his hand there. "I'm not sure what you want me to say, Ellery. There's no one here to watch one of us do the walk of shame. Frankly, there is no need to because, I don't know about you, but I'm not ashamed of what we just did." The boyish grin he flashes should be illegal. "Plus, I'm all out of scarlet letters to pin to your chest, so unless you've brought some with you in your luggage, it's not like anyone else is going to know."

"Why is this so easy for you?"

"Probably the same reason it's so hard for you."

"Meaning?"

"Meaning I've wanted you since that first night. Well, not at first. At first, I was pissed at my brothers and wanted to be left alone. The last thing I wanted was to chat with some random woman. And then you"—he chuckles—"kind of made a shitty situation better."

There he goes again being honest when most men would typically grunt in response.

I open my mouth and then close it. How do I even respond?

"Would it be easier on you if I said yes, it was a mistake? That we had an itch, we scratched it, and now we're sated? That it was a one-time thing, curiosity satisfied, and now we can go on like it never happened?"

He's saying all the things I've told myself in my head, but hearing him say my thoughts aloud sounds ridiculous.

"Sure. Yes." I croak the words out.

His smirk says he doesn't believe a word I'm saying. Neither do I. "Great. Then that's how we'll play this. It was a mistake. An immoral, egregious, *satisfying* mistake." He leans forward and for the briefest of moments, I hold my breath, anticipating one of his mind-numbing kisses. I tell myself I don't want it, but damn if I'm not disappointed when his lips find my ear, his warm breath tickling the skin there.

"Ford—"

"The best part about mistakes is sometimes you have to make them a couple times to know if they're good ones or bad ones. I'm not picky, Elle. I'll take either one when it comes to you." He leans back and nods. "Now if you'll excuse me, I need to go find a place to sleep for the night." I slowly exhale as he steps away, eyes still locked on mine. "Good night, Ellery."

I watch him move toward the door. My head, my body, and my reasoning feel like it's all on spin cycle so I can't find my footing.

"Ford," I say when he reaches the door. I stand as he turns around to face me.

"Hmm?"

"I broke it off with Chandler weeks ago." I shift on my feet, my fingers twisting together in front of me. "I'm not sure why I feel the need to tell you that. But I did. I'm the one who ended things."

"Why?" It's a single syllable and yet I feel like so much is riding on my response. I can't read the look in his eyes across the distance, and for that I'm grateful.

"That's the part that doesn't make any sense to me. *The why.*"

He drops his head for a second and then looks back up. The playfulness that was there moments ago is now gone. "I was keeping my distance because you belonged to someone else, and I'm not a cheater. Perhaps *you* need to explore *the why.*"

Our eyes meet again as lightning flashes.

When he turns on his heel to walk away, it takes everything I have not to chase after him. To explain. To justify.

But I know why I don't.

I know if I say it out loud then I'll have no other choice than to face the truth myself.

And I'm not ready to do that just yet because it scares the shit out of me.

CHAPTER TWENTY-FOUR

Ellery

Twelve Years Ago

"ELLERY?"

"What?" My eyes are bleary and after staring at the computer for hours, I feel like I have a pound of sand in them. My finals are brutal this year. Aren't they always? But nothing but the best is allowed in the Sinclair/Haywood household. Not even when they're the last finals I'm ever going to take as a high schooler. Sullying the Haywood family name with mediocrity isn't something that will be tolerated as I was once so blatantly told. "I said *what?*" I snap.

I know I'll be reprimanded. Garland Haywood always demands respect. Being snippy or talking back isn't deemed *respectful* even if it's two in the freaking morning.

"Elle?" His reaction is the exact opposite of what I expected. It's quiet when I expected loud. Subdued when I anticipated agitation.

When I look up, I know something is wrong.

My fingers pause on my keyboard.

My body tenses.

And before he says another word, I already know. I've had this feeling once before.

"Mom?" Her name is a hoarse whisper, and the world slowly falls out from under me.

"Ellery—"

"Stop saying my name," I shout, hoping I'll never hear it again. Ever. He starts to speak, but I cover my ears like a little girl. Like I did when my mom told me that my dad was gone.

He steps into my room, his eyes locked on mine, and for a man normally devoid of all emotion, the lone tear that escapes and drops down his cheek confirms what I already know.

No.

No.

No!

This can't be happening.

Why is this happening?

Not again.

Please not again.

Don't do this to me, Mom.

Don't you fucking leave me too.

I rise from my desk. Each step he takes toward me is another I take backward, head shaking, the word no on repeat.

"I'm sorry, Elle. There was a car accident. A drunk driver crossed the median . . . I'm so sorry." My fists beat against his chest as he tries to gather me against him.

I don't want him.

I don't want his comfort.

I just want my mom.

Mom, how can you leave me here too?

I can't. I can't do this again. This constant, never-ending pain.

Why did *you* leave me?

I've done this before. I know the drill. The steps to go through. The words to say to pretend I'm okay. The pain that comes when the door closes . . . and everyone is gone. The feel of warm tears sliding down my cheeks and onto the pillow.

The pretending that everything *is going to be* okay . . . when you know your world is irrevocably, tragically changed.

I'll never go through this again.

There's no one left to lose.

Now, I'm truly alone.

Everyone I've ever loved has died.

Numb.

There are no other words to describe what I feel. I don't even have the power to ask *how*. I feel . . .

Gray.

The world has been leeched of color without her to brighten it up.

Everyone leaves.

Loving me is simply not enough of a reason to stay.

CHAPTER TWENTY-FIVE

Ellery

THE NEXT FEW DAYS ARE COMPLETE CHAOS.

There's a reason construction sites follow a set schedule of when specific trades perform what. Where their work falls in the scheme of things. If they're on-site simultaneously, the site is too crowded. Accidents can happen.

But we're not a normal site.

We have so many different phases going inside our little world. Some rooms are stripped to the studs while others are being overhauled and prepped for new paint and flooring.

All the trades are here, everywhere at once.

I welcome the chaos. The shouting that someone is in someone's way. The questions about how the hell is this feasible. The cacophony of sound that pulls me here and there and everywhere.

And being busy is good. Not having a single second to think is wanted at this point in time because every time I have a free moment, my mind goes right back to him.

To Ford.

To a few nights ago. To the sensations he evoked and to the open-ended question he left me with. To the clarity it roused and the questions still unanswered.

Is that why I've been *pulling a Ford?* Avoiding him? Keeping my distance? Making sure we're not alone together for more than a few supervised seconds around tradesmen?

And is that why he's on the same page? Or at least I think he is, because every time I go to the kitchen area after everyone has left or flip the

TV on for a few minutes of mindlessness, he suddenly needs to be any-where but with me.

The irony is, he's making himself scarce, which is only serving to make me want his company more.

And not just for sex, although I wouldn't object to more of that once I straighten my own head out.

But more for his friendship. For our easy conversations that can be deep or shallow but that make me laugh and feel valued.

The absence only reinforces the fact that I'm often alone here. Lonely. Isolated in a sense.

At home, I have friends. While I never let them in too much or let them get too close, at least I have someone to meet up with for drinks after work or grab a coffee with on a lazy Sunday morning. I never realized how much that companionship mattered until I didn't have it.

But here it's me. It's Ford. It's an inn that's in complete disarray. There's very little outside contact other than a quick drive to the supermarket across town or an absent conversation with the food delivery driver.

It's Sunday and, for the first time since we "broke ground" so to speak, the inn is void of workers. Because of our accelerated schedule, different crews are here around the clock. And while that commotion is overwhelm-ing, it also prevents any downtime. It prevents me from realizing the sol-itude in the silence, something I seem to be an expert at. Especially since I lost my mom.

I glance up to the rooftop bar in the making. To where Ford has made his pseudo flat—where he sleeps and works. To where he's currently oc-cupied with his other job—Sharpe International stuff. A conference call with people on the other side of the world—or Mars, for all I know. Or maybe he's doing nothing more than sitting in the same solitude I am but enjoying it.

Fordham Sharpe.

He was supposed to be off limits. Supposed to be a look-from-af-ar-but-don't-touch. And now I can't stop thinking about him, and in the odd times that I'm able to, of course, that's when he needs to speak to me.

But I'm old enough to know how this story ends. And it's not a hap-pily ever after like the one I got to in my book but didn't finish last night.

Then again, I'm not into happily ever after. I'm into the now. Into some good sex and enjoying the moment. I'm into the presumption that the couple I'm reading about will stay together.

Maybe that's why I never read the epilogues. Maybe I know that love ends in pain, in being left behind, and I want to suspend disbelief that it won't for my fictional friends.

And even in knowing this, in acknowledging that the physical is all I'm ever after and never the emotional connection, why is it that sleeping with Ford scares the hell out of me?

Is it because for the first time in forever, I have someone on my side who believes in me? *Maybe I value that more than a fleeting orgasm.*

Then again, why can't I have both? The support and the great sex?

It is the twenty-first century, after all.

I take a sip of my wine and stare out at the ocean and its never-ending horizon. Seagulls squawk. The waves crash. My thoughts run as the notion takes hold.

I want Ford again.

"Hey, you."

Ford takes a seat beside me, leaning back with his elbows in the sand and his feet crossed at the ankles, before I can even respond.

"Hi."

"It's weird for it to be so quiet inside," he says as he reaches up and tugs on my ponytail.

"I know. That's partly why I'm out here."

"Does the other part have anything to do with me?" He lifts an eyebrow as our stare holds, and I shrug. "Fair enough."

"I know the answer to *the why*, Ford. Maybe I just don't want to say it out loud because it sounds ridiculous."

"Like I said"—he shifts so that he's propped up on one hand while his other hand tucks a loose strand of hair behind my ear. It's an oddly intimate gesture that he seems to do so casually—"*Fair enough.*"

The sexual tension is still there. That one night did nothing to abate it. In fact, I think knowing what he feels like, how he made me feel, made it even stronger.

Why do I not want him to say *fair enough*? Why do I want him to demand an answer and then drag me upstairs and fuck me seven ways from Sunday?

Maybe I want to be heard.

I reach out and run my hand over the scruff on his jaw. His nostrils flare at the touch of my hand and his lips part, just in time for my thumb to graze his bottom lip.

"Ellery," he murmurs, his eyes darkening.

Without preamble, I make the decision for us that we've been tiptoeing around. I lean forward and press my lips to his. The kiss is soft, tender, and he lets me take the lead. It's my tongue that seeks access first. It's my fingers gliding up his shoulder and threading into the hair at the back of his neck.

There is no rush like the other night, no urgent hunger in the kiss. There's pleasure. Reverence. A cautious testing of the waters we've already swam in but now fear we might drown in.

I fall into the moment. The possessiveness of his hand on my lower back. His groan in the back of his throat. The warmth spreading through my body from his kiss. The ache of desire burning between my thighs.

The kiss ends, his hands now on both sides of my face, as our foreheads rest on each other's. We sit like this for a few seconds, no words exchanged, almost as if we're still figuring out if this is right or wrong or somewhere in between.

And just as I'm about to lean away, to break the sudden softness of the moment, Ford speaks.

"Let's go," he says, standing without warning and grabbing my hand to help me stand. He links his fingers with mine as we make our way across the sand toward the back of the inn.

For some reason, nerves rattle. I can handle the hungry sex. The animalistic. The lust gone wild.

But if the kiss we just shared is any indication of the sex we're about to have, it unnerves me.

I expect to go in the back door of the inn and am surprised when Ford tugs my hand to keep walking on the boardwalk.

"No. I'm taking you somewhere," he says cryptically as he turns the corner of the building and heads toward the parking lot. When he opens the car door for me, I just stare at him. "We've lived, eaten, and breathed this place for two weeks. It's time we had a break."

"Where are we going?" I ask as I climb into the passenger seat.

He steps between my knees still angled out the door and angles his head to the side as he studies me. "We're feeling things out."

"What does that mean?"

"It means we've kissed." He puts a hand on my thigh and squeezes gently. "Let's sit with that for a bit. Escape this prison. And once it digests, we'll figure out what we want after that."

"Like?"

His smile is shy, but his eyes are alive. "Like maybe another kiss. Maybe, it remains to be seen."

"What if I already know the answer to that?"

He leans forward and presses a kiss on my forehead. "Then humor me, will you?"

CHAPTER TWENTY-SIX

Ellery

"H OW DID YOU EVEN KNOW THIS WAS A THING?" I ASK AS THE breeze tickles my cheeks. The sound of water lapping the dinghy's hull nearly lulls me to sleep.

"Some of the crew were talking about it. I guess it's a town tradition. Something about reliving the founder's first steps or something." He shrugs and brings the bottle of beer to his lips before setting it back down and holding the tiller again. "I thought it would be nice to get on the water and away from the site for a bit."

"It's most definitely nice." I look around at the line of boats before and after us. We look like ducks following each other in our twelve-foot sailboats. Some boats have four people on it, others just one, and a few young kids manning the helm by themselves.

Chatter can be heard from one sailboat to another, community members who clearly know each other. On the shore to our right, the townspeople who don't have a boat or a ride in one are barbecuing and setting up for a night of festivities apparently.

I turn my attention back to Ford, who looks completely at ease with the halyard in one hand and the tiller in the other. Or at least I think that's what they're called because he threw a lot of terms out at me, and I don't exactly remember which is what.

He looks good with the setting sun on his face and the evening breeze in his hair.

"You have a smudge of dirt on your forehead," he says. "Here, let me get it."

"It's not dirt." I scrunch my nose up as my cheeks turn red and wave my hand at him. "Don't ask."

"You know I'm going to ask after you say that." He angles his head to the side. "What?"

"It's a bruise."

"Okay." He stretches the word out. "From?"

"I was reading last night in bed," I say as if that should explain it all, but when he just furrows his brow in confusion, I continue. "I fell asleep and dropped my Kindle on my face."

He belts out a laugh that I'm sure has other sailors looking our way. "You what?"

"You heard me."

"I wasn't aware there were hazards in reading. Well, was it a good book at least?"

I think of the chapters I flew through. The hero fighting for the heroine. The push. The pull. The incredible, hate-fuck scene that followed where I admit—embarrassingly—that I was picturing Ford and me as the characters.

And then the *thunk* followed by my yelp as it hit my face when I dozed off.

"Very good."

"Why are you blushing, Ellery?" He angles his head to the side and stares at me, his smile widening as if he already knows.

"No reason."

He laughs again, his stare unrelenting. "Maybe I should read this book of yours."

The red on my cheeks darkens. "I don't exactly picture romance as your genre of choice."

"You never know. I'm full of surprises. Maybe that's one of them." He stretches his foot out and bumps mine with his, his grin widening. "Regardless, maybe you should take up less hazardous ways to occupy your time."

"Like what?"

My question is answered with a hundred-watt grin and a long, languorous appraisal of my body that has me smiling and shaking my head in return. "I can think of a few things."

I walked right into that one.

"I'm sure you can."

An airhorn sounds to our left as someone shouts and then jumps off their bow into the water. Clearly there's an abundance of alcohol on that boat, but it's entertaining to say the least.

"Do you want to try?" he asks, pointing to the till.

"Try what? Sinking us?"

He chuckles but reaches out and tugs on my hand. "Come on, I'll help you."

I crawl on my knees toward him, terrified that if I stand, I'll rock the boat and lose my balance. "Where do I—"

"Right here." He directs me so that I sit between his spread legs, leaning my back against his chest. He moves us out of the parade of boats before spending the next few minutes directing me on what to do. He does this by covering my hands with his to show me when to steer the tiller or swing the jib. After a bit, he lets go so I can do it on my own, but he remains where he is.

"There you go," he encourages as I take control of the jib for the first time by myself and the boat turns in the water. He rests his chin on my shoulder. "You'll be a pro in no time. Then again, it seems you're good at everything you do so there's no surprise there."

"Whatever." I roll my eyes.

"I'm serious. You are, and it's not a bad thing."

"Who taught you to sail?" I ask, changing the subject off me as I contemplate if I'm turning too sharp. "You seem pretty comfortable on the water."

"My father. It was a requirement for the Sharpe boys to be schooled in all things," he says with a hint of sarcasm in his voice. Or was that melancholy? I can't quite tell.

"Tell me about him," I say.

His sigh is a clear indication that he's uncomfortable with my request, so I don't push. I just let him rest his chin on my shoulder and settle into the silence.

"He was a good man. Fair but strict. A man who started from nothing and made a whole helluva lot of something. But Dad being *Maxton Sharpe the mogul* is all I really remember, with each year elevating his status even higher than the last."

"I meant, tell me about him as your father," I say, not caring in the least about the businessman because clearly, he was good at what he did. "Did he attend little league games or barbecue in the backyard? Tell me about *him*."

I can feel Ford's body tense, almost as if the question surprises him. "He was there as much as he could be. Being a single father with three teenage boys isn't exactly easy."

"I can't imagine."

"But yeah, he made it to everything he could when he wasn't off conquering the world. At the same time, he tried to make up for us not having a mother by being over the top at everything." He chuckles as if he's remembering something, and I can only assume what over the top means when it comes to a billionaire.

"Tell me," I prod as I turn the boat a little more. But since the breeze has died off some, it just kind of stops.

"On the outside, birthday parties were ridiculous. A box suite at Yankee Stadium. Skydiving for our eighteenth. Christmas was spent skiing or overseas. Anywhere but in our house where we could be reminded of the mom we missed."

"I'm sorry."

"She was the love of his life. He had girlfriends after her, but even up until the day he died, we still knew she was it for him. There was never a doubt in our minds that we were the result of that love."

"That's beautiful," I say, my throat thick with tears because I understand that love. I saw something similar with my own eyes. "Doesn't that scare you though?"

"How so?"

"That he had that love and then lost it? That it's so easy to lose?"

Ford wraps his arms around my waist and pulls me back more to relax against him. I can virtually feel the weight of my question weighing on him. "My brothers have both taken the plunge toward marriage over the last few years, and they seem abnormally, sickeningly happy." His sigh says everything he's not saying—how much he loves them despite whatever arguments they may have. "I mean, having wives didn't stop them from being the assholes they are, but loving their wives, creating their own worlds with them, seems to have made them better men. So yeah, I believe that some risks are worth taking."

"Hmm," I say in response as I try to drown out the memories. The loss. The loneliness that comes with losing your parents.

Sure, I had Garland, Joshua, and Gregory as my family, but it was nowhere near the same. Just like my mother said that day—her marriage to Garland was different from my dad. So was the patchwork-quilt family they created.

Harsh words weren't spoken, but I never felt that all-encompassing love from Garland like I did when I was wrapped in my mother's arms. He was a father figure to me, but never a father. He provided for me, but never thought beyond the monetary needs to my emotional ones.

It wasn't a cold house by any means. We managed. We lived side by side and shared experiences, but it was nowhere near the environment I remembered growing up with my dad.

And then after she died, I became an add-on. A secondary thought. And while it was never explicitly stated, I was kept part of the family out of duty. Because of a promise made to my mother on their wedding day and the six years I lived under their roof.

Sadly for me, it was all I had and so I accepted it. I needed it. The hand-me-down scraps of family I was offered were taken because I had nothing else to accept.

And the shares of a company I never thought I'd be a part of became my lifeline to a woman I missed so fiercely, and the only way I figured I'd be able to hold tight to her was to be a part of the only other thing she'd created besides me—Haywood Redesigns.

I kept friends at an arm's length for fear of being hurt or left behind. I still do.

I had boyfriends who I let in only to shut them out when they got too close.

It became so much easier to think of relationships as transactions—something that is mutually beneficial until it's not—in lieu of being devastated again.

In lieu of finding out if the epilogue of life could really be all that happy because from my experience, that notion is a crock of shit.

Hence my situation with Chandler and my acceptance of a marriage based on mutual interest instead of love. If things went awry, it's easier to walk away from an emotionless contract than to be devastated by one where your heart is invested.

But then the storm happened.

Then Ford happened.

And I'm just not sure how it and he make me feel when I've been so resistant to feeling at all.

"*Hmm?*" His lips vibrate against my scalp, interrupting my thoughts I shouldn't be having right now. "What's that sound supposed to mean? You don't think love or the possibility of love is worth the risk?" he asks, pressing a kiss to the side of my head. I'm not used to casual affection. To random kisses pressed to reassure. To a head leaned against mine in comfort.

And every time he does it, it stops me in my tracks. It makes me realize how very different, how very genuine—in the best kind of way—Ford is.

"I don't know. I'd think watching your parent experience that kind of loss would make you fear getting close to someone."

He nods, his chin bumping my shoulder as he does. "Or it could give you hope. What about you—"

"And your mom? Do you remember much about her?"

He gives a soft laugh. "She was larger than life, and that's saying something in comparison to my father. I remember vague things about her. Her smile. Her laugh. The way she'd 'try' to watch action movies with us only to point out every unrealistic thing about it. And I remember how she loved. It was as if she knew she was going to die young. She was hugs and words and actions. We all knew we were loved."

"That's beautiful."

"It was. It still is." He clears his throat. "My dad tried to live up to that standard, but he wasn't my mother. And yet, I idolized every single thing about him. And I don't mean the man who ran Sharpe International. That man I admired. The man I idolized was the man who we saw behind closed doors. The flustered father trying to do his best and the devoted husband he always remained." His hands fist and his voice clutters with emotion. It sounds like so much more than the pain of having lost his father.

"Ford . . . I don't even know what to say."

"Share then. Tell me about your parents. About—"

We both jump as a bullhorn siren goes off on the sailboat to the right of us. "Time to get to shore, everyone. The party is about to start."

"We wouldn't want to miss the party," Ford says as he puts his hands over mine to help me take the helm again.

I'm not sure why I breathe a sigh of relief for being saved from having to answer.

But I know a lot of it has to do with how both of us have endured the same loss . . . but have ended up on different sides of the spectrum.

And I'm still trying to process how that is. *And whether I could ever have the courage to change.*

CHAPTER TWENTY-SEVEN

Ford

"C'MON, CELERY ELLERY," I CHIDE AS I WALK OUT ONTO THE makeshift dance floor. Lights are strung across the park's concrete square, a cover band is playing on the stage to our right, and an array of booths and food is everywhere else.

"You're telling me that you, Fordham Sharpe, dance?" Her eyes are wide, her smile lighting up her face.

This was a good decision. To get out of the inn. To experience the town and something other than work together.

She was feeling trapped. I could tell it in the look on her face, and her short fuse when talking to contractors.

But it was more than that. It's whatever has been weighing her down. Whatever happened with Chandler? Sleeping with me? Something with her brothers and stepfather? I don't know and she won't volunteer it.

The woman is a closed book. I'm just having to work at it to slowly crack her open.

And tonight's a start.

There's fire in her eyes, much like that first night we met. A sass to her tone that's been missing.

And God, how I want to kiss her again.

"I didn't say I could dance well . . . but I have no problem making a fool of myself. None of these people know me. Few I'll ever see again, so what do I care?" I grab her hand and pull her onto the dance floor. Her head falls back, and her laugh carries loudly as we move to some cheesy pop song.

We dance for what feels like hours. We laugh for what feels like the best kind of eternity. It's like being off the property has lifted a weight off our shoulders we didn't know we were bearing. Roles we *had* to play fell to the wayside.

Here at some simple county celebration, we aren't partners or co-workers. We are friends . . . and a little bit more.

Her kiss earlier took me by surprise. No complaints by any means because the woman could kiss me any time, and in any place, and I wouldn't complain . . . but it surprised me.

Especially after we've purposely kept our distance from each other over the past few days.

And painfully so on my end.

Every whiff of her perfume. Every echo of her laugh. Every sound of her sigh in frustration cemented her mark on me.

My space in the soon-to-be rooftop bar is as far from her room as possible—and it's still not far enough.

I want her. Plain and simple.

"Cookies and cream and jamocha almond fudge?" I ask as I peer through the glass case that houses the ice cream.

When I look over, Ellery's nose is scrunched up. "Eww. No. Mint chocolate chip and chocolate and peanut butter."

"That's a weird mix."

"So is yours."

"Okay. What about, chocolate ice cream and cookies and cream?"

"Really?"

"Really," I say.

"No. That's boring. Mint chocolate chip and cookies and cream."

"Is that your final proposal?" I ask as I tuck a loose strand of hair behind her ear. Her smile lights up the night as she remembers how we got here. The other final proposal I made.

"Yes. Final proposal."

"You drive a hard bargain, Sinclair, making me forfeit one of my favorites."

"It's only fair that we each get something and each forfeit something."

"True." I nod. "Fifty-fifty."

She throws her head back and laughs while I fish money out of my pocket to pay the cashier as the ice cream is being scooped.

"I told you this was a good combination," Ellery says around a spoonful moments later as we stroll down the sidewalk.

"So . . . there is one thing we need to talk about," I murmur as I motion for her to sit on a park bench. She does while we watch a group of kids see whose sparkler makes the best circle when spinning their arms.

She leans her head back on my arm resting on the back of the bench, a laugh falling from her mouth. "No talking about work when I'm tipsy." She pushes one finger against my chest. "That's taking advantage of me."

There's a whole helluva lot I'd take advantage of right now when it comes to her, and it has nothing to do with work.

"You're the one making proposals over ice cream," I tease and take another bite. "It needs a name."

"What does?" she asks, but I see the recognition as soon as she says it. "I thought you wanted it to be a Sharpe Signature property?"

"I do, but it still deserves an *actual* name."

"You mean you're going to let *me* help name it?"

I stare at her, her brilliant blue eyes and flushed cheeks, and hold myself back from leaning forward and kissing her. "Of course, I am. Fifty-fifty, right?"

"I just . . . I mean good business sense says for you to slap the Sharpe name all over it, so I'd resigned myself to that. I didn't expect—"

My lips find hers despite telling myself not to. It's just a brush of connection, but it sends such a charge through me that it takes everything I have to drag myself away and leave it at that. "Fifty-fifty," I murmur. "So start thinking of a name for it."

The hitch in her breath is audible. I love knowing I do that to her. That she's affected by my kiss.

It's a fucking turn-on.

"Okay." She nods, her teeth sinking into her bottom lip as we stare at each other, goofy smiles on our faces. "Thank you. For this," she whispers.

"It was good to get away for a bit."

"It was."

"But it is getting late," I say. But neither of us move. "And it might take a while to get an Uber in this town with everybody drinking like us tonight."

"I know, but I don't want to go back just yet. I want to sit here on a bench with you under the stars, with the sound of laughter in the air, and the moonlight on our faces."

"Why, Ellery Sinclair, are you a romantic?"

It doesn't fit her. First the romance novel, now this? The woman is a mess of contradictions, none of which I'd expect to be a romantic, and I love discovering them one by one.

"A romantic?" She snorts. "You have to believe in love to believe in romance."

"Whoa. That's a big statement."

She laughs and plays it off with a shrug.

Then again, who's *not* cynical after ending a relationship?

"But you read romance books?"

"Those authors write some good sex."

"I should have figured." I bark out a laugh. "You still read them though."

"But not the epilogues," she says, holding up a finger to emphasize her point.

"Wait. What? Why don't you read the epilogues? What's wrong with them?" Our eyes meet as her tipsy smile fades and something flashes through her eyes. Almost as if she let that slip without thinking about it. It's only a split second of time, but it's enough to see that guard of hers fall. I know there's pain hidden behind it. "Elle?"

The wall is refortified in an instant and is smothered behind an unapologetic smile. "I'm joking. It's a joke. I mean, what *is* romance really? Grand gestures that are over the top so the guy can win the big-dick contest when he brags to his friends and she brags to her friends about how much he loves her?" She waves a hand my way and then finishes the seltzer in her hand.

Clearly, Chandler wasn't doing it right.

But I leave the thought unspoken, just as I don't question her further on her epilogue comment. I stand and hold out a hand to her.

"Love and romance aren't mutually exclusive. And it's not always grand gestures."

She rolls her eyes and pushes against my chest. "Show me a man who knows how to do that and I'll marry him." She laughs and jumps up, holding her hands out to me. "One more dance before we go?"

We head to the dance floor and move to the beat.

Her body against mine.
Her laughter in my ears.
Her words in my head.
She doesn't read the epilogues.
She doesn't believe in happily ever afters.

CHAPTER TWENTY-EIGHT

Ellery

How did he know this is what I needed? A night out. Some time away. A little bit of entertainment, some horrible-for-you-food, and laughter. *So much laughter.*

I let the feeling suspend me on the drive home. My head's on his shoulder, his hand's on my thigh, and our rideshare driver isn't bothered by the silence or our laughter every few minutes when Ford pokes my ribs.

It's been forever since I've felt like this. Carefree. Lighthearted. And not that I'm always serious, but it takes a lot for me to feel comfortable enough with someone to let my true self show. To let my guard down and just be me.

And now as we head toward the inn, our home, I know I want more out of tonight.

I want him.

"Stupid lock," Ford mutters as he jiggles the handle and it doesn't budge.

"Let's try the back."

"I don't have a key for the back one. It was just replaced and hasn't been rekeyed." He looks at me and we both burst out laughing.

"Seriously? Are we locked out of our own property, Ford?"

He stands back and braces his hands on his hips, his lips twisted, and his brow furrowed in concentration. "I know."

"What? Are you going to break in?"

He shakes his head exaggeratively. "No. But, the windows on the second floor aren't locked."

"Are you crazy?"

He turns to me, his grin huge, his eyes alive. "Only for you," he says with a bark of a laugh before running down the sidewalk to the side of the building.

"Wait." I scurry after him, the world spinning a bit beneath my feet. "You can't climb that," I say, pointing to the side of the building with its attached trellis that Ford is already making his way onto.

"Why not?" He turns and grins. "We know the owners. Live on the wild side, Sinclair."

"I'm not reviving you when you fall off and break your back."

"That's the most romantic thing I've ever heard," he says through a laugh before pressing a chaste kiss to my lips.

Without another word, and with a lot of laughter, Ford manages to climb the side of the building and push open one of the newly installed windows. "Aha!" he yells down to me before he disappears.

I run back to the front door, my stomach hurting from laughing so much, just in time for Ford to open it.

"Voila," he says, bending at the waist.

"You broke into our hotel." I playfully swat at him. He grabs my wrists, holding them against his chest.

"It's hard being this perfect, Elle."

"Oh, please. Don't think so highly of yourself." I roll my eyes but when ours meet again, everything slows down. I feel his breath feather over my lips. Feel his heartbeat race beneath my palms. See the desire darken in his eyes.

"You know what will make me fall from grace?"

"What's that?"

"Making a *mistake*," he murmurs, his eyes devouring me.

"Is that so?" Our bodies move into one another's.

"It is." His eyes flicker to my lips. "I find it's hard to be perfect when you keep making mistakes."

I lean in so that our lips are almost touching. "Then I guess it's time we make another one."

"Is that so?" he asks as I shut the door at my back and lower to my knees. His breath hitches as I look up at him beneath my lashes, a smile on my lips as my fingers work the buttons of his pants. "God, I love mistakes."

Laughter is on my lips as I break his cock free and waste no time taking him into my mouth. His hand fists in my hair almost in an automatic response when the first suck on it takes him all the way to the back of my throat.

"Elle," he groans, and hell if the sound alone doesn't enhance the ache to have him that's burning through me. "Christ, Elle."

I work my hand around the base of his shaft as I suck on the crest of his cock. I'm treated with the salty taste of his precome as his fist tightens. I look up at him with him thick and heavy in my mouth and am turned on by the sight. Eyes drugged with desire half-closed and his teeth sinking into his bottom lip. Tendons taut in his neck and his biceps flexed as he moves his hand with my hand as I work his dick in and out of my lips.

"Stop or I'm going to come." His words spur me on. To suck harder. To take him deeper. I can feel him swell and harden when I didn't think he could get any harder. His next groan has him hauling me up by under my armpits and branding his mouth over mine, swallowing my gasp as his tongue slips between my lips.

His kiss is a mixture of demand and depravity. Of control and chaos. Of want versus necessity.

The man owns my every sense.

My every nerve.

My every thought.

He laces open-mouthed kisses down the line of my neck and uses a hand to squeeze my breast so he can suck on its tip through the fabric of my shirt.

I shiver at the warm, wet heat of his mouth all while trying to shimmy out of my jeans. His other hand helps to push them down and then pushes me backwards until we're against the bar top.

While his mouth's still on mine, he lifts me up and sets my bare ass on the cold counter. I yelp because of its chill and then moan. Before I can even process the thought, Ford has my feet on his shoulders and his tongue running up and down my slit.

"Oh, God." The two words are one drawn-out sound as I prop myself up on my elbows to watch him unravel me with licks of his tongue and his fingers tucking inside of me.

It's erotic. It's sexy. It's damn near sensational. His eyes meet mine from above my mound as he circles my clit with his tongue while his fingers pump in and out of me.

My body coils with each touch, with each lick, with each puff of air he blows on my most intimate flesh.

I tug on his hair and his face lifts with evidence of what he's doing to me glistening on his chin and mouth. "Take me. Now. Please." I pant the words out. Begging. Asking. Demanding.

His chuckle is all I need to know he's ready and wanting too. I yelp when his hand connects with my hypersensitized pussy. The little smack unexpected but so fucking hot that I almost come right then. Right there.

But before my system recovers, Ford is pushing his way into me like a man on a mission.

And I won't complain about that.

He begins to move once I adjust to the fullness. Slow, steady strokes that penetrate deep within me when he leans over and captures my mouth with his. His tongue moving in time with his thrusts.

My nails scrape down the sides of his torso as my body climbs higher and higher. As the ball of desire constricts tighter and tighter.

"Come on, baby," he murmurs against my lips before straightening up. He leaves one hand on my shoulder to hold me in place as he begins to pound into me.

Sensations overwhelm.

Bliss mounts.

Desire detonates into the best kind of devastation.

The coil releases as my cry echoes through the empty room while a tidal wave of pleasure pulls me under. I'm swamped in every way imaginable, the orgasm powerful with both its sensation and sensitivity.

"There you go," he whispers as he moves ever so slowly in and out of me, his thumb rubbing over my clit to help coax the remainder of my climax out of me.

I tighten around him. Over and over and over. My body's spent and soaring all at the same time.

And it's those little pulses around him that bring him to the edge. His groan is feral as he begins fucking me with a fervor and an urgency.

His fingers dig into my flesh. His thighs slap against mine. His cock works me in and out until he can't withstand it any longer.

"Ellery," he groans, the walls virtually shaking at the reverberation of the orgasm that slams into and through him.

He looks like a Greek god between my thighs. Head thrown back. Adam's apple pronounced. Shoulders tense. Lips lax.

And I don't think I've ever seen anything sexier.

I don't think I ever will again.

He collapses on top of me, our bodies misted with sweat, my shirt that's still on dampened from it. He rests his forehead on my collarbone and rocks it back and forth.

"Good God, woman." He presses a kiss between my breasts. "Good fucking God."

I run a hand through his hair, reveling in the feeling of our hearts pounding against one another's. In our chests moving in unison.

"Should I take that as a compliment?" I tease as I twist a strand of his hair around my finger.

"Mm-hmm. Mistakes. They're a beautiful thing, aren't they?"

"Only when it comes to you."

CHAPTER TWENTY-NINE

Ford

Twenty-Six Years Ago

THE WORLD SEESAWS BACK AND FORTH WITH EVERY PUSH OF her foot on the porch. The swing creaks with the motion, and if I close my eyes, I feel like I'm spinning in space. But the smell of the barbecue and the sound of my brothers playing Marco Polo in the pool bring me back to earth before I can even pretend.

My mom's fingers play absently with the back of my neck.

"Please don't tell Dad I cried."

"Ford. There's no shame in showing your emotions." I look over to my mom and shrug. Her brownish-blonde hair is pulled back in a ponytail and her brown eyes hold mine.

"I'm a boy. Boys don't cry."

"That's nonsense and you know it."

"Dad says men shouldn't show their emotions." I sniffle.

"You want me to tell you a secret?" she asks, and I nod. "I've seen Dad cry before."

"Yeah. Right." I roll my eyes. There's no way.

"I'm serious. I can remember the times clearly. The day we got married. He teared up when he saw me coming down the aisle. He was in front of hundreds of people, but he didn't care. He said it was because he knew how lucky he was getting to spend his life with me."

Yuck. Love stuff doesn't count.

"That's once."

"And I remember the day you three were born." I love the look on her face. I don't know what it means, but she looks happy. Like when she was holding her friend's baby and making that weird humming sound as she rocked her. "You were all in bassinets lined up next to each other in the hospital room. He stood in front of you with this look on his face I'll never forget. Love. Pride. Disbelief. Like you were his everything and his greatest accomplishment all rolled into one. He was crying then too."

"Did you cry then?"

"Of course, I did. It was one of the happiest days of my life."

"Do you think it was his?"

"I know it was." She ruffles my hair. "Now do you want to tell me what else is on your mind other than Ledger being mean to you? Because you're moping around here today and it's not because of him."

"Just thinking is all."

"Does that have anything to do with why you aren't out there playing with your brothers?"

Another shrug as she pushes to keep the swing moving. "Maybe."

"Okay." She gives that slow nod of her head that says she's listening. If it's a sharp nod, you're in trouble. If it's slow, it means she's ready for you to talk to her.

But I don't know if I want to talk.

The summers in Sag Harbor are my favorite. There's the beach and sailing and playing anywhere and everywhere so long as we're home by the time the sky is dark.

"Is it your brothers? Are they picking on you again?"

"Nah."

"Then what is it?"

"I read something that bugged me is all."

"About?" She shifts so she can put her arm around me and pull me against her. She smells like the lemons she was just picking from the lemon tree and the soap she was washing them with in the sink.

I pluck at the legs of my shorts as she sits patiently like we have all the time in the world. And I know we don't. My dad needs her. Ledger and Callahan probably do too. But she never makes me feel that way. She always gives me time like I'm the only one in the world.

"About Dad."

Another slow nod. "What about him?"

"About how he's roofless."

Her laugh is loud, and she stifles it when I look at her with confusion.

"I think it said ruthless, honey. Clearly, we aren't roof-less," she says and points to the ridiculously large house at our backs.

"Yeah. Okay. That's what I meant."

"What else did it say?"

"Just stuff." It's easier to study my fingers than meet her eyes.

"Out with it." She squeezes my shoulder.

"It said he was a roof—ruthless person who was a womanizing, patronizing, unscrupulous man who puts the profit before all else."

"Well, you sure got those adjectives right." She laughs loudly and presses a kiss to the top of my head, completely unfazed by the things I just said that I know aren't good.

"You're not mad?"

Mom turns and brushes my hair off my forehead and runs a hand down the side of my face. "Buddy, I'm not mad."

"Why not? You're mad when Callahan calls me a douchebag."

"You're right. I am. But that's completely different."

"How? Why aren't you mad at those people who called Dad those things?"

"I am mad because they're not true. But I don't care if they say those things because they don't matter."

"Why don't they?"

"Because the only comments, criticisms, and words that should matter to you are those that are spoken by your family."

"You say a lot when you're angry," I say and then wince. I can't believe I just said that out loud.

But my comment is met with a laugh and a ruffle of my hair. "True. I do. Most times, words spoken in anger are hurtful. I'm not talking about those kinds of words. I'm talking about ones your family says about you. How they'd describe you to a friend. It's those kinds of comments that matter. Everything else is just noise."

"That doesn't make sense."

"In this world, there will be a lot of people who say things about you. Good. Bad. True. Untrue. You're a Sharpe. We're successful, and it's easier for people to criticize than to admire what we've accomplished. But at the end of the day, when you're old like Grandpa is and are looking back at your life, it's only what the people who you love say that matters.

It's what they think of you—as a person, as a man, as a brother, as a husband, what have you—that is important and shows the true measure of the man you are."

"Shouldn't you care what everyone says?"

Her smile is soft. "You can, but if your family has nothing good to say about you, if they can't say you were a good, kind person who helped better their world, then was the way you spent your life worth it?"

CHAPTER THIRTY

Ford

S HE SMIRKS AT ME FROM BEHIND RODDY'S BACK.

Smirks at me, because hell if he didn't almost catch us this morning.

Note to self: take away all keys from contractors. That way you won't be caught in the act. Just finishing the act. Enjoying the act.

And Jesus, what an act it was. Her lips around my dick. Her cheeks hollowing out. Blue eyes looking up at me beneath a thick set of lashes.

There are perks to having a partner. I just never thought this might be one of them.

"Are you hearing me?" Roddy asks. I give a quick shake of my head as if to clear it from stray thoughts. But they aren't stray at all. They're right where I want them to be . . . despite how distracting they are.

"Yeah. Sure." I chuckle. "We have so much going on at once, sometimes my brain goes a little haywire."

"No shit. I've never seen a site trying to do so much in so little time."

"Time is money."

"It is, but I've got to hand it to Sinclair. She keeps a tight ship with her schedule and makes sure no one's running into each other."

"She does. We're lucky to have her coordinating everything. This project would be chaos without her."

Ellery flashes me a huge grin and waves her fingers before walking down the hallway.

"Yeah. Man," Diego says as he walks up, completely oblivious to the fact that she just walked away. "What I'd do to have a piece of that. Fuck. I bet—"

"Shut the fuck up," Roddy says, slapping the drywaller's chest just as I'm about to say and do the same thing—*or worse.* Fury swims in my veins.

"Bro. We don't say shit like that. She's not a piece of meat, and she sure as hell deserves more respect than that."

"C'mon—"

"Diego." My smile holds absolutely no warmth. Neither does my tone. I reach out my hand to him. "Fordham Sharpe. I don't believe we've met before."

Diego's jaw falls lax, and his handshake needs some serious work to reflect confidence. Then again, it could be the look on my face that says I want to murder him that's making his hand limp and his grip weak.

My last name tends to do that at times. And thank fuck for that right now.

"Sir." He finally finds his voice and clears his throat.

"Listen. I don't know about you, but I was raised to respect women. To admire them. To enjoy their company. Not something you 'get a piece of.' So, let's make something very, very clear here." I lean in closer, my voice low, my hand still squeezing his hard enough that I'm sure his blood might have a problem flowing to his fingertips. "If I ever hear you speak of *my partner* like that again, I assure you that your company will cease to exist." His eyes widen. "Yes, I have that influence. *Understood?*"

Diego stares at me, his lips lax, his head nodding. "Yes, sir," he says just above a whisper.

"Great. Glad we got that cleared up. You can go now," I say and release his hand, which he spreads and clenches as the blood flow returns. I lift a chin toward it. "And you should probably get that circulation checked. It's not looking too good right now."

Diego forces a swallow down his throat and nods again as he trips over a box on the ground, then he scurries away from the balcony bar where we're standing.

"Poor kid needs to check his drawers right now. You scared the shit out of him," Roddy says with a chuckle. "Hopefully that will set him straight."

"One can hope," I murmur. "Thank you, though, for standing up for Ellery." He just earned major points in my book.

Roddy clears his throat and his cheeks flush pink. "She's something else."

Um. Did I just read that right?

"She is." I nod and turn back to the clipboard in my hands, the topic of Ellery Sinclair now over. "Now on the built-ins—"

"I figure if I can keep all the assholes away from her, maybe before I leave the project, I'll finally shoot my shot and ask her out."

I suddenly have a coughing fit.

Major points now completely erased.

They're even falling into the negative about now.

Secondly, the phrase *shoot my shot* never sounded more fucked up than it does right now.

"Wow. Well, okay," I say as stoically as possible while hating the fact that now one of my favorite guys on this site has now dropped rank to Diego status.

Maybe just a little above.

"Do you think I have a chance?" he asks, eyes eager, smile hopeful.

"About as good of a shot as I have"—I nudge him—"and that's not much."

The thought, the conversation, sticks with me the rest of the day. Through phone calls dealing with S.I.N. responsibilities. A call to our resort manager in Japan about our newest resort about to come back online after an extensive overhaul. A run-through of our new marketing campaign to see if a rebrand of our Aspen location is helping to pull in a new demographic. A check-in call with my brothers to make sure we're all on the same page. Between hiring a new resort manager, dealing with a supply chain issue, and a possible union strike at the Napa property, this week has been challenging to say the least. It's pertinent that we know what each other is doing or has done so we can step in for the other if need be.

Then there were the day-to-day items to do here at the inn. A site walk-through with the superintendent where we check off items completed and add things that need attention. Discussions over logistics. The breakup of an argument between a frustrated Ellery and a plumber who refused to take orders . . . and, I'm assuming, take them from a woman, because when I told him what to do, he did them quickly. *Asshole.*

The day has been exhausting yet satisfying. Just like it seems every other day here has been.

Isn't that what I was hoping for when I came here? To work with my hands and see something materialize from that hard work?

And what's even better? To do all these things with a partner, with Ellery, and watch the joy and satisfaction she finds in the process too.

CHAPTER THIRTY-ONE

Ellery

"W HAT?" I PULL MY PHONE FROM MY CHEEK AND LOOK AT it—as if seeing is believing—before putting it back to my cheek. I can't possibly have heard that correctly.

"I said I was reviewing everything for the Revlon job with Gregory, and I am thoroughly impressed with all the prep you did for it. Stellar work. Simply stellar."

"Um. Thank you." What's the catch here? Why is Garland complimenting me now when this is the same kind of work I've always done for Haywood?

"The project is going well, I presume?"

I feel like I've stepped into the Twilight Zone.

"Yes. Very. Most days." I laugh. "You know how projects are. They always have their hiccups, but for the most part, yes, things are running smoothly."

"Good. I'm glad. I hope they continue down the same path."

"Thank you." An awkward silence stretches across the line, and I struggle for something to fill it with. Just as I'm about to speak, he does.

"Her birthday is coming up soon."

My throat constricts at his words and the atypical emotion woven in them. "I know."

Another pause. A clearing of his throat. "It's a tough day for me to get through. I can't imagine how it is for you."

I have absolutely no idea what to say to his comment. He's never said anything of the sort in the years since her death. I open my mouth. Close it.

"I just wanted you to know I'll be thinking about you, Elle. And that she'd be proud of what you're doing because it's exactly what she would have done too."

"Thank you." I can barely get the two words out over the emotion clogging my throat.

"No need to thank me."

When the call ends, I stand there and stare at my cell, replaying the conversation in my head and wondering what it meant.

The skeptic in me would say he's just calling to check on things because he's hoping for a future payday when it comes to S.I.N.

But there was something in his voice, something that the woman who reads romance novels and pretends like she doesn't believe in happily ever afters, heard the faintest strains of.

Garland loved her.

He truly did.

While I may not have understood or seen that love on display in a conventional way, he still did.

Clearly there are more ways than one to love. Not all relationships . . . *look* the same.

You can still be devastated by its loss in the end.

Perhaps that proves my point.

Love is dangerous, something to be avoided at all costs.

CHAPTER THIRTY-TWO

Ford

"I T'S COMING ALONG, ISN'T IT?"

I look over to where Ellery stands in the doorway to the room I've acquired as my quarters. It's a larger room off the balcony bar. I've moved in an old table to use as a desk. The bed is a king but as the constant ache in my back can attest, the mattress completely sucks. My clothes are hung haphazardly in a closet where the door does nothing to protect them from the dust, which seems like it's coating everything. Not my usual living standards, but it will do.

But it's not the room I'm focused on right now. It's the woman in the doorway with her jeans worn at the knees and her red T-shirt partially untucked.

She fits and yet she doesn't somehow.

She belongs in the elegance I know she normally lives in, and yet she's perfectly comfortable with work boots on, dust in her hair, and a pencil tucked behind her ear as she runs this remodel with a perfection I've rarely seen from S.I.N.'s contractors.

She's sharp. She's gorgeous. She's . . . *fuck*. I've got it bad.

"Earth to Ford?" She waves her hands in front of her to flag my attention. Little does she know she already owns it.

"I'm sorry. You standing there kind of made me lose track of my thoughts." Her smile widens. "I'm sorry, what did you ask?"

"I'm hoping the distraction was for good reasons and not because I have paint smeared over my cheek or something."

"You'd still be beautiful even with paint."

"Is someone trying to smooth-talk me?" she asks as she moves toward me.

"Never," I say as I nod. Not unless I need to. "And yes, I think it's coming along. Smoother than I expected."

"Don't jinx us." She laughs. "I prefer things to stay as they are." She takes a slow appraisal of my space. The made bed. The haphazard desk. The little pieces here and there that show I exist. "You know you don't have to stay here, right? I'm sure your house in Sag would be more comfortable and less"—she runs a fingertip along over my table and leaves a streak—"dusty."

"It would be."

"I know you're busy with a lot more on your plate than this place so . . ."

"Are you kicking me out, Celery Ellery?" I ask as I reach out and tug on her waist so that she sits on my lap. I'm more than aware of the tensing of her body as I wrap my arms around her waist and fit my chin onto the curve of her shoulder.

Affection makes her uncomfortable.

It's something I've noticed over the course of the past few weeks since we've been . . . whatever it is that we're doing. Strange for such a passionate woman to be sidelined by touch when it occurs outside the act of sex.

"Not kicking you out. I just thought you might want a break from this place because, God knows, living and working in the same place can make you go a little batty at times."

She's right. It has. But not for the reasons she's thinking. I can live anywhere. Luxury isn't required despite what people think or associate me with.

It's her that's making me batty. My want to be with her all the time. When she's dealing with contractors so I can admire how easily she finesses them. When she's sitting in the dark at the kitchen table eating an ice cream bar where calories don't count. When her butt is planted in the sand, a glass of wine in one hand, and her face lifted toward the sun. When I sink into her and she makes that noise in the back of her throat that sounds like enviable pleasure.

"It can," I say, "but I'm managing just fine."

"I heard you scared the shit out of Diego. I walked in on some of the guys laughing about it, but then they shut up when they noticed me. Care to explain why and what happened?"

I chuckle. "Nah. I handled it. That's all you need to know."

"Why do I get the feeling I should ask more on this?" she asks.

"Do you not trust me to handle the crew?" I tease.

"Now, I *know* I need to ask more."

"He was being disrespectful. I put him in his place with a little incentive for why he shouldn't do it again."

"You know I can handle myself, right? That women being treated like shit in construction is normal?"

"Yes to both, but that doesn't mean I'll allow it on our site. Or for it to be said about you. Call me old-fashioned. Call me a dick. I know you can handle yourself, and I believe I've let you every chance that arises, *but* . . . if I didn't say anything, then I'd be just as guilty as he was."

She nods slowly as she presses her fingertips to my opposite hand and stares at the connection. There's something on her mind. She's a closed book most days. There are times I feel like I talk about everything and anything, but when it comes to her, she conveniently steers the topic to something else.

"What do you want, Ellery?" I murmur, my lips near her ear.

"What do you mean?"

"After this is over." She tenses, and I chuckle. "Relax. I'm talking about business, goals, that kind of thing."

She takes her time thinking of her response, which seems so different than the Chatty Cathy I first met months ago. So, what's changed?

Her sigh comes before her answer. "I want to finish this and . . . I don't know. Will I get the satisfaction, vindication, whatever you want to call it when the project is completed? And if I do, will it be enough to sustain me? Will Garland still think I need to be seen and not heard? Will my brothers respect my opinions as an equal partner?"

"But you said he called and praised some of your work. Maybe the tide is already turning some in that aspect."

She purses her lips and nods. "Perhaps. I don't know."

I can all but feel her conflict.

"Okay, say all of that were true. Finishing the project and it being a success. Spoiler alert—*it will.* But say it is and Garland truly realizes your worth and the dickheads start respecting your opinions. If all of that were true, would you consider yourself successful?"

"That's the question, isn't it?"

"My mom used to tell me that at the end of the day, the only thing that matters in life is what your family says about and thinks of you. I used to believe that wholeheartedly, but to be honest, I've struggled with that as of late. And then we talk, and I watch you battle against the shit your brothers and your dad say. I see you. I know you. I know your worth, and I'm amazed they can't see it."

And isn't that the truth? She's making me realize there is an exception to the rule my mother told me it was important to live my life by.

The question is, how does that newfound knowledge apply to me?

Because I'm starting to realize that part of the reason the biography has produced a sore spot for me is that I always craved those words from him. His praise. His approval. All three of us did. And like with any siblings, when a parent gives one something and not the other, it makes the one who was left out feel less than.

And his lack of discussion about me in the biography did just that—made me feel as if I weren't as important. And my brothers' dismissal of my feelings over it only served to tear open the wound a little more.

But then there's Ellery, a walking example of being an exception to the rule.

To not needing anybody's words to prove her worth.

And I wonder how I can apply that to my life. I wonder if it's possible to step back and overlook what feels like a slight, because if what my family says and thinks about me is to be my foundation for how I see myself, then clearly, I'm lacking.

"Your mom's notion is good in theory, but maybe it only applies to functional families." She laughs. "And God knows mine is dysfunctional in the most normal of ways." She begins tracing my palm with her finger. Seconds pass as we stare at what she's doing. "Why have you struggled with it so much?"

"It's neither here nor there," I say, my chin bumping her shoulder. She's talking. The last thing I want to do is turn the topic to me. But I also find it weird that for the first time, I actually want to talk to her about the biography. My reaction. The invalidation I feel over it. I want to see what she thinks. See if she understands when it seems my brothers think I'm being ridiculous.

"No redirecting," I say and press a kiss to the back of her neck. "You never finished answering the question. What does professional success look like to you? Personal success? I want to know all the things, Ellery, and I'm not letting you off the hook until you give them to me." I squeeze her waist tighter, pulling her against me.

"Professionally, I think I'm still figuring it all out. And I think that's okay. Do I have to work? No. I can phone it in to collect that Haywood payroll check and cash out—but that isn't satisfying to me. Maybe I do another something like this." She gestures to the building all around us. "On a smaller scale so I don't hyperventilate at the sale price."

"You were a little pale."

"A lot pale. Jesus."

"And then I swooped in to save the day," I tease, already prepared for the reaction because, if I know her as well as I think I do, Ellery Sinclair doesn't need anyone to swoop in and rescue her.

Three.

Two—

"You didn't swoop. I don't need swooping."

I throw my head back and laugh. "That was quicker than I thought." She swats at me. "And believe me, I know more than anyone how very capable you are." I kiss her shoulder. "So that's professionally. What about personally?"

"I'd like to travel. My parents were big travelers. I have picture album after picture album that documented their trips. I think it would be cool to do the same. Stand in the same spots they did. Experience the same things. It sounds ridiculous, but maybe it would allow me to feel a little closer to them."

"No. I get it. My brothers and I have all done things to feel a little closer to our parents since they've passed. There is absolutely no judgment or timeline on grief. It's different for everyone. Besides, I think that's a cool idea that you have that history to hold on to."

"We'll see if I ever get to it."

"You bought an inn on a whim. I'm pretty sure you'll get to it."

"Thanks for the vote of confidence."

"When it comes to you, that's a given." Her part snort, part sigh tells me she's about to refute my comment, so I just put a hand over her mouth. "Own it, Ellery. I don't care what it takes, but by the end of this venture, you're going to be nodding when I say that instead of snorting."

Her sigh is all I need to know she heard me. And the slow lick of her tongue over the inside of my palm has blood pooling to my lap that she's so conveniently perched on.

My chuckle is pained as I pull my hand away just as her grin is forming.

I will not be distracted by her seduction attempts. I mean, yes, I'm distracted and will welcome the chance to be again, but after this conversation. It's a fucking miracle the woman is talking so I intend to keep her doing so.

"What's wrong, Ford?" She wiggles her ass over my hardening cock. "Is there something distracting you?"

I close my eyes and suck in a breath as the warmth of her pussy seeps through her jeans and onto my cock.

"Nope." I grit the words out and shift her so she's sitting more on one thigh and less on my hard-on. It's wishful thinking that it'll help with the desire coursing through my body, but it's worth a shot. "Not a thing."

Ledger.

Callahan.

Ledger.

Callahan.

Thoughts of my brothers are a surefire way to give me a reverse boner.

"No kids or white picket fence?" I grit out as she puts her hand down to shift and accidentally grazes my denim-clad cock.

I hiss in a breath as her grin grows.

"White pickets need too much maintenance. Paint and the weather wear on them. Maybe a vinyl fence someday. Or wrought iron. It's a little sturdier."

I laugh. God, this woman. She's something else.

"And kids—"

"You're trying so *hard* to continue this conversation, aren't you?" she murmurs as she traces the bulge in my pants with her fingernail. The sensations ricochet all the way down to my balls and lower abdomen as she leans in, her mouth inches from mine. "How about we stop talking, Sharpe, and you start putting that mouth of yours to much better use?"

"What did you have in mind?" My eyes flicker from her lips to her eyes and then to her tongue darting out to wet her lips.

Whatever it is, I'm sure I'll like it.

She leans in and brushes her lips to mine. "Well, considering we're equal partners—"

"Fifty-fifty," I whisper against hers.

"I do believe you got your fifty this morning, and I'm still sitting here without mine."

Fuck. Is she asking me to go down on her?

She doesn't have to ask twice.

Conversation over.

Libido in overdrive.

"I can most definitely remedy that."

"You can?"

Another kiss.

"What kind of partner would I be if I didn't try to fulfill my responsibilities?"

A momentary slide of my hand between her thighs.

"A horrible one."

A lick of her tongue over my bottom lip.

With my hands on her waist, I help push her to standing while I make quick work of the button and zipper on her jeans. "Then I'm going to need you to sit your ass on this desk right here for me to prove I'm worthy."

Fifty-fifty never sounded so good.

CHAPTER THIRTY-THREE

Ellery

"I NEED YOU TO PICK UP SOMETHING FOR ME."

Isn't that what Ford had asked of me? To run an errand and head to the next town over to help him out?

Can't say that I minded. I've been in a funk the past few days since my mom's birthday, so the chance to roll the car windows down and get some fresh air was just what I needed.

Each mile I put between me and the site allowed me to breathe a little more.

Chaos seemed to be the theme this week.

And I swear it's because Ford jinxed us by saying everything had been running smoothly. This week alone, a pipe burst in the café area, an electrician fell off a ladder and needed medical attention, and we were denied a permit due to some minor technicalities with city ordinances.

Stress upon stress upon stress.

And all of that when we have an impending hard date for the furniture to start arriving.

If the rooms don't get finished, then we have nowhere to put it.

Speaking of schedules, I need to get whatever this is I'm here to pick up and get back.

I glance at the address again on the text Ford sent me and then back to the building in front of me.

Yep. It's the right place. Just not exactly where I'd expect to pick up something for a remodel.

The building is Cape Cod blue with white shutters and flower boxes on the sills. A few women mill about, passing back and forth in the windows. One has a glass of wine in her hand. Another has foils in her hair.

I reach up and touch the ends of my own hair. When is the last time I had it cut and blown out? I've been so involved in the inn, in my time with Ford, that it hasn't even crossed my mind.

Maybe I'll make an appointment while I'm here.

But what do a salon and a remodel have in common? Ford had to have transposed numbers or something on the address.

Me: You sure this is the right address?

Ford: Yes. Blue building. Pink flowers?

Me: Yes.

Ford: Millie has what you need.

I stare at my screen and give a shake of my head.

"Here goes nothing," I mutter as I climb out of my car and up the steps. The inside is airy and sizeable. It smells of the jasmine climbing in the planters. There is the low hum of chatter and blow-dryers as I wait for someone to spot me at the front desk.

"May I help you?" a woman with curly brown hair and a kind smile asks.

"Yes, I'm looking for Millie. I'm here to pick something up for Fordham Sharpe."

Her smile spreads to a million watts. "Isn't that man the greatest? Brains and kindness and looks all rolled into one incredible package."

"Um-yes. I guess," I stutter, thrown off guard by her comments.

She waves a hand at me. "Honey, it's more than okay to agree. There is no judgment here. You must be Ellery."

"Yes. *Millie?*"

"Guilty as charged," she says, her southern accent coming through a little stronger.

"I'll just grab whatever it is he needs and get out of your way." My smile is polite, but I'm not exactly thrilled with this woman fawning all over the man who currently occupies way too much of my time to be considered healthy.

Her laugh draws the attention of everyone around us. "Oh darling, you're not grabbing anything you can take with you."

"What do you mean?" I ask as she extends her hand with what looks like a card in it.

I eye her curiously as I open the envelope and pull the card out.

Elle-

You've been working nonstop. You deserve a break. A little relaxation. Millie has the works set up for you. A massage. A facial. A manicure and pedicure. Other things I don't even know what they are.

And when you're done for the day, there's a nice waterfront condo with your name on it for the night. Food is ordered and will be waiting. Wine is chilling. I've been promised by the owner that some excellent romance novels have been left to aid in that relaxation. Enjoy the time away from the noise and the dust.

Someone once said this place can make you batty. It can. Take this time for yourself to unwind. I'll see you tomorrow.

-Ford

I don't know why tears spring to my eyes, but they do.

"He's not too shabby, if I do say so myself," Millie says softly.

"No. Not at all." I blink away the tears and hate how one escapes down my cheek that I wipe away as soon as it falls.

"It takes a good man to recognize when his girlfriend needs a break from the day-to-day."

"I'm not . . . we're not—"

Her laugh cuts me off. "You can *I'm not, we're not* all you want, but if a man takes time out of his day to make a woman happy who isn't his momma, then I'm thinking you're more than just a friend."

My cheeks flush, and I'm not sure what to say. I nod. "We'll go with more than just a friend."

"Well, it's something all right." She holds her hand out to me. "Phone, please."

"Why?"

"Because if I have your phone, then you'll have a valid excuse why you can't respond to work questions. And because it's what Ford asked me to do, and you know as well as I do there is no saying no to that fine specimen of a man."

I reluctantly hand over my phone, almost feeling like I'm giving her an arm or a leg. As I do so, a text sounds off, but she just smiles and tucks it into a drawer and locks it.

"Now that that's taken care of, let's get that pampering started. Time's a wasting."

I spend the next ridiculous amount of time being treated like I'm royalty. When I ask if I'm supposed to drink water after my massage, I'm told "champagne is made of water so it's okay." When I'm asked what color to paint my fingers and toes, I choose red because I know how much Ford liked my red lipstick the last time I wore it. When I'm asked if I feel relaxed as I head out the door, the tears burn in my eyes as I nod and realize just how much I needed this decadent reprieve.

I tell myself I don't deserve this, all this pampering and attention, but I'd be remiss to deny just how much I'm enjoying it.

Every knot in my shoulders has been kneaded. My skin is glowing. My body's relaxed.

And all because he noticed I needed it when I didn't even notice it myself.

The thought repeats as I walk up the front steps to the condo Millie directed me to.

I'm like a giddy teenager as I unlock the door and look at the luxurious bed and huge clawfoot tub to soak in. I run my fingers over paperbacks by some of my favorite romance authors and revel in thought over how whoever brought them knew what I liked. A charcuterie board is set up on the table. Beside it is a box of chocolate-covered strawberries, a bowl of Chex Mix without the pretzels, and a bottle of the cabernet I like. The doors to the balcony are open, looking at the same ocean our inn does, but for some reason—maybe it's my relaxed state, maybe it's the day I've had—it sparkles even bluer.

I dial Ford the minute I finish taking it all in.

"So, I take it you didn't have any problems today picking up what I needed picked up?" Ford asks by way of answering.

"Ford." My voice breaks. Why does this feel like the nicest thing anyone has ever done for me? Seeing that I needed a break. Giving me that break. Not being put out that he's taking the brunt because of that break. "I don't even know what to say. Thank you doesn't even begin to cover it."

"There's no need to say thank you. I just hope you relaxed rather than thought of ways to escape."

"Why would I escape?"

"Says the woman who put the capital A in Type A?"

"You're so full of it."

"I am? Because I bet you that bottle of wine you're pulling the cork from right now that you struggled with giving someone else control for the day, even when that someone was me."

I burst out laughing because he is so right. I did worry about not being there. About someone needing me when I couldn't be reached.

"See, I know you well. That's why I had Millie take your phone away."

"Apparently." I pause and it dawns on me. "Oh my God. Something happened today, didn't it?"

"Stop frantically scrolling through your texts. Nothing happened. And if it had, do you not have any faith in me?"

He's right. I'm not alone. I have a partner who is more than capable.

"Okay. Panic attack averted." I sit on a cushy chair and put my feet up. "Seriously though, that, *this* . . . everything was so thoughtful. I truly think it's one of the nicest things anyone has ever done for me."

"Well, that's a shame because that is a drop in the bucket on the things you deserve, Ellery."

Silence falls on the line. It's not awkward, but I feel like there is so much unspoken in the space of time that neither of us are comfortable putting a voice to.

"Should I be jealous of those books you plan on reading tonight?" he teases.

"Whoever picked them has good taste."

"Is that code for they have great sex scenes in them?"

"Something like that." We both laugh. I'm not sure why I half expected to hear a knock on the door and have him be talking to me on his cell from the other side of it.

But there is no knock.

There are no expectations.

And I'm not sure if I like that he doesn't expect anything in return for his kindness or if I'm disappointed that he didn't come share this night with me away from the inn.

"Thank you," I say softly. "You doing this . . . it means a lot to me."

"I meant what I said. You deserve the break and so much more. Thank you for letting me show you that. For letting me spoil you. Now go enjoy your night. Soak in the tub. Dance naked because nobody's watching. Fill your glass back up. And then I'll see you in the morning."

Jesus. Someone needs to write that in one of my romance novels.

No. Wait. I don't want them to because this moment is mine.

And I don't want it to be taken away from me.

"Good night, Fordham the University."

"Good night, Celery Ellery."

CHAPTER THIRTY-FOUR

Ellery

Seven Years Ago

"I DON'T UNDERSTAND." I BLINK OVER AND OVER AS IF EACH CLOSURE and opening of my eyes will change the scene before me.

Will make me hear something different.

"You don't need to understand, Elle. All you need to know is this, us . . . it's over."

He's going to propose to you tonight, Ellery. Josh Fitzpatrick is going to ask you to marry him, and then you'll live happily ever after and be ridiculously in love.

Was it only hours ago that my best friend told me that in her singsong voice? How did I go from that to this? From elation to devastation? From getting a manicure so my nails looked perfect in pictures to show off my new ring to staring at the polish and wanting to vomit?

"Josh. I—don't—"

"I met someone else."

"What do you mean you met someone else?" I shout, tears welling in my eyes and the hollowness of my voice echoing in my head.

"Just like it sounds. I met another woman."

I scrub a hand over my face and try to process the last few minutes. "You cheated on me?"

"A relationship shouldn't be this much work. You either love me or you don't, but I shouldn't have to try and coax it out of you. I shouldn't have to try this hard to make you love me."

"But I gave you everything I could. I gave you everything I'm capable of giving." I take a step toward him, and he takes a step back.

Fight for us.

"Look, I know you've been handed a shit sandwich in life . . . but your abandonment issues aren't my problem."

Fight for me.

"I gave you everything I could."

I'm worth it—the fight, the effort, the trouble—I promise.

"Look, I thought I loved you. I thought I could cope with you not saying it back to me. But then I met someone . . . and I realized that what you gave me just isn't enough." Josh hangs his head for a beat before looking back up to me. "Goodbye, Ellery."

I watch him leave when I want to beg him to stay. His broad shoulders. His tall frame. Then the closed door itself.

I love you.

I loved you.

I forced myself to believe when the thought suffocated me. I allowed myself to think of possibility before the fear.

I let you in, Josh.

I let myself hope.

I let myself believe.

I let myself love.

Even when I was terrified of loving because I know the pain that comes with it.

I let myself love.

I thought maybe this time would prove different. That I was worthy of the love everyone talks about. That everyone gets to experience.

But clearly, I'm not.

"I realized that what you gave me just isn't enough."

I'm done. Broken. Sure, my mom was strong enough to try to love again, but I'm not her. She only lost my dad.

I lost him.

Then her.

And now Josh.

Love leads to loss, even when you try your hardest.

And especially when you're someone like me.

"I thought I loved you. I thought I could cope with you not saying it back to me. But then I met someone . . ."

He's right. He deserves the love I can't give him freely. The same love that is a double-edged sword for me. I can't fault him for wanting more.

For leaving me.

I tried.

I opened myself up and really tried.

Lesson learned.

Just like everything else in my life I've ever loved . . . it's gone.

Never again.

CHAPTER THIRTY-FIVE

Ford

"S O WHAT'S THE REAL REASON YOU DECIDED TO FLY OUT HERE and visit me today?" I ask, cutting straight to the point we've been tiptoeing around for the last few hours.

I was shocked to hell to look up and see both Ledger and Callahan standing in the foyer of the inn, assessing the progress.

We only tag-team when shit's serious. Don't they know I know that? And they're tag-teaming me.

What's the fucking deal?

Why are they here? Because they sure as fuck haven't let on as to the why during the tour of the site. Nor during the lunch they pulled me away for. And definitely not during our catch-up session where Callahan bragged about his daughter and Ledger puffed his chest at his soon-to-be born son.

Lord help us that soon there'll be a miniature Ledger running around. One is more than enough.

The two of them look at each other and then back out to the ocean beyond from where we stand on the balcony bar. Neither will look at me.

They are so obvious it's ridiculous. "Which one of you is the good cop, huh?" I ask.

"Isn't it enough that we just want to see our brother?" Callahan asks, his smile unconvincing.

That tone. I know it, and I don't trust him as far as I can throw him.

"*You're* the one playing good cop?" I bark out a laugh and nudge Ledger. "Seriously? Callahan?" Callahan lifts a middle finger my way. I shake my head in return. "So what gives, since clearly the two of you are here for a reason?"

"You're not answering our calls," Ledger says. Always all business. I'm surprised it's taken him this long to get to the point.

"I answer plenty of them." Just not the ones I don't want to deal with.

"I'll rephrase. You're being selective in which calls, which texts, you respond to. Is that better?" Ledger asks.

"You know you missed us," Callahan says.

"I did. I always do. Sometimes. Except for when you're bullshitting me. Which is now." So much for having each other's backs. Sure, we went through some struggles a few years back, but once Callahan got his shit together and lost the chip on his shoulder, I was certain we were headed in the right direction again. That we were there for each other. But now . . . now there's this. The biography. Their disregard for how it has affected me. And now we're right back to the animosity, to the agitation, and fuck if I have a clue how to fix it. The last thing I want is for them to bring it all here. It's about time they head back home. "Get to the point. I've got shit to do."

"I'm sure you do." Callahan snorts.

"What the fuck is that supposed to mean?"

"Testy. Testy," Ledger says as he crosses his arms and studies me.

"And off come the gloves," Callahan mutters.

"Let me guess. We need to show a unified front and do a press tour for the book. Heaping praise while having fake smiles plastered on our faces," I say.

"Well, on the whole, the book *is* good," Ledger says. "Neither of you said otherwise when you received your advanced copies."

"You're fucking kidding me," I mutter. Has he not been listening to me? Has he not been hearing me when I speak?

"No. I'm not. We don't have to like every single sentence in there, but overall, it was a fair representation of who Dad was. The man he was. Why wouldn't we want to praise it? To promote his legacy? It's not like the author fabricated a bunch of bullshit. These are Dad's words. It's a living piece of history that's allowed us to get to know more about him. It's a way for our kids to see the man he was in his own words. Do you not see that?"

I clench my fists and scrunch my nose.

I see it.

Of course, I see it and understand it and find truth in everything he just said.

But doesn't that make the sting even sharper? Ledger's kids will know about his dedication to be just like their grandfather. Callahan's will learn about his rebellious ways but how my father admired that streak in him.

And mine? Mine will know their dad as *Just Ford*. The man who was so unremarkable his father didn't have much to say about him. *And because of Mom's words from long ago, it's Dad's opinion of me—or lack thereof—that is tearing me down.* And nothing I do can change that now. He's gone. I don't get a second chance.

"I see it, all right. I see it and then some. The problem is you're not seeing it either. Or rather, you're not seeing what's not there." He holds my glare and gives a slow nod. "Discussion over. Call Miguel to fire up the chopper. I've got a shitload of work to do, and I'm sure you're about ready to head home. You came all this way for nothing."

Callahan's chuckle is low and taunting. "Not exactly for nothing. I mean, it's good to know we were right about one thing."

"Let it rest, Callahan," Ledger warns.

If they wanted my attention, they sure as fuck have it now.

"What the fuck does that mean?"

"C'mon, man. The sexual tension between you two is so fucking thick it's muggy in here."

"There's nothing there," I groan. We were around Ellery for a whole twenty minutes. There's no way they noticed anything. He's bluffing. Plain and fucking simple. "Nice try, though."

"My God. You are so full of shit." Ledger's laugh grates on my nerves. "Do you think I don't know you, Ford? Know your moods?"

I step into his personal space, my voice cold. "If that's the case, why can't you understand why promoting the book is a slap in my face? Why being made to feel like I didn't matter is reason to be pissed?"

"Because it's asinine, that's why," Ledger says. "We lived this life. We know Dad. We know how he felt about each one of us. That's all that should matter. Isn't that what Mom taught us?"

"Yeah, but he sure had a helluva lot to say about you, didn't he?"

"Will you two stop acting like little old ladies? There are more important things to discuss, like how Ford here needs to get laid so he can chill the hell out."

"Fuck off," Ledger and I say in unison and then look at each other

227

and start laughing. And despite everything—their trip to gang up on me, the biography, their requests for press—it feels so damn good for the pretenses to be gone and to simply laugh with them.

"Hallelujah!" Callahan glances at his watch. "We have a breakthrough. It only took five hours to get there, but we'll fucking take it." He grins like he's the mastermind when he's far from it. "So what's the deal with Snaggletooth? Is it on? Is it off—"

"Have you stuck it in?" Ledger asks and then chortles like a teenager, proud of his lame joke.

It's not lost on me that weeks ago I almost punched Diego for saying something similar. Now I'm laughing at my brother and flipping him off.

"How about no?"

"How about you're a lying motherfucker," Callahan says. And there's the triplet telepathy. I don't have to say a word, and they already know the goddamn answer.

And maybe I don't want them to know the answer.

Maybe I want to figure this shit out on my own.

Besides, the minute they know anything has happened, it's open season for them. The last thing I need is for Ellery to get spooked when she's already skittish enough.

"I believe I only saw one bedroom. *One bed.* Tell me how exactly that's working out for you," Ledger says.

"One bed on the first floor. One bed up here. That's how it's working for us," I chide.

"So you have variety. Beds. Tables. Floor. The sand. That's always good for the sex life," Callahan says and shrugs nonchalantly. "I mean, Sutton and I try to make sure we go somewhere new at least once a—"

"TMI. I do not need to know about Sutton's and your sex life," I say, holding my hands up in surrender. "Just like you don't need to know about mine."

"So there is one then?" Ledger asks.

"Go away, Ledge," I groan.

"If you're not going to answer, then I'll just go ask her. You know me. I'm not shy." Callahan stands up.

"Don't you fucking dare."

"Huh. That would be a yes." Callahan flashes a gloating grin. *The smug fucker.* I can't believe I walked right into that one. "Good to know I was right."

"Look. She just came out of a relationship. We're having fun. Can't that be enough for now?" I ask but know it's a bit more than just having fun.

Like I want her in my bed every night. By my side every day.

"He's in deeper than he's admitting," Ledger says to Callahan like I'm not even in the room.

"Definitely deeper. He's on the defensive, in protection mode. Definitely deeper," Callahan says to him.

"Aren't you guys the ones who said some shit like rebounds can be good? Great sex? No attachment? Did I miss something?" I ask.

"Yeah. You missed a lot." Callahan snorts. "Hey, Ledge? When's the last time Fordy here lied about any woman he's dated?"

"That would be never, Callahan," Ledger says in a mocking voice.

"Your point?" I ask.

"You're already in over your head. Take it from a man who has been there." Callahan raises his hand, and we all laugh.

CHAPTER THIRTY-SIX

Ellery

M AYBE YOU, OF ALL PEOPLE, CAN MAKE FORD COME TO HIS SENSES *instead of doing something he's going to regret.*

Ledger's parting words as he strode out of the inn, clearly frustrated with Ford, are on repeat in my head.

What exactly did he mean?

And why would he think that I, of all people, could help?

When I talked to the three of them, things seemed fine. They asked questions, they murmured approvals about how they really think this Sharpe Signature idea could lead to something, and they engaged in conversation with me as if I belonged as part of the four of them.

To say I was a little envious of their sibling bond is an understatement. I've never had that. Only rivalry. Only disregard. Only competition.

So that's why Ledger's comment when he left took me by surprise.

Maybe I should ask Ford what his brother meant? Then again, it's none of my business. If he wanted to talk about it, he would. Besides, asking him means getting involved in things outside of this little universe we've created here at the inn. And I'm not one hundred percent sure how I feel about letting the outside in just yet.

"You were no help," I say to the wooden stick in my hand, now devoid of the ice cream and chocolate that was on it moments ago.

Regardless, maybe there's something going on and he needs . . . comfort? Space? *Me?*

Me.

Why would a man like him need me when clearly, he has a handle on everything himself?

Between S.I.N. business and the inn, the man works nonstop without complaint or fanfare. Some days he'll take off in the chopper for the office in Manhattan at five in the morning, to return by noon, and then put in another eight or so hours here at the site.

He typically knows the answer to every question a contractor asks—even on issues or details I'm in control of—and I don't believe I've ever heard the man ask for help.

He's a one-man show, and it's incredible to watch him from the sidelines and learn from him by standing at his side.

So what is it that Ledger thinks Ford might regret? What is it that he isn't telling me?

Clearly he has the business side handled, so whatever it is, it must pertain to his personal life. Family, then. Because it doesn't seem like anything else exists for Ford outside of work and family . . . *and me.*

I sit on that thought for a bit and am more than reminded of all the kind things he has done for me.

Of course, there was Millie's salon and the condo. But there were also flowers left on the kitchen table after I mentioned how there was nothing alive in this inn. A meal delivered when I was sick of eating the same food we have stored in our makeshift pantry at the inn. A laundry service to come and take my dirty clothes. A walk down the boardwalk when Roddy pissed me off to no end and he knew I needed to cool off. Quiet nights when I read my book and he perused the Internet on his laptop where we found comfort in the silence.

Simple things that at the end of the day, make me smile. Make my day a little better.

It's high time I do something nice for him. The question is *what?*

I jump at the sound at my back. So lost in my own thoughts over the man who made the sound, that I didn't notice him.

"Sorry. I didn't know you were in here. I didn't mean to scare you," he says distractedly.

"You okay?"

"Yes. Yeah. Sure." He opens the refrigerator then closes it. Does the same to the freezer before sitting and then standing back up and going to the window to look into the darkness outside.

"Can't sleep?" I ask.

"Kind of. I don't know. I . . . I just don't know."

Something's wrong. *Is it what Ledger was talking about?* I wish I knew. Clearly Ford is distracted and unsettled.

Just like that first night we met.

It feels like a lifetime ago, but the expression on his face and the discord in his eyes are so much the same as back then.

I want to help him, but I'm not sure how to.

That doesn't mean I'm not going to try.

"Ford?"

"Hmm?" He keeps staring straight ahead as I rise from the seat, all thoughts of having a second ice cream gone. Without thinking, I move through the darkened room to him, slide my arms through his, and wrap them around his waist.

The kiss I press to his shoulder blade is so unlike me and yet . . . strangely, it feels so right, like something he would do to help comfort me.

"Tough day?" I whisper against his back. He shrugs in return. "When I was little and had a tough day, my mom would let me sneak into her bed. She'd tell me there's nothing a good cuddle can't fix."

The memory hits me out of nowhere. My mom's huge bed. My head on her chest with her steady heartbeat beneath my ear as she played with my hair. The soft melody of her voice as she told me silly stories about me as a baby. About her childhood. About my dad. The muted laughter we'd share. The calm I felt as I drifted off to sleep to the quiet lilt of her voice.

He slides his hands over mine where they encircle his waist. I'm jolted back to the here, to the now, but my mom's warmth is still wrapped around me, still cocooning me when I haven't felt it in so very long.

"Wanna come cuddle with me?"

Ford's body tenses momentarily. Almost as if he knows how much that question just cost me. As much as I've enjoyed—*and, oh, how I've enjoyed*—the sex with Ford, I've yet to stay overnight in his bed with him. Or let him stay in mine. Because that just seems too . . . intimate. That makes things too real. So my offer even surprises myself. "You sure?"

"Mm-hmm."

We make our way through the inn toward my room. We don't speak. Not as we brush our teeth. Not as he strips down to his boxer briefs and me to my tank top and panties. Not as we slide into my bed. Not as he rests his head on my stomach, arm heavy on my thighs, and I toy absently with his hair.

This feels . . . dare I say, *normal?*

Even the silence that settles around us isn't awkward. I'm not sure why I thought it would when we've lived day in, day out, with each other for the past two months, but it clearly doesn't.

Ford's breathing slowly evens out to the point that I think he's fallen asleep.

"My brothers are pissed at me," he says quietly, jolting me back from the beginning stages of sleep.

"I'm listening," I say.

"The biography about our dad. They want me to support the book. To participate in the promo tour and press junket for it like they are. I don't want to."

"Is there a particular reason why you don't want to?"

His sigh weighs down the room. *This* is what Ledger was talking about. Ford's lack of participation and his possible regret.

What the hell do I know about giving advice about this?

"Truth be told, the biography is great," he says. "The author did an incredible job bringing my dad to life. He was often misconstrued by the public as is often the case when someone finds success like he did. Rumors and gossip and supposition. But the author was able to weave together everything he learned from his interviews with my dad to show him as the man that Callahan, Ledger, and I knew him to be."

"What an incredible gift to have a piece of your dad alive in a sense."

He mutters something incoherent, but I get the gist that he's struggling with something more.

"There are things in the book I never knew about him. Stories about him and my mom that I'm so grateful to know. More about events we only knew bits and pieces of."

"Then why are you so upset by it? Is it because you've lived with him in the public eye your whole life, that you wanted to keep those last, new things you've learned about him as private?"

"I never thought about it that way. But no. Our lives under the microscope and in the spotlight is all we've ever known. Every success, every failure, has been documented on some society page somewhere. Hell, there are pictures of us at our mom's funeral out there. It's a big montage of the grieving triplets that some paparazzo sold for a ridiculous amount of money. Nothing seems to be off limits."

"I'm sorry. That had to be rough trying to cope and grieve and be in the public eye at the same time."

"It is what it is. What we didn't get in privacy we had in privilege. We know that. We've come to terms with that."

"So what is it, then, about the biography that's upset you so much?"

"There's a chapter dedicated to our dad talking about us. I'm not a fan of what is and isn't said. Callahan and Ledger don't understand why it upsets me. They think I'm being a pussy and should get over it."

I want to ask so many more questions but don't. Clearly he's telling me an abbreviated version of what he wants me to know, of how it's made him feel. If I were in his shoes, the last thing I'd want is to be given the inquisition over it.

"Your feelings are your feelings regardless of what others think. You don't need to justify them to anyone. I know for me that when someone tells me I shouldn't be one way, it only pushes me further the opposite way."

"You buying this inn is case in point."

"Very true." I laugh into the silence as I twirl a piece of his hair with my finger.

I can still recall very vividly Gregory and Joshua's reactions when I met them after signing the papers at the auction house. The disdain and disbelief that etched in the lines of their faces when they'd learned I'd unexpectedly partnered with Ford, a man they were clearly jealous of.

When I'd taken something for myself, with someone else, and their say would no longer matter. Not that it did anyway, but in their own heads it did.

"It's laughable if you think that Fordham Sharpe and his egomaniac brothers will accept any of your ideas on that godforsaken inn. He won't take you seriously, and where will that leave you? Broke and at his mercy? A fucking laughingstock of a failure?"

Being backed in a corner is all I've ever felt before I took on this project. Before I took this leap. I know what it feels like to have your back against the wall, knowing the only way to step forward, to be heard, is to come out swinging.

That was my life. Is my life.

And maybe knowing intimately how that feels will allow me to comfort Ford some.

"This disagreement isn't the same reason you fought the night of the storm when we met, is it?" I ask.

"It is."

"Then I'll tell you now, what I told you then, but in simpler terms. *Fuck 'em.* You have a right to feel how you feel. To be what you want to be. End of story."

"In theory your advice, your plan, is flawless. Somehow, I don't think it's going to work, though." He chuckles, sleep audibly edging closer. "And why is it that we're always talking about me, Celery Ellery? Why do you always get off the hook?"

"I'm far from off the hook."

"Bullshit."

"I'm an open book. Just ask me. Too bad there's nothing interesting on the pages to read." I chuckle.

"That's one of your many party tricks."

"What is?"

"Deflect, dodge, and then change the subject when it veers toward you. Make a joke. Laugh it off. Why are you so afraid to let someone get too close? To know you?"

"Don't be ridiculous. I don't do that."

But I know I damn well do. He's just the first person who's called me on it in a very long time.

Possibly because he's the only one I've let get this close since . . . since Josh.

"Whatever you say, Elle. But at some point, people stop trying to know you when you won't let them."

His words hit me almost as hard as the unexpected memory of my mother. She was the one I had shared everything with. And just like my dad, she left. That was all the proof I needed that it was better to keep myself distanced from people. Because if you don't love them, if you don't allow yourself to love them, then there is no loss when they leave you.

"But at some point, people stop trying to know you when you won't let them."

Those words replay in my head as we talk about everything and nothing. Favorite sports teams. Bucket list items. Pet peeves. First loves.

We laugh. We grow quiet. We get to know each other on a level we haven't before. And only when it's two in the morning do we decide it's time to get some sleep.

"Good night, Celery Ellery."

"Good night, Fordham the University."

It's comforting having the heat of his body behind mine, and the weight of his arm over my waist.

And suddenly, despite the yawn on my lips, I can't sleep.

All I can do is think. About Ford. About tonight. About everything he did and didn't say. About how close I feel to him.

"Hey, Ford?"

"Hmm?"

"I know the why."

"I'm glad you do."

I love that he doesn't ask me what it is. That he doesn't press me when most would. I think that's the only reason I decide to tell him.

That's a lie.

I tell him because it's important for him to know.

"I broke up with Chandler because I agreed to marry him for the wrong reasons. I never recognized it until the night I met you." I take in a deep, steadying breath. "I felt more in one night talking to you, listening to you, laughing with you, than I ever did with *him*, a man I was going to marry. I left him because I never knew that feeling existed, and the thought of possibly never feeling it again scared the hell out of me."

The admission takes my breath away. For a woman determined not to let herself feel, I just committed a cardinal sin and admitted how much he made me feel.

How much I wanted to feel again.

And while I'm scared as hell over putting it out there in the universe that has been so very cruel to me, I might even feel a tad bit of relief over saying it too.

And in perfect Ford fashion, he responds in the way I need him to most. He picks up my hand and presses his lips to my palm.

"You deserve everything good, Ellery Sinclair. Laughter. Happiness. Love."

If only I could truly believe that was true.

CHAPTER THIRTY-SEVEN

Ellery

DAYS BLEND TOGETHER.

Mornings into days. Days into nights. Moments spent together working . . . and enjoying each other in every capacity.

What I didn't expect was that one night I invited Ford to sleep in my bed to be the start of him being there every night.

It just sort of happened.

The next night he came to talk to me before bed. We both needed to shower, so logically we decided to conserve water. And then we may have lain in the bed with towels wrapped around us and talked for hours before drifting off to sleep.

And then the night after that, I called him in to look at an idea I had on my computer. He gave his input. He told me he trusted my decisions. And then he never left.

There was no conversation about the transition. No, "Hey, what do you think about me moving into your bed on a permanent basis?" It just happened.

And it happened in a way that didn't allow me to freak out about it.

Even weirder is the self-admission that it's rather nice to wake up with him beside me. There's a comfort in him being there. A sense of companionship. A lack of loneliness.

"We can stay at the Sag Harbor house if you want," Ford says, his shoulder leaning against the doorjamb. "I know it's a drive, but if we do it together, it won't be too bad."

I inspect the freshly set granite in one of the suite's bathrooms. The edge detail is right. The cuts are clean. The caulking straight. The edge detail craftsman quality.

I'm impressed. The installer did a great job.

Now to inspect fifteen more just like it but in different grain patterns. No two suites here will be alike.

"I appreciate it. It's a good thought in theory, but even without traffic, we'd spend two hours a day commuting. That time could be better spent here."

He nods. "I figured you were going to say that, but I wanted to put it out there. They do need to start work on your room though. How do you want to handle that?"

"I'll move my stuff out. There's not much. I can float from space to space that's not being used or—"

"Or you can stay in my luxurious accommodations with me upstairs. Didn't we agree that will be the last room since it has the least amount to change?"

I nod, my heart pounding in my chest. How ridiculous is it that it's okay if he sleeps, *stays*, in my bed, but the thought of moving into his room makes me panic?

I'll answer for myself. *It's completely ridiculous.*

My smile is tight. "Sure. That will work."

His laugh echoes around the empty bathroom. "Your expression looks like I just asked you if it was okay to amputate your arm or something."

"It did not."

"It did too," Ford says as he moves toward me. His forefinger is on my chin, tilting my eyes up to look at him. "I would say I promise I don't bite . . ." His lips brush against mine and have me reliving his nip to my shoulder last night. "But you know that's a lie."

The chuckle he emits vibrates into the ache forming between my thighs.

Who thought a love bite could be such a turn-on?

"Are you trying to distract me, Ford?"

Another kiss.

Another slide of his hands to squeeze my ass.

"Am I doing a good job of it?"

"I'm not completely distracted yet. I'm noticing that the grout line over there has a void spot between the fourth and fifth tiles."

His hand slides inside the waistband of my jeans and heads straight for that ache. "Void spots are a travesty."

I bite back a gasp as his fingers find my clit and slide into the wetness beneath.

"And the toilet needs to be reset. It's not perfectly level. Sitting on an uneven toilet is uncomfortable."

"Details. You're so good at noticing them." He nips my earlobe as his fingers tuck inside of me.

I'm helpless to my moan. There's no fighting that as he hits that rough patch of nerves inside.

"That sound says you're distracted now," he says and then runs the tip of his tongue down my neck.

"The shower enclosure needs to be caulked in the far right corner."

A lick of his tongue up my neck. "I know what else can be *cocked*."

I laugh.

It turns into a mewl as I sag against him, fingernails digging into his biceps and forehead resting on his chest, as pleasure begins to build. As the coil twists tighter. As his harsh breaths and attentive hand bring me to the brink and then push me over the edge without any goddamn warning.

"Jesus, Ford," I pant as my body absorbs the wave of sensations he just provoked. "What was that for?"

"I had to convince you why it was worth it to move into my humble abode." He winks.

I swat at him as my breathing evens out.

"Sinclair?" a voice calls out down the hallway as the two of us jump apart.

"I thought everyone was gone," Ford says as he removes his hand from between my thighs and I quickly button up my pants.

"I did too," I whisper-yell.

"Ellery?" the voice calls again, closer.

"This bathroom smells of sex," Ford says, looking around as if that's going to help rid it of the scent of my arousal.

"Great. Good. Why don't we get out of here so whoever that is doesn't come in here?"

Ford pushes at my back. "You go first."

"Yes. Great. *Hi, whoever you are* with the post-orgasm flush on my cheeks."

He starts laughing. Isn't that all we can do at this point?

"Well, I have you on my hand, so I'm no help getting rid of the sex smell." His grin says he's enjoying this.

"I'm in here," I yell out from the suite, pushing Ford behind the bathroom door and out of sight just as Roddy passes.

"Oh, there you are," he says, stopping and studying me with an odd look on his face. "You okay? You look kind of—"

"I was just making a punch list for this bathroom. Hot flashes hit at the strangest times." I wave a hand in front of my face to sell the lie. "Want to walk to the next one with me?"

His eyes narrow. *Come on, Roddy. Let it go.*

"Sure. Yes. Okay."

"What are you doing here? I thought you'd left for the night."

"I did." He blushes as he fiddles with his keys before holding them up. "Found them."

What am I missing here? Why does he seem so nervous?

"Found what? *Your keys?*" But if he'd lost his keys, how had he driven his truck home when he left earlier? Why is he lying to me?

"Yes. Keys. These keys." He nods again as we enter the only other suite on the floor. When he doesn't speak, I begin to assess the bathroom installation in case he thinks I'm lying about what I was doing. A guilty conscience and all.

"Did you need something else?" I ask and look up to him when I finish making notes on the punch list for the suite.

"No . . . but I'm glad I came, though. The same lady who was nosing around earlier is out there again. I told her she was on private property and needed to leave or we'd call the police for trespassing."

"What lady?" I ask, completely confused.

"The reporter who was here earlier? Or at least she says she is. I would have figured Ford told you about her since she was camped out there for so long."

"No. He didn't." *What the hell?* "What does she want?"

"She wants an exclusive with him. Or at least that's what she's gunning for."

"Over the inn? Over the book—"

"Yeah. The book. She wants to know why the other two brothers are promoting it and he's not. She's playing the 'there must be trouble in paradise angle' or some shit like that."

"Um. Okay. I had no idea." Nor do I have any real answers as to why he's not.

"Ford knows about her. He was the one who told us to turn her away earlier." He looks around the bathroom and then back to me. "So, see? Losing my keys meant I came back and saved the day." The joke falls flat but his nervous chuckles echo within the empty suite.

Something is off here.

"Anything else you need?" He shifts back and forth on his feet and keeps averting his eyes from mine. "Roddy?"

"No. Yes." He rocks on his heels, clearly unable to stand still, and gives me a strained smile. "I've really enjoyed working with you on this project."

"As have I with you."

"And since there are only a couple of weeks left before we open to the public, I was wondering if maybe you'd like to go out and celebrate a job well done?"

"Of course. I was already planning on doing a little something for everyone who's worked so hard on this. Great minds think alike."

"That's not—Ellery." He looks at me and then looks back down as it dawns on me. The fidgeting. The nerves. The showing back up here for *lost* keys. "I meant you and me. Just us."

My recognition of what's happening takes longer to process than him asking, and so I stare at him, blinking with my mouth lax and surprise owning me.

"Um. I—Roddy—"

"Hey. Rod. What are you doing here? Did you need help with something?" Ford asks as he walks into the suite. Either knowing or not knowing that his timing is perfect in this most uncomfortable situation.

Roddy startles and jumps back. "*Ford.* I didn't know you were here. I didn't see your car out front. I—"

"It's parked next door. The lot was full earlier." He looks at me and then back to Roddy. "Everything okay?"

"Yep. Just left my keys is all." He holds them up and then accidentally drops them. They clatter on the floor as he bends over and fumbles to pick them up. "I was—I was just chatting with Ellery about how the project's almost over."

"Crazy how fast it went," Ford says. By the way he's looking at Roddy, I know he heard what he asked. That he asked me out.

And I'm not one hundred percent certain how I feel about the jealousy firing in his eyes.

Normally it would piss me off. I don't belong to anyone.

But for some reason, the look on Ford is sexy.

"It is." Roddy takes a few steps back and checks the door for what seems like the twentieth time. He's more nervous now than before.

"Thanks again for earlier. The reporter."

"Not a problem. She was here again. I got rid of her."

"See? I knew we could count on you to look out for everything to do with this project." Ford's smile is electric. "I'll walk you out."

And as the two men clear the doorway, Ford looks back at me and gives a shake of his head.

He overheard Roddy all right.

And since there are only a couple of weeks left . . .

Roddy's comment repeats in my head.

Is that what's been bugging me? Why I've been kind of bitchy this last week? Because like it or not, Roddy's right. There are only a few weeks left here on the project. Then what? What do I do next? How can I go back to the life I lived with people who didn't believe in me when I've spent the last few months with someone who has done just the opposite?

Ford has let me make decisions. He's let me struggle and applauded me when I've figured out the solution. He's let me succeed and told me he knew all along I could do it. He's looked to me for my suggestions and allowed me to bend his ear when I'm trying to find my own answers about a problem or a situation.

He's let me grow in ways no one ever has before. And when I've doubted myself, he's looked me in the eye and either given me the tough love I deserved or the soft words of encouragement he somehow knew I needed.

And that's only touching the professional side.

Personally? How do I unpack that?

He's been my friend. My confidant. My lover. All three combined have been something I've never experienced before.

What does the future hold for us? It's not something we've talked about while we're in "project land" where we don't have to think about beyond this.

But *beyond this* is coming.

Beyond this is only weeks away.

Then what?

I can't imagine him not being a part of my life. It's just that simple. It's like he convinced me to do this project with him, has held tight, and hasn't let go.

It's almost as if I've fall—

"Well, that was awkward," Ford says with a huge grin when he walks into the room. But his feet falter and his eyes narrow when he sees the expression on my face. "Elle? What's wrong?"

No.

No.

No.

This can't be happening.

I can't be—I haven't—there's no way I've fallen for Fordham Sharpe. It's impossible.

I don't do that. I don't fall. I don't love.

I don't let myself love.

This is sex.

This is companionship.

This is loneliness mixed with a forced proximity combined with great sex and a good friendship.

"Nothing is wrong," I assert forcefully. "I've just got work to do."

His chuckle is low and taunting, oblivious to the internal war I'm simultaneously waging and freaking out over. "That's not what you said about fifteen minutes ago."

"You're right. It's not." I emit a nervous chuckle. "But Roddy and his asking me out kind of killed the mood."

"Love the guy but not in particular right now."

"Please tell me you didn't get mad at him for—"

"I didn't say a word. Acted like I never heard a thing. Didn't want to embarrass the guy."

"Good. Great." I go to walk past Ford, and he grabs my hand.

"What's going on?"

"I said nothing."

"C'mon, Sinclair. Lay it on me. What are you not telling me?"

"Nothing."

His face is a foot from mine, and I have nowhere to hide. I try to keep a straight face, but I'm certain there's panic in my expression. Desperation.

I need space. Time. Distance. *Anything* to have a few minutes to build that wall back up that I clearly let slip.

I am *not* in love with Ford Sharpe.

That's absurd.

Ellery Sinclair does not fall in love.

Correction, Ellery Sinclair *will not* fall in love.

He nods. His lips are pursed. His eyes searching. "Okay. I'll accept that answer. *For now.* But I know you well enough to know something's going on. I just hope you trust me enough to tell me what."

Emotion I don't want to acknowledge clogs in my throat. *Trust and love go hand in hand.* So no, I don't want either it seems. I clear away the emotion and straighten my spine.

Deflect.

Dodge.

Redirect.

"The book? What's bugging you? The reason the reporter is snooping around?" I shrug dramatically. "It appears the same thing could be said of you, Ford."

And with that comment, I turn on my heel and walk away.

CHAPTER THIRTY-EIGHT

Ford

THIS IS RIDICULOUS.

It would be one thing if she gave me an all-out cold shoulder for whatever she's pissed off at me about.

But she hasn't.

We work side by side. We sleep side by side. We fuck . . . well, we fuck in all different positions that are anything but side by side.

Yet . . . something is off with her. And the only clue she's given me was the whole comment about the biography and what I haven't told her.

Not exactly sure I believe that.

When my phone rings, I look at the screen and groan. "I'm not in the mood for your shit," I answer in greeting.

"Wow. Hello to you too," Callahan says.

I take a step outside of the inn for some privacy away from the craftsmen crawling all over the place.

"If you're calling to rehash the same bullshit Ledger called about yesterday—"

"Yes, but . . . for other reasons."

"So, we're back to good cop then?"

"No. I'm the brother who says you have a right to be pissed. Hurt. Whatever it is you want to be. But I'm also the brother who is going to give you a little tough love and say those things but also be part of this with us."

My hand pulling down on my neck eases some. "What was that?"

"You heard me, you fucker. Being nice is a rarity so don't make me repeat myself."

"*Why?*" It's the same question I asked Ellery weeks ago. I have a feeling this answer will be just as important to me.

Callahan's sigh is heavy. "Because we're the only family we've got and we don't like doing this without you. Look, I'll be the first one to admit Dad was a bastard at times. It's not exactly like the two of us got along all the time . . . and yet, *he's still my dad*. I still love him. Just like I know you still love him too."

"Callahan . . ."

"I know. Believe me, brother, *I know*. But you're letting what someone wrote—what someone chose not to write—come between the three of us. Mom would be fucking pissed at that."

I stand in silence before emitting a long, drawn-out sigh and moving to a set of chairs just delivered for the café. "You know what's the hardest?" I finally ask. "I know you guys know what Dad felt about us, but it's embarrassing for other people to know too."

He barks out a laugh. "Dude, the whole world knows what a fuckup I am. How I dropped out of Wharton. How I was a challenge who rebelled every chance I could and got in trouble more times than not. He even retold that story about how he caught me screwing that intern on the desk."

"That was so bad." I laugh. I can't help it. And it feels so good to. "I forgot that was in the book."

"Yeah. I didn't. And neither did Sutton. *Christ*," he mutters. "That was a fun one to explain."

"Like she was surprised by it."

"You're right. She wasn't. She knows my past." He chuckles. "If you're desperate for the world to see you, there's always the leaked sex tape angle. That always works getting your name out there."

"Fuck off." But there is a smile on my face.

"Make one. We can have a housekeeper at your house accidentally find it and sell it to the tabloids. Isn't that how it's supposed to work?"

"Like I said, fuck off."

"Speaking of sex," he says, completely unfazed, "you and her still good?"

I pause for a beat. "Yeah. I think so."

"You *think* so? Now, *that* sounds convincing."

"No. It's . . . I don't know what it is."

"Has it run its course? I mean, that happens sometimes. No shame in that."

"No—"

"Is it just like a project fling? I've had a few of those. A little fun while you're on-site that ends when your job there ends."

"That's not it. It's—"

"Just sex. A good bang but no verbal agreement on the monogamy side. If that's the case, man, make sure you jacket up. I mean, always jacket up but—"

"Goddamn it, will you let me get a fucking word in edgewise?" I shout at him, frustrated that of all the scenarios he's painted, none of them describe what Ellery and I have.

"Or there's a lot more there and either one or both of you are too chickenshit to just come out and say it. Or you have and the other isn't sure how they feel about it—which is fucking brutal to say the least."

"Callahan," I warn, my voice steely as I pinch the bridge of my nose and begin to pace the small and newly landscaped garden area on the western side of the property.

"Then there's the chance that you just flat-out love her or she loves you . . . and you don't know what to do about it because love wasn't on either of your radars."

My feet falter.

I know the answer. I think I've known for quite some time.

It still doesn't mean it doesn't stagger me.

I stand there with my phone to my ear and the ocean before me, but I don't see a single thing in front of me.

"Sometimes it just happens when you least expect it," Callahan says, his voice softening. I don't have to speak or explain or refute, because he's my brother. He already knows. "It was the last thing on my radar, that's for fucking sure, and then it hit me like a sledgehammer. That I—selfish, egotistical, asshole Callahan—was in love with someone."

"I didn't say a word," I finally manage.

"You don't have to. I know, brother. *I know*," he says in quiet commiseration.

"*Fuck.*" I run a hand through my hair.

The woman had a silent freak-out when I asked her if she wanted to sleep in my room for a few nights. I don't exactly think falling in love with me was part of her plans.

But it wasn't mine either and look what happened.

"If I can give you one piece of advice—and I know it's hard to hear coming from your little brother, but just listen and use what you want. You can't force love. You either feel it or you don't. And not acknowledging it doesn't mean it didn't happen. But once you put it out there, you can't exactly take it back. You have to live with the consequences of it. Maybe you tell her once you've wrapped your head around it. Maybe you don't tell her at all. Maybe you wait for her to come to you. The worst thing in the world is to give someone your love and for them to shun it. That hurts like a motherfucker."

My smile is faint. "Look at you. When did you become an expert on this shit?"

He chuckles. "I haven't. No one's an expert when it comes to love. That's the beauty and the pain of it."

"I've gotta get going."

"No, you don't. You're going to stand wherever you are for the next ten minutes and try to analyze and then refute but eventually accept what I've just said. That's how you are, but I'll let you lying to me about it slide." He pauses. "Ford? This is what I meant. We're always here for each other, a unified front. We help each other when we need to. It sucks not having you be a part of this with us."

"Noted, man. Noted."

"Love you, bro."

The call ends and I stay where I am for a good few minutes. Or as Callahan stated, ten minutes there about.

My mind spins. At the things Callahan said and the truths hidden behind them.

Maybe you don't tell her at all. Maybe you wait for her to come to you. The worst thing in the world is to give someone your love and for them to shun it. That hurts like a motherfucker.

So what the hell do I do about this?

CHAPTER THIRTY-NINE

Ellery

"WE STILL NEED A NAME FOR THE INN."

I look over at Ford sitting beside me on the beach. "I know. I'm working on it. I just haven't found anything catchy enough that goes with your regal-sounding half of it."

"Oh, please." He rolls his eyes and playfully tugs on a piece of my hair. "There's nothing regal about Signature Sharpe Collection."

"Uh-huh. Well, it seems to be everywhere right now. Too bad we can't have the remodel finished and this place open to help cash in on all that visibility." Ford blanches at the comment but doesn't say anything. So I continue. "You're still mad about it?"

Talk to me, Ford.

"More like indifferent at this point."

I purse my lips and nod, guilt overwhelming me about the lie—or rather the omission—that I'm making.

I know why you're hurting.

The biography is well-written. Its stories and insights about the larger-than-life Maxton Sharpe have held my attention for the past three days since its release. It's not exactly my normal read, but I've surprised myself by how much I've enjoyed it.

In fact, I was plowing through it, one chapter after another, loving learning the relationship his parents had. Laughing at Callahan's rebellion and antics. Amazed by Ledger's drive and focus. I was eager to learn more about Ford through his father's eyes . . . but the stories never came. The insight was not there. In fact, there was nothing more than a few generic sentences that painted Ford to be nothing close to the spectacular man that I've come to know.

And to add insult to injury, the author included a quote about how Maxton referred to him as *Just Ford*.

That's it. Just. Ford.

Ford's eyes hold mine, and I completely understand why he's indifferent. Why he's harboring hurt. I would be too.

I just wish he'd talk to me about it.

"Okay," I murmur. "Indifferent is okay." My smile is soft as I take a sip of my wine and hold his eyes over the wine glass.

"Have you figured out what's next for you yet, Celery Ellery?"

I shrug. "No. I need to sit down and have a face-to-face with Garland."

"Have you talked to him or your brothers at all?"

"My brothers? Beyond the obligatory normal check-ins? Not really. But I was quite surprised that Garland has called me a few times to ask for my input on several things."

"What's that about?"

"Absence makes the heart grow fonder?" I joke and then roll my eyes. "But seriously, there were a few things he wanted to ask me on some of the ongoing projects, things, details, what have you, that I've done on past projects."

"Things your brothers took credit for, I presume?"

"Yep. You got it. And when they couldn't answer him, he figured that out."

"So he had to call you and now he knows you were the mastermind behind all of the good things there?" Ford asks, grin widening.

"Well, when you put it that way . . ." I chuckle and brush imaginary dust off my shoulder.

But it'd felt damn good when he'd called to get my input. And even better when right before I hung up, he subtly commented about how my absence there was noticeable.

I may have fist-pumped the empty room.

I might have skipped a step or two as I went back to work.

"And how exactly do you intend to use that to your benefit when you go back?" He lifts his eyebrows and waits for an answer while my brain is still focusing on *go back*.

On the notion that this is all going to be *over* soon.

"On one hand, I know I can show him what we've done here and that's all the proof I'll need that I'm capable and experienced—"

"More than capable."

"But on the other hand, I almost don't want to taint what we've done here by using it to get a better footing there." I twist my lips and look at the waves breaking on the shore. It's as if I don't want to share this with them.

"Then don't," Ford says as a Sharpe can. He nudges me and winks. "I know someone who can give you a great reference."

"Thanks." I chuckle. "What about you? Do your brothers already have you scheduled out for the next year?"

I hate that we're talking about next steps like strict business associates. Like there is nothing more between us than this project and seeing it come to an end in the next two weeks.

But isn't that what I want?

Isn't that what I've tried to convince myself this is over the past week?

"We haven't really talked about it, to be honest. They're not exactly thrilled with me at the moment. They're working double time between S.I.N. and the press junket and they don't feel I'm contributing."

"But you're working double time too. For S.I.N. and here."

"They don't exactly see it that way."

"Do you think you'll regret it? Not being part of everything surrounding it? The public representation? Preserving his memory, and all the rest that goes with it?" I ask as if I have no clue why he doesn't want to participate.

"Only time will tell. Does it sit like a rock in my gut every time I think about what they're doing, what I'm not, and the biography? Yes. I won't deny that." He shifts in the sand and clears his throat as the sun sets, and the sea's end begins to blend with the darkening horizon.

I wait for him to say more. I silently plead that he does, that he trusts me enough to ease the burden that's weighing on his heart and soul, but he doesn't.

"You asked what was next for me," he says, switching topics. Clearly he's been around me for too long and has taken notes on avoidance. "I have my normal duties with S.I.N. . . . and maybe I'll look for another property to convert into a Signature Sharpe one."

"Really?"

257

He nods. "I've been mulling it over. I like the niche. The idea of it. Of course, I'll have to have some returns from this one first to see if it's financially viable, but I've had fun doing this. Enjoying the hands-on part has been rather unexpected for me."

I smile and don't voice the question that's on the tip of my tongue. Do you want a partner on the next one too?

"You were a pro in every sense of the word, Ford. You blew my expectations out of the water. I seriously would have never known you hadn't done this before."

"Same can be said for you." He taps his glass against mine and holds my gaze with the funniest expression on his face. Like something he wants to say is on the tip of his tongue. But as quickly as it's there, it's gone. "I was thoroughly impressed, Sinclair."

"We make a good team," I say and rest my head on his shoulder.

"We definitely do," he murmurs.

And this is what I'm going to miss when this is over.

Our peaceful unwind sessions after a long hard day.

His little pep talks that make me feel validated. Included. Wanted. Heard.

In simple terms, *him*.

CHAPTER FORTY

Ellery

"WHAT? NO ICE CREAM BAR CELEBRATION?" FORD ASKS, interrupting a rather juicy part of my book, as he walks into our newest room we're staying in since where we were is now under major overhaul.

"There is no way I'm eating in here." I look up to find him standing in the doorway, fresh from the shower with a pair of gym shorts on and everything else left wonderfully bare for my eyes to feast on.

"Because?"

I motion to the suite around us. It's the nicest, cleanest, most comfortable place we've gotten to sleep and live for the past few months. "The last thing I want to do is dirty it up." He snorts with a glance to the bed that has me smiling in turn. "Of course, you'd think that."

"I'm a guy. Do you expect any less? But you do realize in less than a month's time, people will be ordering room service and eating in here, right?"

"I'm well aware." I internally huff and set my Kindle down on the bed beside me. I guess the hate-fuck about to occur in my book will have to be revisited and enjoyed in a bit. There's nothing worse than being interrupted mid-sex scene.

"Are you feeling okay?" he asks. "It's late, and you're opting to read versus sneak non-caloric ice cream."

"I'm opting to enjoy the softness of this bed." I lean my head back against the headboard and revel in the feel of the mattress. "Remind me to give Katarina a raise," I say of our interior designer who helped us pick out all the furniture and décor. "She did a hell of a job selecting mattresses."

"Really? Let me see." He falls back on the bed and sighs, much like I did when I first sat on it. "Talk about heaven, but then again, I think anything would feel like it at this point after sleeping on what felt like ply-wood the last few months."

"I told you to stay in Sag Harbor."

"And I told you that if I go, you go, and you refused to go so . . . we stayed."

"Stubborn man."

"Hardheaded female." We both chuckle, but as the silence stretches, Ford's eyelids grow heavy. "We did good today, Elle."

"Really good."

"Every last item of furniture has been delivered save for those two broken barstools. Both kitchens passed inspection today. The exterior was painted. So many things. I feel like it's so close."

"It is, but we still need a name so we can get the signage ordered."

"I know. I know."

Yes, each day brings us closer to the grand opening, but it's also bit-tersweet too. Every item checked off our punch list, every trade finishing and clocking out for the last time, every walk-through of the inn in com-plete awe at the transformation is more than bittersweet.

It's a reminder that this is ending.

It means . . . who knows what it means for Ford and me? We've yet to even broach the subject.

"I've been thinking," he murmurs, his eyes still closed, his arm stretched out so his hand is on my calf. His wet hair is leaving dark marks on the comforter beneath his head.

"About?"

"What if we partnered up again?" he asks as my heart leaps in my chest. "I mean, I'm more than certain your stepdad would jump at the chance for a long-standing contract with S.I.N. Who wouldn't?" His arrogance knows no bounds, but he *is* right.

Isn't that what I had leveraged to get the okay to come here in the first place?

"I know the financial burden of something like this could be over-whelming. S.I.N. could buy the properties and take on the fiscal responsibil-ities, and Haywood Redesigns could do the improvements with the caveat that I'll work with you and no one else. Garland would be handcuffed, and you'd continue to get to do what you love and are incredible at. I mean, that is if you're interested in working with me, Celery Ellery?"

I stare at him and his closed eyes, my mouth agape. How can he just say something like that so casually and not freaking look at me?

"Hear me out," he says, mistaking my shocked silence for hesitation. "I'm not saying S.I.N. would take you out of that picture. You'd get a percentage of ownership in each property. I get that you think it'll come off like you slept your way into the position, or that I'm only asking you because I feel obligated to or out of plain pity to stick it to your brothers, but that couldn't be further from the truth. You're talented and crazy good at what you do. Besides, you've spoiled me. I don't think I could do this with anyone else. So that's why I'm asking you."

Excitement at the thought of getting to do this again bubbles up. Of doing it with him, even more so. The "yes" I want to shout from the rooftops is sitting on my tongue. I wish I could say it, but don't we need to address the white elephant in the room? Or rather, the fact that we're on the same bed, his hand on my leg, and basically living together?

I mean, I was going to marry and live with Chandler with a whole lot less than there is between Ford and me . . . so why am I hesitating?

Or rather, why are we not addressing it?

Do I really want to know? Do I really want to be told that in two weeks this "fling" or whatever it is will be over? Or is it better to just stick my head in the sand?

I pick up my Kindle and flip to where I was at.

Just call me Ostrich.

"You're not responding." Ford tilts his head back so he can look at me. "Wait a minute. I ask you to partner up with me, and you opt to read your book instead of responding?" he teases as he sits up. "I'm thinking I should take that as an insult." And before I can react, he twists around and plucks the Kindle from my hand.

"No," I yelp, eyes wide as he taps the screen and words come to life.

And my freak-out is for more than a few reasons.

One, oh my God. He's going to know what I've been secretly reading most nights while he taps away on his laptop. And it's not that I'm ashamed, but . . . now *he's going to know.*

And two, Maxton's biography is on there. In my library. And at this point I'm more than grateful that I had the forethought to open and close several of my other books so that the memoir is buried farther down the library on the off chance that he might see my screen. But still, it's on there.

"You're ignoring me for . . . *Oh. Wow.*" He sits up straighter as his eyes widen. His eyes flash to mine, a ghost of a smile painting his lips before he looks back at the tablet.

I gulp, and my cheeks turn what feel like ten shades of red.

The scene I was reading was damn good. Descriptive and dirty and thigh-clenchingly sexy.

He clears his throat. "This is really interesting stuff, Ellery. Even more fascinating is that you bookmarked the page." He meets my eyes before reading out loud. "'*Her cry fills the small space as I slide my tongue up her slit then back down before burying it inside of her. Before owning every inch of her. Before licking her and pleasuring her with my fingers until her legs buckle, and my name falls from her lips over and over as I bring her to the brink.*' Whew." His Adam's apple bobs. "Should I see if you've bookmarked any of the other sex scenes?"

"No." I swipe at his hand, but he yanks the Kindle away. All I can do is laugh.

"Don't be embarrassed. Sex. *Wanting sex.* Wanting sex *with me* . . . it's completely natural. Completely logical. And this? This is . . ." He grins at me. "*Incredible.*"

He says that as if sex with him isn't of the same caliber.

Because it is.

It definitely is.

I yelp as he tugs on my leg with one hand and pulls me flat, climbing over my hips to straddle me.

"Let's see," he says as he touches the screen. He sucks in a breath and groans. "This one is hot. '*Ah, Lilly. This ass is perfection. I want it pink from your punishment. I want it violated by my fingers. I want it filled while I fuck you long and deep with my cock in that willing pussy of yours.*' Jesus." He barks out a laugh that is strained. His eyes meet mine. One hand holds my Kindle, his other runs languorously up and down the midline of my chest. Under one breast, his thumb just skims my nipple, before moving on to the other one. His cock is thick, heavy, and hard where it presses against the seam of his shorts. "I definitely need to read *this* book. It's . . . yeah." He coughs out a laugh as his cheeks flush. I love that he's slightly embarrassed by it.

It lessens the fact that I am.

Who am I kidding? It doesn't.

"What else have we bookmarked in here? Should we look?" He grinds his hips over me and my body burns a little hotter. "Eeny. Meeny. Miney Mo. Oh. Damn. Here's one."

He leans forward and teases me with a kiss, but when I try to deepen it, he pulls back and simply tugs on my bottom lip.

He clears his throat.

"Hands on the wall."

"Only if you fuck me," she says in a broken voice.

"We're getting there." I laugh, but then groan as she jolts when I slide the head of my cock right into her opening.

Every part of me tenses. I try to fight the violent desperation to take her with abandon. To pound into her. To chase my own bloody pleasure now that I know she's found hers.

My hips thrust ever so slightly into her. Her warm, wet heat grabs my cock inch by inch, until I bottom out and see stars.

Fuck.

Heaven.

Hell.

Just fuck.

My hands grip the sides of her hips as she flexes those muscles around me. Once. Twice.

"Lennox," I warn, as her chuckle fills the room.

She's in control now. She owns me in this moment. With her pussy. With her confidence. With how damn good she feels.

And I snap.

Control lost.

My hips slam against hers. I thrust over and over in a punishing pace encouraged by her words. Oh my God. Harder. Yes. Right there. Faster. Don't stop. I'm coming again. Rush. Rush.

And when she tightens around me this time, I lose the battle but win the damn war. I empty myself into her, my hips jerking, my vision going black, her name a groan of bliss on my lips."

"I lose the battle but win the damn war. That's rather poetic when talking about fucking, don't you think?" He chuckles. "Look at me, Ellery." He pauses and adjusts his hips so I most definitely feel how hard he is, how turned on he is, pressing against my lower belly. "*Look. At. Me.*"

"Hmm?" I flash my eyes up. He's so goddamn gorgeous it hurts to look at him.

"You're telling me, I can talk dirty to you, I can run my tongue over and in every inch of you, but you squirm when I read these hot-as-hell scenes to you?"

"Ford." I sigh his name out as he leans forward and tugs on my ear, the warmth of his breath sending chills over my body.

"Do you want me to do this to you, Ellery?" A nip of my bottom lip. "Does it turn you on?" A tug of my nipple through the fabric of my tank top. "Do you want to act out this scene?" He leans back and slips his hand between my thighs to feel the heat there, the arousal soaking through my shorts. "Well, well, well. It appears you do."

"Ford," I repeat on a strangled moan.

He leans forward again, his lips taunting mine with an almost kiss. "I'm only in trouble when you say my middle name after it . . . and I don't think I'm in trouble right now."

I already want him. I'm already more than wet for him, but I startle when his hands rest on my ass and squeeze.

That action is followed by him burying his nose into my slit and taking one long slide of his tongue from my entrance back up. My breath catches. Every muscle affected by the lick of his tongue tightens in anticipation. Every part of me wants.

"I'm going to fuck you, Sidney." Another lick. "I'm going to bury my cock in this tight pussy of yours." His breath hot against my tender flesh. "Then I'm going to slip my finger into your ass." The soft press of his thumb against my rim of muscles. "I'm going to fuck you with both so that when you come, every single damn part of you does." The slide of his tongue into my pussy so that every part of his face is buried against me. "Do you understand?"

I nod, the dark promise of his words an aphrodisiac poured on top of the seduction he's already plied me with.

"Uh-uh-uh," he murmurs as he fists my hair in his hand and gently pulls my head back as he runs the tip of his nose up the length of my spine. His finger slips into me just as his mouth reaches my ear and his dick presses against my thigh. "No nods." He works his fingers in and out of me, the sound of how wet I am filling the room. "No easy way out." They slide back out and the trace of his coated fingertip travels up the crease of my ass and then down. "I want you to make noise, Princess." The tug of his teeth on my ear as his fingers tuck back in and curve against my G-spot. "I want you to scream." A soft tug of my hair. "And I want to know you know who's making you scream."

"I'm sensing a theme here." His eyes are heavy with desire. His breaths shallow. His fingers run up and down the seam of my shorts so that the fabric is now damp. My pussy's already swollen with desire. He rises from the bed. "Take off your clothes, Ellery."

CHAPTER FORTY-ONE

Ellery

HIS WORDS ARE LIKE PUTTING GASOLINE ON A FIRE.
I'm already primed, already turned on, and now he's going to order me around? Yes. Please. There's something to be said about a man who likes to take control in the bedroom.

And I'm all for it.

I take my time stripping my clothes off. My tank top. My shorts. I take pleasure in watching his eyes darken and nostrils flare as I do so, followed by a lick of my lips and the slide of my hand between my thighs.

The sound of slick flesh in the room as I let my head fall back and moan. He's primed me all right. Now he just needs to finish the job.

"Ellery." His voice breaks, and it's the only sign he's affected—well, besides his rock-hard cock he's currently stroking. His thumb capturing the precum and rubbing it around the head. "Turn around on your knees and grab the headboard."

"Grab the headboard?" I ask coyly.

His teeth sink into his bottom lip as he crawls onto the bed, cock still in hand.

"Mm-hmm. You're going to need something to hold on to." He reaches out and squeezes my breast ever so slightly. "Don't make me ask twice."

"Or else?"

Before I finish the words, I'm flipped over on my stomach and he smacks me on the ass. "Or else I get mine before you get yours."

Jesus. Who knew Ford had this side to him?

I'm all for it.

"Now up on your knees and spread them wide so I can admire what I want to fuck."

I do as I'm told, my ass in the air, my hands on the headboard. I jolt at the warmth of his mouth on the back of my neck, and the feel of his body as it ghosts mine where his erection presses between my ass.

"You like these books. These scenes. How about I prove to you that what happens in books isn't just fiction? That you can have it in real life too." He nips my shoulder and then sucks on the sting of it, all while reaching around and rubbing his fingers over my clit.

I lean my head back on his shoulder as he plays with me. As he preps me. As he readies me to be fucked and owned by him.

I moan as the pleasure takes over. As his fingers work and his tongue licks and as his dick swells against me.

"You're so fucking beautiful, Ellery. Your body. Your mind. Your determination. This pussy." He whispers each word against my skin. Each word further turns me on. "On your hands. Show me that pretty ass of yours."

I obey, the cool air of the room hitting the wetness at my core, illustrating how vulnerable I am to him. How much I must want him to allow him to demand and for me to comply.

A gasp. That's all I can manage as he unexpectedly slides his tongue into my center before running it up and over the tight rim of muscles there.

"God, you turn me on." His teeth sink gently into my ass cheek.

"Ford."

And before the word leaves my lips, Ford pushes into me in one, determined stroke. Our dual cries fill the room—pleasure personified.

"The best part about this position? I can fill you deeper than any other way. Do you feel that? Can I fill you any fuller?" He groans as he pushes in a bit more and grinds his hips against my ass.

I drop my head and absorb the pleasure as he begins to move. In. Out. His hands gripping my ass and spreading my cheeks farther apart so he can push deeper in.

My body rides toward that high. My arms and legs begin to tingle as my core tightens with every push in and pull back out.

He licks his tongue up the line of my spine. "You're so fucking hot," he murmurs against the back of my ear. "So. Fucking. Hot." Each word's accentuated with a thrust into me.

I can't concentrate. I can't think. It's only him in the moment. Only the sensations. Only the pleasure.

He drags a hand back down my spine where his tongue just was, and he straightens up. I emit a garbled moan when he presses his thumb against the tight ring of muscles right above where his cock is working me so masterfully.

My hips buck against his thumb, causing him to play with me a little more. Push a little harder. Stimulate a little more.

"You like that," he grits out. "I knew you would."

"Ford," I mewl as I begin to lose all control. My arms weaken. My legs tense as my body detonates into a million tiny explosions that ricochet throughout my entire body. A jolt of electricity that whips from my center out to my fingers and toes before slamming back into me again where he keeps touching and sliding and masterfully manipulating the nerves in my body.

"Ah, that's it. Tighten around me. *Fuck me, Elle*," he says as I push my ass back and forth on his cock to milk my own orgasm. To prolong it. To ride it out and absorb every ounce of pleasure from him.

"God, yes," I moan as another orgasm slams into me completely unexpected. I collapse beneath the weight of its strength, but Ford holds my hips in the air as he drives into me over and over until it's his guttural cry filling the room. Until it's his release that's owning us.

Our bodies ride the high as we come down ever so slowly. Ford releases my hips, but I'm able to keep them right where they are because I don't want him to pull out just yet. I don't want to lose this feeling.

He presses a tender kiss on my spine as his cock slowly softens inside of me. "God, yes?" He chuckles. "Should I take that as a *yes, I'll partner with you, Ford?*"

My body shudders with the waning pleasure. I'll give him anything he wants if I can have whatever we just did again. "Consent under duress can't be taken seriously in a court of law." My voice feels sex drugged. Sated.

"Duress?" He hums, and it sounds so sexy as it rumbles through the room. "Baby, that was anything but duress. But if you need me to do it again so you can contemplate the merits of yes under pressure, I'll be more than happy to give it a go."

"What?"

"Do you want me to fuck you again?" And in an instant, I'm on my back and his head is between my thighs. When he looks up at me with a grin on his lips, he whispers, "I dare you to tell me no."

CHAPTER FORTY-TWO

Ford

SHE'S GORGEOUS.

I can't sleep. My mind is reeling—too many thoughts, too many emotions to process in this early morning hour—but the one that's constant is, *she's gorgeous*.

But isn't that what I think every time I look at her?

It is, but it never gets old. *Never*.

Her hair has fallen over her cheek, and I itch to push it off but don't want to wake her just yet. I'd rather enjoy these few moments where I can study her without her being self-conscious.

Then again, how can anyone be self-conscious after how fucking hot that was earlier?

The woman is incredible. And a turn-on in every sense of the word.

And her books? Those scenes? One word. *Fore-fucking-play*.

My sigh is deep as I relive the fun we had. The laughter. The sex. The falling asleep sated and satisfied. The . . . asking her to be my partner.

Was that my chickenshit way of keeping her close without admitting to her I'm head over fucking heels in love with her? Without scaring her away?

Unequivocally, *yes*.

And I have no shame in doing so. None. I'm not ready to give her up just yet. Or to admit how I feel and have her run the other way.

Too bad life isn't like that romance novel, right?

But she said yes.

And for now, that'll have to be enough.

I roll onto my back, the next few weeks on my mind. What is going to happen with Ellery and me in the in-between—the end of this project and the beginning of the next one? There's only so many bullshit meetings I can call before she'll catch on.

Just tell her you want this to be a thing, Ford. You don't have to tell her you've fallen for her. You don't have to admit you want so much more than a fling. Just tell her you don't know what this is between you two and you want more of it.

In the morning. It can wait till then. Until the sun has risen and she has woken up.

I'll do it when she has that sleep-drugged voice and pillow creases on her cheek. When her lips are swollen and these thin sheets cover her body.

I give her one last look, determined and feeling slightly surer of myself.

Decided, I try to will myself back to sleep. To quiet my thoughts. To count fucking sheep. Nothing works. Insomnia is something I deal with on the regular. I thought the sexhaustion would help tonight. That the several orgasms would lull myself to sleep.

I was wrong.

Because other than the shadows dancing on the ceiling and the bathroom light we accidentally left on, it's just me, a sleeping Ellery, and not a single Z for me in sight.

Scrolling through my cell it is then. But when I go to reach for it on the nightstand, I notice her Kindle where we left it.

That scene was hot.

I opt for the Kindle instead of my phone. For the sexy scenes in her books over the cold, hard facts of the business and stock market apps on my phone. I go to tap on the screen and practically drop it on my face—clearly, they *are* hazardous. In my attempt to catch it and not end up with a battle scar, I somehow push buttons or the screen or whatever and end up in her library.

Romance novel upon romance novel fill the screen. I scroll through the covers, laughing at the titles, comparing the image I have in my head of my abs with those of the men on their covers and wondering if I'm close, and then just as I'm about to click back on the book, I stop.

Maxton.

My dad's face looks back at me. His book is in her library with a "Read" in the corner to say she's read it in full.

What the fuck?

With a lump in my throat, I press on the cover. The book pops up to the last place she was reading, and there is one sentence highlighted on the bookmarked page and one sentence only.

"He's . . . just Ford."

I stare at the words colored in yellow and a myriad of emotions charge through me. Anger. Betrayal. Confusion. Hurt.

She knows? And yet, she hasn't said a word?

"Ford?" Ellery's sleep-drugged voice asks beside me.

I don't respond, too involved in my head and trying to hold back from lashing out at her.

The bed dips. The covers pull some. And the hitch of her breath cuts through the room when she sees what I have in my hand. When she takes in the words and their highlights that blanket the screen.

When she reaches out and squeezes my forearm, my whole body tenses. "You wouldn't tell me what was wrong." She sounds like she's talking to a wounded animal and that only makes things worse. "You're putting a wedge between you and your brothers, and I thought if I knew what that wedge was, I might be able to help."

"So, you invaded my privacy?" I can't look at her. I don't want to see the pity in her eyes or hear the *Poor, Just Ford* on her lips.

"It's not private if it's public information."

"It's none of your business," I shout and yank my arm out from her grip.

"Bullshit it isn't." She sits up and pulls the comforter around her. "I'm the one here, remember? I'm the one on the other end of it all. Your mood swings every time you see a news clip. The comments your brothers made before they left when they were here. Your silence when a reporter shows up or hounds your assistant for a reason why you're not on the publicity tour. So yes, it affects your day-to-day. You may think no one else sees it, but I do, Ford. *And I'm the one here.* So it is my business because I'm the one waiting with bated breath for it to hit you out of the blue. And I will help hold your pieces together since you refuse to get it all out, fall apart, and then go from there."

"Leave me the fuck alone, Ellery."

"Really? That's all you've got for me? *Leave me the fuck alone?*" She throws one hand up. "I'll tell you the same thing I'm sure your brothers have told you: who cares what some random person on the street thinks about you?"

"You're not a random person on the street, though. You're . . ." *The woman I love.*

"I'm *what?*" she demands, but when I look at her through the dim light of the room, when I'm more than certain the truth flashes in my eyes, she shakes her head as if it's going to erase what she just saw there.

That I'm in love with her.

"No, no, no." She rocks back and forth before getting up out of bed and pulling the comforter with her to cover herself. "Don't you dare say it. Don't, Ford. Not now. Not here. Not . . . just *please*, don't." Tears well in her eyes that I don't understand but wish I could.

There's undisputable fear there. Genuine panic.

Why, though? Why does the idea of someone loving her terrify her?

"Then what do you want me to say?" I ask, my own words sounding defeated.

She paces back and forth, her head shaking with each step, almost as if she's talking herself out of something. She stops and stares at me, eyes pleading but voice resolute. "I think you're forgetting what matters the most. The real relationship you had with your dad. You're so busy allow-ing the outside noise of someone else's perspective to ruin and taint the memories you have of and with him."

"Here we go. Here's what you really think of me," I counter, crossing my arms over my chest and leaning back against the headboard with a smug smile on my lips. "So, you think I'm being a chickenshit?"

"No, Ford." She shakes her head and sighs. "I think you have every right to be upset about what's not said, but in the same breath, you get the chance to pay homage with your brothers to the man you wanted to be like. The man you idolized. *You. Have. The. Chance.*"

"And your point?"

She growls in frustration. "I'd kill for a quarter of that opportunity. To let the world know just how incredible my mother was. To have siblings who I can lean on. To know why my dad . . . *left.*"

Her words connect right where I don't want them to connect. In my gut. In my heart. She's lost both of her parents too. One in an accident. One by suicide.

I hear what she's saying. I feel what she's saying. But just like my brothers, that doesn't invalidate how I feel.

What I feel.

Two damaged people trying to hurt each other more.

"Those are just words. Easy to say when you're not in someone else's shoes."

Her bottom lip quivers as she glares at me. "Quit being so goddamn selfish."

"*Selfish?*" She's calling me fucking selfish?

Like she's one to talk. A woman who shows every bit of love but can't see past herself to let me own it.

"The book isn't about you. It's about your dad. It's about letting the rest of the world admire and respect the man in a way that only the three of you do. So yes, quit being so selfish and making it be about you when it's about him."

"So, at first this is about my relationship with my brothers. Then it's about my dad." I stare at her and shrug, itching for the fight. Itching to take this anger out on someone. "Who the fuck are you to give advice? Are you really going to lecture me about relationships and how to foster them and take part in them while you stand there and deny that we're in one? *Fucking classic, Ellery.*"

"Don't do this, Ford." She takes a few steps back and forces a swallow down her throat. That familiar panic flickers through her eyes.

"Don't do what?" I shout, flinging my arms out to the sides. "Talk about what's staring us in the face? What we've been doing for months and you refuse to even acknowledge?"

"This isn't about us."

"No? Really? My bad. I didn't realize it was okay for you to stick your nose in *my* business but not when it's *our* business."

"This is about *you*, about *your* family."

"Of course. Isn't that what it's always about? I mean, it's never about *us*. Or *you*. Every time the topic turns to *you*, you change the subject, making sure it comes back to me. You hide from revealing any little part of yourself that God for-fucking-bid makes you vulnerable."

She stands there, bottom lip trembling, but her eyes cold as fucking ice. "Go to hell."

"Why don't you read the epilogues, Ellery, huh?" I ask, needing to hurt her like she's hurting me. Needing to push her away since she's hitting so damn close right now. "You want me to give answers, it's high time you do the same. Why don't you read them?"

I ignore the hurt glancing through her eyes, my own hurt jading my thoughts.

"Leave me alone, Ford."

"Oh," I say and chuckle condescendingly. "*Now*, I'm supposed to leave you alone."

"Stay out of my business."

"No. Not on your life. Why don't you read them? Are you too afraid to find out what happens after they fall in love? Is that what it is? You self-sabotage yourself and so—"

"Shut up," she shouts at the top of her lungs, her voice breaking. Tears well and slip down her cheeks. Her head shakes from side to side yet her eyes lock on mine. The expression on her face guts me and yet her words hit even harder.

"Why? So you can run and hide from answering the question?"

"Like you? The man who ran here, who partnered with a random woman he's only met one other time, just so he could stick his head in the sand and avoid his daddy issues?"

If she's aiming for the bullseye, she just fucking nailed it.

Motherfucker.

My chuckle is low and haunting. "That's a low blow, Elle. But that's what you were aiming for, right? To piss me off so I drop it and let it go? Because that's way easier than you actually talking to me. Than actually having to face fucking facts about us—"

"The only thing to talk about is why you're not on your way to the city to be on the morning shows with your brothers right now."

Of course. I told her about the damn interviews last week and now she throws them in my face? Fuck that. Fuck this.

"You're telling *me* to leave? Fine. You got it." *Fucking unbelievable.* "You win. I'll leave in the morning. I'll go do the morning show circuit with my brothers while you stay here and be boss of everything but what matters."

"Fine."

"And then when that's fixed, when I've been *unselfish*, you have to do the same. You'll have to be unselfish and figure out what the fuck you want here, because I'm sick of not knowing. Deal?"

"Fine."

"Say something else besides fucking *fine*," I thunder, my voice reverberating through the room, my frustration at epic proportions.

She stares at me with that hollow, fearful look in her eyes that I wish I weren't the cause of but know I am. Her nod is slight, but there as she opens her mouth and then closes it again. I know I may have pushed too far.

But don't I deserve to know where *I* stand? Where *we* stand?

She blinks away tears and whispers, "Fine," before walking out of the suite, the comforter still wrapped around her, and shutting the door at her back.

It takes everything I have not to go after her. Not to rush down the hall, press my lips to hers, and tell her that whatever it is, whatever is scaring her, we can figure it out. We can work through it.

But I don't.

I stay where I am, staring at the closed door, and know it shouldn't be this hard to love someone.

"Shit," I mutter to an empty room.

If I was looking to push her into acknowledging we were something, that sure as shit just fucking backfired.

CHAPTER FORTY-THREE

Ellery

MY CHEST ACHES.

Deal?

From the words he didn't say but that I could see in his eyes.

From the fight that I picked because I needed space and time to think. To make him realize I'm not that girl. That he can't love me. That this can't be any more than it already is.

From the tough love I had to dish out so he could see what he has when so many others would kill for it. What I would kill for.

From the truth behind his question: *why don't you read the epilogues, Ellery?*

And it continues to ache all night as I sit in the empty rooftop bar, wrapped in the comforter, staring out at the moon, high over the ocean. I watch its reflection ripple with the swells as they ebb and flow. I listen to the muted sound of the waves crashing on the beach below. I sink further into my own thoughts as the new framing creaks and settles all around me.

You'll have to be unselfish and figure out what the fuck you want here, because I'm sick of not knowing. Deal?

Is that why I ran away? Or rather ran to the bar, which sounds ridiculous in and of itself?

Because, God yes, he's gotten too close. And when someone gets too close, I panic? Is it because I'm mad at him for having a family I could only dream of and not wanting to preserve it? Some of one, a little of the other.

Or is it because I'm afraid to believe that I could actually deserve that happily ever after? That *he could be* my happily ever after? And I'm terrified to hope, terrified to believe, that if he is, he won't be ripped away from me too?

Or is it simply that I'm questioning everything about last night? His promise to partner up. His suggestion to tie my stepfather's hands so that I have a stake in what is rightfully mine.

Was it all legitimate? Does he really want to partner up with me, or was he trying to bind me to him in some way so that I can't run? So that I don't have a reason to walk away?

But then again, the binding would only be of our companies since he would front the capital.

And how do I feel about that? Less than? Bought? Bribed?

I scrub a frustrated hand over my face as the questions spin and spiral out of control, the doubt not far behind them, as the dark night turns into the early morning hours.

Where did my resolve go? When did my willingness to just have fun and enjoy him disappear?

I was willing to marry a decent man for what boils down to helping our business prowess. What is so wrong with dating a man and working with him at the same time? A man I'm crazy about no less?

Fordham Sharpe.

So much more than *Just Ford*. I just wish he'd understand that.

Maybe having the night to our own thoughts will help us realize the truths we're refusing to face. Maybe it will help us find a middle ground where we can meet and agree. One where he sees that he needs to go to his brothers and that I'm not a happily-ever-after kind of girl—while *I* realize it's okay to be with him without freaking out.

Time settles everything down.

Time gives clarity.

At least I hope it does.

The sky begins to lighten to that miserable morning gray before the sun thinks of rising.

More than anything, we need to clear the air before we face a hotel full of workers trying to finish this monstrous task in such a short amount of time. We have to be able to work together even while at odds.

It's something we've yet to face during this entire project—adversity between each other—but isn't that what a true partnership is about? What a true relationship is about?

Because that's what this night has allowed me to accept. Ford and I are a thing. What type of *thing* is the question, but I'm willing to acknowledge that and make that conclusion.

I'm willing to admit to him there is more here than I've ever felt for someone before and that's huge. I'm hoping he'll let me leave it at that. I'm hoping he'll realize and accept that I'm not an *I love you* type. That he'll realize as Josh did that what I can give isn't—will never be—enough for a relationship. That eventually, Ford would want to leave me too.

Professionally?

Yes, it's a deal, Ford.

It was last night when I told you.

With the comforter still wrapped around me, I make my way back to the suite. I need to get dressed before the crews start arriving, but more importantly, I need to talk to Ford. I need to tell him that yes, I'll make that deal. That if he goes and fixes things with his brothers, then I'll let him know where we stand. That we're in a relationship . . . but that I can't give him what I think he needs. What he deserves. But that I can be everything but.

It's something, right? While it might not be exactly what he's looking for, at least it's a jumping-off point.

With each step I take downstairs, I rehearse the words in my head. The phrasing. The reasons behind it. The everything.

But when I walk into the suite, the sheets, sans comforter, are pulled up as if the bed is made, and Ford is nowhere in sight. His laptop is gone. His keys are too.

Panic vibrates through me.

He left.

We argued. He left.

I go through the room like a mad woman, only to find his clothes still there, his toiletries on the counter, random work notes strewn about on the dresser.

Relief hits me like a battered tidal wave.

Maybe he just needed space too.

But he didn't leave me.

He didn't walk away.

Tears of relief fall while I'm in the shower. It's the only moment of weakness I allow as I reassure myself that he's coming back.

That he's still fighting for us.

I spend the next hour getting ready because even though Ford and I had a fight, the show must go on here. Contractors need to be directed. Problems need to be solved. The day must move on.

Maybe he drove to Sag Harbor for the night. To gain that same distance I did.

But when I'm outside showing Roddy how the awnings need to be fixed over the café's door, we're all distracted by the sound of a helicopter.

It's a common sound out here in the playground of the rich, but this one is especially low.

And when I look up and see the black chopper with the gray letters S.I.N. fly overhead, I know Ford is showing me that he's keeping his end of the bargain. Just like that. No additional discussion. No negotiations. No final proposals. He did what he said he was going to do. He's keeping his word.

He's also warning me that when he returns, I'm going to have to keep mine.

CHAPTER FORTY-FOUR

Ford

SHE'S TINY AS WE FLY OVER.

Her hands over her eyes as she looks up and takes in the chopper.

As she realizes I'm keeping my word.

I watch her until I can't watch her anymore because I fear this might be the last time I ever see her.

I worry that whatever she's scared of is stronger than the love I see in her eyes when she looks at me.

And hasn't that been the crux of the matter this whole time?

CHAPTER FORTY-FIVE

Ellery

"YOU EXPECTING GOOD NEWS OR SOMETHING TODAY, BOSS lady?" Roddy asks as he walks by me.

"What do you mean?" I ask, turning to look at him.

"You've been checking your phone every ten minutes today like you're expecting your sister to be having a baby or something."

I laugh. "Considering I don't have a sister, that might be a long wait."

"Touché." He stops and narrows his eyes. "But all is good? No problems with the project or permits or shit?"

"No. Nothing like that. Just waiting for an email to come through on the canopy deliveries for the café," I lie, suddenly feeling ridiculous that I've checked my phone enough today that someone noticed.

"They have my number too. That's not something you should really have to deal with. You've got enough on your plate as it is. Let me handle that."

So much for that lie.

"There. No more distractions." I make a show of taking my phone out of my pocket and turning on Do Not Disturb. "If I'm going to preach about being attentive on the job, I guess it's only right that I do the same."

He laughs and winks before getting called into the café to help with something.

I sigh and lean against the wall. Despite my lack of sleep last night, today has been a good day.

Am I still hurt and confused about the things that were said last night? Of course, I am. I'm not a robot.

The comment about my phone, though? It's because I can't stop seeing headlines and Instagram notifications hit my screen. To say there is a buzz over the first interview with all three Sharpe brothers together is an understatement.

Clearly by Roddy's comment, I'm too caught up in it.

Is it weird to be proud of something that's not even something you're part of? I'm sure it is, but I am.

The media is having a field day with the visual alone. Three attractive men, identical in their sinfully good looks, successful in the American dream kind of way, all sitting in one camera shot. Their smiles alone must sell ratings, but it's the passion and love with which they speak about their beloved father that will win the public over if they haven't already.

And only the trained eye of someone who has spent almost every minute of the last ninety days with the middle brother would notice the slight blanche on some questions. The hitch is so fleeting.

In the clips I've seen, I've been moved by their love for their father. Their complete admiration and adoration of the love between their parents even years after their mom passed. The connection the three of them have is heartwarming to watch, even from afar.

I've sent Ford a few texts saying as much. I'm a big enough person that even though I am struggling with how to fulfill but not fuck up my end of the bargain when he gets back, I can't deny him the right of knowing how proud I am of him for stepping up.

And even though he hasn't responded, I know he's proud of himself too. It shows in the smile he flashes. In the laugh he emits. In the shy shake of his head when his brothers tease him blatantly, making it clear their father loved Ford just as much as them, regardless of what the book doesn't show.

Yes, I've spent that much of my workday obsessing over it, frequently under the guise of trying to track down a missing shipment and deal with grand opening-day issues that have arisen.

If anyone would have questioned me on it further, I would have been caught flat on my heels.

But they didn't, and for that, I am grateful.

As the day continues, my anticipation to see Ford grows. My resolve is stronger. I realize that I want something more with Ford than I ever wanted with Chandler or Josh. Its definition though, I can't give or even know yet. I just hope he'll be able to accept the limits.

I keep myself busy with my endless list of things to do to get this place ready to meet our deadline.

My to-do list gets shorter in some rooms and grows longer in others. It's not until I walk into the bar upstairs that I see everyone huddled around a phone and then scatter when they notice me.

Furtive looks are exchanged back and forth between the workers.

"What?" I ask, standing in the middle of the room, throwing my arms out. "What is no one telling me? Do I have dirt on my ass? Is there a sex tape I've never made on the Internet? What. Is. Going. On?"

Not a single man smiles at the laugh I'm angling for.

Hank is the poor soul who meets my eyes. "You." I shove a finger at him. "What is going on?"

Hank glances at another finish carpenter and then back to me, clearly dreading whatever it is he knows.

Now suddenly so am I.

Hank shuffles forward, his shoulders hunched, his cell phone outstretched.

It takes a minute for my mind to process the TMZ headline on his screen timestamped ninety minutes ago. My mind stutters and my heart drops as the world falls out beneath me.

Helicopter Crash in the Hudson

My gasp is audible as I yank the phone from Hank's hand and read. Only certain words register.

Fordham Sharpe on the manifest.

Heading out toward the Hamptons.

Downed in the Hudson.

Search for survivors underway.

I can't breathe. *Is that normal?* I can't breathe. I can't think. I feel like there are a million things I need to do—call his brothers when I don't even know their numbers. Get to New York City when the only way to get there quickly is via helicopter, and there's no fucking way I'm doing that right now. Have a panic attack because, while it won't solve anything or answer my questions, it sure as hell will allow me to feel something. Because right

291

here, right now, I feel everything and nothing all at the same time. How is that even possible?

I stagger backward until I collapse onto a chair. I don't care if I'm showing my cards to our crew. I don't give a fuck if my gasp and the blood draining from my face shows them that Ford and I are a thing and not simply partners.

Roddy is at my side, and I don't even know how he got there. He pries my fingers off the phone. "Breathe, Sinclair. Breathe."

"My phone. I need my phone," I croak.

"In your back pocket. Right there." He points, and I yank it out.

The screen is a mess of texts. From my Garland. From Ledger. Messages I never paid attention to because I had muted my phone.

I stare at them until my eyes blur, fear of what they might tell me preventing me from unlocking my phone and reading what they say.

A glance up tells me everyone is watching me. Everyone is holding their breath just as I am, and the concern etched in their faces is devastating.

"Everybody out," Roddy directs, swooping his arms in a shooing motion. I don't look up. I don't meet their eyes, but in my periphery, I can see them slowly shuffle out of the room. "Do you want me to stay or go?" He squats in front of me, hand on my knee, and waits for an answer.

"I need . . . alone, please."

He nods and squeezes before standing and walking out.

I'm the one who pushed him to go. I'm the reason he was on that flight. I'm the reason . . .

No.

He has to be alive.

He's Ford. Larger-than-life, stubborn-as-hell, Ford.

When the door shuts, my exhale is shaky as I swipe open my phone and prepare for what I read.

But before I can, my cell rings. It's an unknown number, and I answer it as fast as I can, hoping it's Ford.

"Hello?" I gasp into the phone.

"Ellery? It's Ledger." The solemnity in his voice cuts me to the core. The grief wavering in it is indescribable. Fear and panic are woven into every fiber.

"Please . . ." It's one long, drawn-out syllable. Please let him be okay. Please tell me he's alive. Please tell me he's standing in front of you.

"Search and rescue." He chokes the words out. "They have him."

My heart breaks.

Not they have him and he's okay. Not they have him and he's alive. Just *they have him*.

"Ledger," I croak, the salt of my tears hitting my lips when I didn't even know I was crying. "Please."

Seconds feel like hours as they tick by and all the air is suctioned from the room, leaving the pulse pounding in my ears the only sound that I hear.

"He's okay." It's his voice that breaks this time. It's his hiccupped sob that shudders through the connection. His words allow me to breathe for the first time in however long it's been—minutes that feel like hours.

My sob follows right behind it. "Have you talked to him?"

"No. Not yet." His voice is hoarse but relieved. "It went down. Our pilot was able to set it down. The blades. The water. I don't understand how they made it, but they're okay."

"I need to get there, to see him . . . to . . . I can't get in . . . I can't fly there." I choke the words out.

"I know. I know. We're . . . Callahan and I are in the car. On the way to see him."

"Please," I plead. "Please have him call me."

Please. I can't lose someone else.

Not again.

293

CHAPTER FORTY-SIX

Ford

"I CAN'T BREATHE." I PUSH AGAINST MY BROTHERS, BUT THEIR ARMS stay locked around me in the type of hug I haven't had from them in years. *Since Dad's funeral.*

"Fuck you," Callahan mutters.

"Double fuck you for scaring us like that," Ledger adds in.

And when they step back and I meet their gazes, we're all looking at each other with tears in our eyes. "Relax. It's too much fun being a pain in your asses to leave you fuckers just yet."

Their laughs aren't believable. They hold no amusement, only relief.

I close my eyes and stagger to a seat. I know they want more details than I gave them on the phone. A play-by-play to explain everything, but all I can focus on are the thoughts that ran through my head in those fleeting moments between our pilot telling me there was a technical failure and his words "brace for impact."

My mom. Her soft smile. Her warm hugs. Her lasting wisdom.

My dad. His unyielding ways. His affection you knew you'd earned when you were on the other end of it. His legacy I feared I wasn't going to have the chance to carry on.

My brothers. The other pieces of me. The ones who make me whole. My rocks when I can't be one.

And Ellery. *I love her,* and I never got the chance to tell her.

I love her.

I won't make that mistake again.

"I need your phone," I say to either of them.

Ledger holds his out. "It's already ringing."

I take the phone and just as it hits my ear, I hear her voice and it brings me to my knees. "Ledger?"

"Ellery." My voice breaks saying her name.

"Ford? Ford!"

I don't know who breaks first. Her or me or both of us, but a tear slips down my cheek at the same time a sob escapes her.

"I'm okay."

"Ford."

"I'll be home soon."

CHAPTER FORTY-SEVEN

Ellery

THE WORLD STILL FEELS LIKE IT HAS STOPPED. IT DOESN'T matter that I've talked to Ford. It was brief and he was quiet, surrounded by his brothers, but it was the best sound I've ever heard in my life.

I'll be home soon.

Leave it to Ford to act like surviving a helicopter crash is nothing.

Leave it to him to be fearless in hopping back on another one to get to me as fast as he can.

When his car pulls into the lot, I'm running out the front door and jumping into his arms—legs wrapped around his waist, lips planted firmly on his. He staggers backward under the force of my weight, and his chuckle fades with the kiss I give him without thought or care to who can see us. To who knows.

The kiss says so many things. I miss you. I was so scared. Never again. Words I'm still so goddamn fearful of even thinking.

And when the kiss ends, when my feet are lowered, I beat my hands against his chest. "Don't you ever, ever, ever do that to me again."

His laugh rings out. "Just another day at home with you beating me up one way or another."

"Shut up." I push him and then press my lips to his again. Another taste to affirm he's alive. That he's okay. That this is really him, here, in my arms.

His hands are on my face. His eyes are locked with mine. His half-cocked smile owns my heart.

"I love you, Ellery Sinclair. I love you, and I'm sick of not saying it. I love you, and all I could think about as the chopper went down was that I hadn't told you. So I'm telling you now. I'm telling you so that you can do what you want with it, but nothing is changing my feelings now. You got that? Because I'd rather make a mistake in telling you than it be a travesty that you didn't know."

I hear his words. I understand what he's saying. But I'm so overwhelmed by everything that there is. Lost in not losing him that his words are there, but my need for him to be alive dro2wns everything out.

The fear.

The panic.

It's just him.

Just us.

Just another tomorrow for us to figure this out.

CHAPTER FORTY-EIGHT

Ford

THE DREAMS NEVER STOP.

One after another. What could have happened. What did happen. And each nightmare shook me awake to find Ellery's face on the pillow beside me. Her legs intertwined with mine. Her even breathing and steady heartbeat beneath my palm a reassuring reminder that they were just that. Nightmares.

And in between the terror and fear was the reminder of what happened last night. Of me pulling her onto my lap. Of us holding on to each other. Of her lips meeting mine as she sank down onto me.

As she loved me—with her body and the emotion in her eyes—but never with words.

We moved in the silence.

Reacting to each other's touches. Each other's moans. Each other's pleas.

Reacting until it became almost painful to breathe knowing that I almost lost this. Lost her.

When I pulled back to look at her, to watch what she looks like awash in love, a lone tear slid down her cheek. I kissed it away. I murmured that I was okay. That I am okay.

And that I loved her.

But the pleasure became lost when the next nightmare hit. When it scared the shit out of me.

I think the dream jolts me awake. Or did the door just click?

The first thing I notice is the room is starting to lighten from the early dawn breaking.

The second is that Ellery isn't beside me. The bed is cold.

I scrub my hands over my face and swing my legs over the side of the mattress. "Elle?" I ask toward the partially opened bathroom door.

Maybe she's having the same nightmares I am. Maybe she needs a reminder that I'm okay.

But when I peek in the bathroom, she's not there. I head to the hallway, and when I look down it, her back is to me as she rolls her suitcase behind her.

Panic strangles me. Does she have a meeting I forgot about? A conference call she needs to be on?

But I know the answer is no.

She's running.

"Ellery?" I jog after her, but she doesn't look back at me.

When I move around her in the hallway, blocking her path, it's only then that I can see the tears streaming down her cheeks. See the utter devastation etched in the lines of her features.

"Baby. Please. Tell me what's wrong?"

Her expression remains stoic despite the tears staining her skin and the subtle shaking of her head. "I'm so sorry," she whispers.

Those three words fucking devastate me. Obliterate every bit of hope I'd held on to.

"Don't do this. I'm not letting you go," I say as my pulse races and my disbelief riots. "Not after everything. Not after yesterday. Not after . . . *us.*" I don't even recognize my own voice right now. The pleading in it. The fear woven in it.

"This isn't right," she murmurs as she tries to step around me. I move to block her. "This can't happen."

"What can't?"

"This. Us." She looks down and tears splatter the new carpet between us. "I refuse to let myself . . ."

"To let yourself what?" I demand. To hope? To want me? To . . .

"To love you," she whispers as her eyes look up and meet mine.

"Why? Why can't you love me?" I challenge, my hands on her shoulders, desperate to give her a shake and knock some sense into her. But she's scared enough already.

Just as I am.

But my fear is because I know what I want and am afraid I won't be able to have it. And her fear is because she's never had it and she's terrified to feel it.

"Because I can't." She swallows over a sob. "I just can't."

"I deserve more than that. A better reason, Ellery, and you damn well know it." I draw in a deep, fortifying breath to calm myself. "Why can't you love me?" My voice breaks.

"Because . . . because everyone I've ever loved has died. Has left me. And I just can't . . . I can't lose you too. I almost did yesterday. *I almost lost you.* And I'm terrified of loving you and then losing you. I can't put myself through that again."

I stare at those sapphire eyes that own me. At those lips that can say anything and I'd do what they'd ask. At the woman who has my heart fully in her trembling hands.

"*Son, when a woman's temper makes you love her even more, when her defiance makes you want to challenge her, and when her smile makes you want to earn each and every one, then you know she's worth the goddamn fire.*"

My dad was right.

It is in this moment that I know I'd crawl over coals, risk the singe and the burn, to pull her against me and take away that look on her face.

God, how he was fucking right.

Fire's got nothing on love.

On what you'd do for it.

On what you'd give for it.

On how bad you'll burn for it.

"I just want you. Any way I can have you, Ellery. We're worth the fight. You're worth the fight. Everything else is just noise. We can work on the rest."

She takes a step back and out of my grip, her eyes on everything but me. "I have to go, Ford."

That tear last night . . . it was because she knew she was saying goodbye.

With that, Ellery Sinclair walks around me and out of the inn.

And with what I fear is out of my life.

CHAPTER FORTY-NINE

Ellery

THE TEARS DON'T STOP.

Neither does the ache in my chest or the pain in my heart.

I love him.

I love Fordham Sharpe when I swore I'd never allow myself to love him.

And I almost lost him.

The dreams never stopped coming. The panicked gasp when I woke to find him there, alive, his chest rising and falling, only scared me more.

Everything I love dies.

Everything.

I can't curse Ford with that. I can't curse his brothers with that.

I wipe another tear away and then trace the engraved letters on my father's headstone.

His face flashes through my mind. His big laugh and warm hugs. His strict discipline but effusive praise that made you feel like you were on top of the world when he gave it. His unwavering support and distinct advice that I still hold close even today.

Mom's shoulders shudder as I try and hold on to them. As I try to comfort her like she has me.

But no hug is going to help this hurt.

No kiss on the boo-boo is going to make this go away.

I squeeze my eyes shut. It's easier than looking around and seeing everyone pretend they're not looking at us. Their eyes full of pity. The it's such a shame murmured to one another. And my eyes being closed is ten times better than looking at the shiny black casket above the ground in front of us.

Is he cold in there?

Is he still in pain?

Is he wishing he hadn't done it because he sees how much we're hurting? How much we miss him?

Mom tries to pull away from me. To reverse the roles back to where they should be with her as the parent and me as the child. And one look at her face—eyes sad, face swollen, nose red—tells me what I already know: nothing will ever be the same again.

She slides me over and onto her lap. Her chest heaves against my back and the sound—the mewling sound she's fighting back—I hope I never hear again. I put my hands over my ears and try to make it stop. To try and pretend this isn't happening.

It's the sound of devastation.

Of my life changing.

Of a little girl irrevocably changed.

Why did you do this, Dad?

It hurts to breathe.

You broke us.

My head dizzies.

You broke her.

My eyes burn so much, but I have no more tears to cry.

What if I can never put her back together again?

I hate you for this, Daddy.

"I don't hate you," I murmur. "I just don't understand though. Even all these years later. I don't understand."

The tears fall past my eyelashes, the hurt so strong. Even though it's been two decades since I was forced to say goodbye.

No, I don't hate my dad. How could I? But I'm pissed he robbed me and Mom of more years with him. Of more time. *God, I've missed you, Dad.*

The breeze picks up and a leaf tumbles across his plot until it lands on my mom's.

I smile. It's almost as if he's telling me it's okay to leave him for my mom. I press a kiss to my fingers and touch his headstone before shifting and looking at my mom's headstone.

It's more elaborate than his. Garland went all out on it. What was it like for him to bury the woman he loved next to her first love instead of somewhere the two of them could be together?

I never really thought about that. About what he gave up so he could give her this. About how he loved her even while knowing she'd always loved another man more.

The thought sits with me as I rearrange the flowers I brought for her in the permanent vase affixed to her headstone.

I don't think I could do the same. I don't think I could love someone like Fordham while knowing he loved another woman more.

Maybe I've been so jaded by grief for so long that I never stopped to consider the kind of man Garland is. The person he was for her when he probably needed and wanted so much more.

"He still thinks about you, Momma. Just like I do. Every minute of every day."

I stop fussing with the flowers and shift to lean against the marble slab.

I hate this place.

I hate that it's here that I learned all about true and utter loneliness. About devastation.

I hate that it's peaceful here. Peaceful in a way that lulls you to sleep with a gentle breeze in your hair and the rustle of leaves overhead.

Because it shouldn't be peaceful.

It's the place where dreams are broken and hearts are shattered.

It's where you realize more than anywhere else in the world just how dark and lonely death is. How permanent it is. How many scars it leaves behind. *Every time.*

I hate this place.

It makes every part of me riot inside—my heart, my soul, my being.

Garland stands beside me, his sunglasses on, with one hand resting on the mahogany coffin. He doesn't move. He doesn't cry. He doesn't speak. He just stares at his hand in silence before dipping his head ever so slightly in one last goodbye before taking a step back.

He pauses and squeezes my shoulder before walking away to give me time with her.

To let me do the one thing I'm not prepared to do—say goodbye.

I've tried to hold it together. I've tried to be the adult once again in a situation I should have never been in once, let alone twice.

But as I stand here and stare at the casket, all I can think is what I would give for one last hug. To listen to her whisper "I love you" in my ear as we did. To lean back and see the pride and love in eyes that are the same color as mine.

"Why did you leave me?" I whisper to the wind. "You were all I had left. What do I do now? How do I go on? How do I . . . live?"

The tears come. It's no use holding them back. I've already screamed and yelled and cursed God and everything in between for taking her. For having to go on without her.

I lean over and press my lips to the wooden lid, warm from the sun's rays. I hate how much she'll miss. How much I'll miss her. How I'm supposed to live without her. Because this time, I have no one to hold me while I cry.

There are no shoulders to lean into.

I can feel the loss sink into me. The fear to love without dreading the loss that comes after, enveloping me.

Because why try?

"I know you were brave enough to love again, Mom, but I'm not. I'll never be as brave as you were."

I never want to feel this way again.

Ever.

The breeze picks up again and the leaf that tumbled by earlier comes back the other direction and hits my leg.

"You trying to tell me something, Mom?" I smile through the tears, wondering what she would have looked like now. Fine lines and gray hairs she'd fuss over when they peeked through. Rumblings over why I'm not married and when I'll give her grandkids.

Normalcy.

Things I've been robbed of.

Things I fear more than anything.

I met a man, Momma. He's kind and funny and handsome . . . and he believes in me more than I do sometimes.

I love him.

I love him, and I'm so damn terrified that by loving him, I'm going to lose him. I can't do this to him. To his family.

I just can't . . .

The tears come harder now as I lean my head back and let the warmth of the sun dry them from my cheeks. But I don't think they'll ever stop. They never have in a sense.

There's such an irony that this place brings me such peace when it's also the place where my life fell apart. I watched my mom's face and body crumble as we said goodbye to my dad here. I had to say goodbye to her here too.

This is where I learned that love was too dangerous for your heart.

This is where I accepted that I would never let myself love anyone again.

I open my eyes to see the leaf picked up by the wind so it dances through the air a few feet off the ground.

I smile because in watching it, I can hear her voice. It's faded over time, but right now it feels so real and loud and alive.

It's okay to love him.

It's okay to fear losing him.

But it's not your love that's causing this.

It's not your fault.

I shake my head as if this is a two-way conversation and not just in my head. My fingers continue to trace, my thoughts continue to spin, and my heart still aches.

"If that's true, then give me a sign, Mom. Give me a sign."

CHAPTER FIFTY

Ford

"Y OU OKAY, BROTHER?" LEDGER ASKS. "YOU SOUND LIKE SHIT."

"She left."

"Like to go to the store?"

"No. She left, left."

"Left, left?"

"Yup," I say with a sigh.

"What the fuck did you go and do this time?" he asks with a chuckle.

"I almost died."

His laugh is louder, almost as if I'm joking. "Bullshit."

"No. I'm serious. Everyone she's ever loved has died, Ledge. Everyone. It wasn't until she said that to me that I'd thought about it."

"So she's afraid if she loves you, she's going to lose you again and—"

"And she can't handle losing anyone else."

"Jesus. I don't even—"

"The goddamn epilogue . . ."

"What?" he asks, confusion laced through his tone as I finally put the missing piece into place.

"Nothing, it's just . . ." *She's afraid to believe in happily ever afters. She can't read them because after the declaration of love in the last chapter, she's afraid to see what happens next. She's afraid to see if they're still together. That's why she doesn't read them.*

"It's just what?"

"Nothing," I repeat.

"Well . . . shit."

"Yeah. You're telling me," I mumble. The past few days have been miserable. She's my other half here in everything . . . and now that she's gone, I'm fucking lost.

"What are you going to do?"

"What can I do? I can't fix years of her thinking one way."

"Sure you can."

"You don't know how stubborn she is."

"You're telling me you've given up? That's not the man I know. The brother I know."

"I haven't given up. I love her, Ledge." I sigh and run a hand over my stubble. It's rough. I'm fucking rough. I look like the walking fucking dead. Roddy must think I'm on a bender, still shaken from the chopper crash with my bloodshot eyes and grumpiness.

But I can't sleep.

I can't eat.

I just want her back where she belongs.

Here.

With me.

"I just need to give her something to make sure she understands I care about her fear, but that it doesn't scare me away in the least."

"If you need our help . . ."

"I know, brother. I know."

And I did know.

Ellery had been right. Dad's book was about Dad—*his* life. His achievements. His failures. His challenges. His relationships with Mom and us. The short amount of time I spent doing the press release put that in perspective for me. Even more importantly, that day helped heal the rift that had formed between my brothers and me.

I know the love he held for me. The love they have for me. And in the end, that's all that matters.

So when Ledger says they'll be there if I need their help, I know they will be there. Just like I was when they needed help with getting Asher and Sutton. *Because that's what you do for those you love.*

And I love Ellery.

The question is: what do I do to prove to her that I love her and I'm not going anywhere?

When the call ends, when I lie back in a bed that smells like her, surrounded by things that she had a hand in creating, I know I'll do anything to get her back.

Even walk through fucking fire.

CHAPTER FIFTY-ONE

Ellery

I T TAKES EVERYTHING I HAVE TO STEP OUT OF THE CAR.

The inn is before me in all its remodeled glory. How ironic I stood here months ago with a pocketful of hope and no idea what this chance would offer me—if anything.

It gave me a new sense of myself, a confidence in my professional skills I never knew I had, and now a huge project under my belt that I can use as a reference.

It gave me a chance to see that I'm capable of feeling. Of receiving love . . . and now . . . now I need to steel myself for the person I want to love but am terrified to allow myself to.

And maybe that's why I'm still sitting in my car, one foot out of the open door, the other in the footwell, as I summon the courage to face Ford for the first time in two weeks. Sure, we've talked through emails. Through conference calls with multiple people on the line.

But I haven't seen him. I haven't had a one-on-one conversation with him.

Until now.

Today is the contractors' walk-through. The day where the people who made my dream come to life, get to see the finished product, what their work contributed to, before it opens to the public.

I wouldn't miss it for the world, even if it means facing Ford before I have answers, or a sign, or whatever ridiculous thing I'm waiting for to tell me it's okay to love him.

That it's okay to be afraid but still love him.

I stare at this new beginning for me. Think about the memories we made inside. The partnership I cemented. And I miss him more than I ever thought possible.

"It's a day for a lot of new things, Sinclair," I murmur to myself as I take a deep breath and exit my car.

The inn looks incredible. The exterior is stunning with its lush landscape and newly made stone perimeter wall. My smile is automatic. My vision came to life, and I feel a sudden pang of regret over missing the last two weeks here. Over not being a part of the little nuances and problems that probably caused Ford and Roddy to scramble to figure out. Of not being here to finish the job Ford and I started together on a whim.

I just need space.

Isn't that what I told him the first and only time we spoke after I left? When I told him that I was working remotely with Roddy to make sure my presence was felt in my absence? Isn't that what I kept saying in my head every night as I cried myself to sleep? Isn't that what I repeated on the drive here only to have it go out the window the minute I pulled in?

It was so much easier to heed my own request when I was away from Ford. But now that I'm here, and I'm more than certain he's in there, I'm a mixture of every emotion imaginable as I move one foot after another toward him.

There are still a few things that need to be fixed or finished. Even now, I can't shut off my brain from looking for them. The right shutter on the fourth floor, three windows over from the right is slightly crooked. A plant near the left corner has already died. The planter by the front door isn't centered the same on the right as it is on the left.

And there is no signage for the inn's name.

I guess that would be my fault. He asked and I never delivered an answer. Maybe I felt like I didn't deserve to, or that he'd moved on and did it himself. Or maybe I was afraid to permanently place my mark on something we'd never share again.

Stop thinking that way, Elle.

Start thinking positively. Take this next step forward. *You've already negotiated with your stepdad and have officially bound yourself to S.I.N. for the foreseeable future in the hopes that Ford will see you're ready to commit to something with him.*

If he'll still have you.

I push open the front door, expecting there to be a flurry of contractors and their significant others milling about the halls.

But I don't see anyone.

I move from one location to the next, the silence of the inn deafening, and I check my phone to make sure I didn't mess up. That this is the time the invitation said.

It is.

"Hello?" I call out, feeling like a stranger in something I own.

Partially.

Fifty-fifty.

The thought brings a ghost of a smile to my lips as an "Up here" calls back to me.

I make my way to the rooftop bar expecting the party to be up there but walk into a completely empty space.

My breath falters as I hold my hand to my mouth. It's done and absolutely gorgeous. This was the last place to be finished and so I missed seeing it come to fruition, but . . . wow.

"It's incredible, isn't it?" Ford asks from behind me, and my heart swells in my chest.

I hang my head for a beat, steeling myself for the visceral reaction I know will happen when I see him.

I only last seconds before I turn around to face him. He's standing in the doorway with a Henley and a nice pair of jeans on. His hair is messy like I like it, and the hope in his smile owns every sad, scared, *hopeful* part of me.

I love him.

I get the chance to love him.

It's the same thing I've repeated over and over for the past few weeks. The same phrases I've been teaching myself to not wince at or be on the defensive when I say them.

Because it's true. As much as it terrifies me, I love Fordham Sharpe.

"You did a great job," I say, starting easy.

"No, we did a great job." He smiles softly. "You look good, Celery Ellery."

"You too, Fordham the University. Where is everyone?"

He chuckles, looking down at the floor and then back to me. "They'll

319

be here in thirty minutes. I may have changed the time on your invitation so I could see you first. You know, I'm selfish like that."

"Ford—"

"It was a joke, Elle. Aren't we past that yet?"

"Yes." *Please still love me. Please tell me it's not too late.* "So you've seen me first, now what?"

"Several things."

"As in?"

He motions to the bar top, to where papers are laid out to the far right. I'm not sure if I'm happy that he's being all business—buying me more time—or upset. What did I expect after I hurt him? For him to pull me into his arms and tell me he loves me after I rebuffed him once already?

I take a fortifying breath as doubt starts to creep in. Did I wait too long? Has he moved on? Am I too late?

But when he turns and looks at me, that smile warming up his face as he motions for me to move to where he is, I know it's going to be okay.

He has a way of doing that to me. Soothing away the panic.

Curious, I move toward the papers, graphics really, and then gasp when I see the entirety of the renderings. On the bar are about ten different mock-ups of possible logos and signage for the inn.

But it's not the masterful designs that bring tears to my eyes. It's the name of the inn itself that Ford has selected.

Azure. A Sharpe Signature Collection.

I try to blink tears away but fail as I stare at a name that means so very much to me. "Ford? Do you know—"

"I do," he murmurs as he moves beside me. "Delia Azure Sinclair-Haywood. Mother of one Ellery Jean Sinclair. I thought it only fitting that since I have a way of honoring my father with the inn's name, that you should have the same opportunity."

"So you named it after my mother?" I ask.

"I did, yes. I hope you don't mind."

I asked you for a sign, Mom, and this was a huge, flashing one that I couldn't miss. Literally and figuratively. Thank you.

"Fordham . . ." I whisper as I reach out and run my fingers over the designs as if I can feel them before turning to look at him. "Thank you. It's perfect."

"Don't thank me. This is half yours too. Remember—"

"Fifty-fifty," I say.

"Fifty-fifty. And I figure the next one can be a nod to my mom somehow. Then the one after, a nod to your dad . . . and so on. I want to find a way to honor those we've loved and lost, not just exist with the loss."

"You're serious?"

"I am."

"But why . . . I mean . . ."

"You asked for space. I gave you space. But rest assured, I wasn't letting you go. Not on your life." He purses his lips and plays with the corners of one of the renderings as words unspoken drift between us. "I even went so far as to call Garland and speak about a new partnership with Haywood, but apparently someone beat me to it."

He looks at me now, a ghost of a smile on his lips and hope flooding his eyes.

"I did. You see, you're not the only one who was afraid of letting go."

He nods, almost as if he wants to say something, but refrains as if he's afraid to ruin the moment.

It's my turn to talk. It's my turn to lay it out there for him.

I have speeches prepared. Explanations and excuses and everything but a Venn diagram basically.

But when I go to speak, only one thing comes out.

And it's the one thing that matters.

"I love you, Fordham Sharpe." His breath hitches, and I hold my hands up to let me get through what I need to say. He nods. "I love you, and it terrifies me to death that by me loving you, I've put Fate's target on you. I love you, and it scares me because I've never known this kind of love before, and I'm not sure what to do with it. Do I offer it to you after I've pushed you away and hope that you accept it? Do I tell you 'here it is' and then say you don't have any choice because I'm never letting you let me walk away? What do I do, Ford, because I'm lost, and I'm terrified that it's too late and—"

He steps up and presses his lips to mine.

"Ford. I want the epilogue now. To read it. To love it. To live it out."

"You sure?"

With my teeth sunk into my bottom lip, I nod. "I'm sure."

His smile lights up his face. "What changed?"

Fair question. One I've thought about a lot.

"You. You're what changed me. Your unwavering belief in me. Your relentless love for me. Your patience. Your friendship. Just you, Ford. You're what has changed me."

"I'm going to kiss you now."

"Why are you telling me that?" I laugh.

"Because it's going to be romance-novel worthy. The kind you write one hell of an epilogue after," he murmurs against my lips.

"Bring it on."

Two weeks is a long time to go without his taste. Without his touch. Without his love.

How did I think I could walk away? That my fear of loss was greater than the strength of this love?

Because fear does that.

And somehow, Ford has taught me that love counters that risk.

When the kiss is over, when I'm thoroughly reminded of the havoc the man can wreak on my system, and how very much I missed him, he pulls back and frames my cheeks with his hands.

"Let's get one thing straight. You, Ellery Sinclair, have not put a target on me. You have not cursed me or hexed me or whatever you think you have. You have completed me and done it in ways I never expected. With your love for germ mix and your penchant for ice cream bars. With your thirst for knowledge and your love of romance novels. From wanting to read my father's book to better understand me. With the way you look at me from across the room and make me feel like I'm the only one in it. And with the way you're not afraid to dish out tough love—even if it's to simply protect you from getting too close while sending me to a tragic death in the Hudson."

"Hey—"

"Just kidding." He laughs and holds his hands up in surrender before cupping the sides of my face again. "You . . . you are the biggest pain in my ass and the greatest love of my life." He presses a kiss to my lips. "My father once told me that I'd know *the one* when I'd be willing to walk through fire to get to her. These past two weeks feel like all I've been doing is walking through fire while I waited for you. And you know what? I'd gladly do it all over again times a thousand just to hear you say those words to me again."

"What words are those?" I tease, earning me a swat on the butt and another soul-searing kiss. "I love you, Fordham Sharpe. Now. Always. Even when I'm scared. Even when I fear them. Even when I feel like I won't be able to love anymore, I love you."

"What? Just like that? There's no negotiating?" He chuckles as he tucks a strand of hair behind my ear. "You're getting soft on me, Celery Ellery."

"What is it you want to negotiate?" I narrow my eyes as if I'm serious.

"Things. So many things." He presses another tender kiss to my lips. "Things like when we get back to the city, how you should move in with me."

I should say that I'm shocked, that my natural response would be to say no, but aren't we already living together here?

"Live with you?" I ask. "Only if we can get a dog."

"A dog?" he laughs out.

"Yep. A dog. That's a requirement."

"Okay." He nods. "What else?"

My mind is buzzing a million miles a minute. How hard it was to accept this love and now that I have, how damn easy it is to fall headfirst into it.

"I'm not sure yet, but I reserve at least three more things that I can throw in there once I can think properly."

He draws a finger down my back, lifting the hem of my shirt so it can skim across my skin. "Why can't you think properly? Is something distracting you?"

I laugh. It feels so good to. "Maybe. I might need some more distracting." I lift on my tiptoes and kiss him.

"Distraction commencing." His groan is all I need to know his body is as wired as mine is right now. Is as needy and wanting. "Now I'm wishing I'd have scheduled everyone else to come an hour later instead of thirty minutes."

"Why's that?"

"Because I want to make love to you for the first time, Ellery." He grins. "That's such a cheesy thing for a guy to say, but to hell with it. I'm using the word *love* every chance I get so you get used to it. So you are no longer scared by it."

"Move in with you. Get a dog. *And* immediate lovemaking. *Wow, Sharpe*. I don't know," I tease, my smile turning up against his lips. "Is that your final proposal?"

"Baby, I'm just getting started." He chuckles as he leans back to look at me, the grin he flashes making my knees turn to jelly. His words even more so. "No. You'll know when I propose." A chaste kiss. "And there will be no negotiating the answer on that one."

CHAPTER FIFTY-TWO

Ford

Three Months later

"YOU REALLY THINK THAT'S THE BEST OPTION?" ELLERY LOOKS over to me. She's propped up against the headboard of the bed, in my—er, *our*—penthouse. Her laptop is on her thighs, her hair's piled on top of her head, and her face free of makeup.

Jesus.

Sometimes the sight of her staggers me. How did I get this lucky? How did I get her to choose me?

"Why are you looking at me like that?" she asks, eyebrows narrowed and lips pursed.

"No reason." I grin. "Sometimes it just hits me. This. You. Us." I shrug.

"Fordham Sharpe, are you getting all soft on me?" she teases.

"Not where it counts." I wink and she laughs before I motion to the laptop. "Yes to your question. Park City is the winter playground for the wealthy. It's a great place for the next Signature Sharpe. Expensive. Exclusive. And if the success of Azure is any indication, people like to flaunt their 'unique' experience."

And boy, have they.

Azure is booked through the next eighteen months, and we've only been open for two. Word spread fast among the elite and celebrity circles. And thank fuck for that.

Of course, there have been a few snafus, as happens with anything that is new, but we've managed to mitigate those and correct on the fly.

And I won't lie, I just might throw its success in my brothers' faces every chance I get. Just as they would in mine.

"Okay." She nods as she bites the tip of a pen. "Park City it is."

"I knew you'd—" The doorbell rings and our rescue mutt, Chex, lifts her head as if she's figuring out if she gives a fuck before deciding she doesn't and lays it back down.

The only people who come up without the doorman announcing them are my brothers. "What the hell are they doing here?"

"I don't know," she says as she pushes the laptop aside and rises from the bed.

Within seconds, I have the door open and am staring suspiciously at both Ledger and Callahan standing in my entry. "You're tag-teaming again. What should I be worried about this time?"

Here we go again.

"We have something for you," Ledger says, moving past me toward the family room as if he owns the place.

"Hello. How are you today, Ford? Are we interrupting anything? Can we come in?" I tease as I follow them. Ellery's laugh sounds off behind me.

"Trust us," Callahan murmurs, and fuck if that doesn't make me worry.

I glance over to Ellery, and she shrugs.

"Can you use AirPlay from my laptop to the TV?" Ledger asks, knowing I damn well can.

"Sure, but . . . do you mind telling me what the hell is going on?"

Callahan's grin concerns me. The last time he grinned like that was when they showed me CCTV footage of me in an elevator with a woman I was dating. They thought it would be hilarious to critique my technique.

Fucking assholes.

"It's not that," Ledger says and laughs.

"It's not what?" Ellery asks.

"You're better off not knowing," I say and press a kiss to her cheek that definitely makes her want to know more.

"Take a seat," Callahan says, but when I don't, he guides me and pushes me to sit on the couch.

"What in the hell . . ." But my words stop the minute I hear our dad's laugh fill the room and see him on the screen. He's seated in a chair, one ankle set on the other knee. He's leaned back, his arms on each side, his lips pursed.

My heart leaps into my throat. To hear that sound, to see him . . . I look at Ledger and Callahan, and they just motion for me to look at the screen.

"Tell me about Fordham," a person off camera asks, and I know exactly what this is.

The interview tapes for the biography.

My father's smile is wistful, adoring, and tears spring to my eyes simply because of his response when he's asked about me.

"Fordham is . . . he's an incredible kid. Hard-working. Dedicated. The hugest fucking heart. If you're looking for juicy stories on him, there are none. He kept his nose clean except for when he was trying to take the fall for something Callahan had done." He chuckles and runs a hand over his face much like I'm doing right now.

It makes me smile.

"Thanks for that, man," Callahan says with a pat on my shoulder. "I still owe you for those." I was so enthralled with my dad on the screen that I didn't notice both Ledger and Callahan were sitting on either side of me.

"Carly and I used to joke that Ford was the rock of our family. If you needed help, he was there. If you needed to talk to someone, he was there. If we needed someone to mediate between Callahan and Ledger, he was there. Fordham cracked the best jokes at the times we needed them most. He can read a room better than anyone I've ever met and would know what comment to make to either diffuse a situation or put someone more at ease. He worried about everyone because he wanted everything to be okay at all times. He wasn't bothered by taking a back seat to his brothers because his own light shone through regardless."

"He sounds like a great guy."

"The absolute best." My dad looks at the interviewer and smiles in a way that seems like he's looking right at me. "Carly and I used to joke that he was the kid who knew what to do in every situation. He was *Just Ford*. Humph." Another smile as a memory clearly flashes through my dad's mind by the far-off look in his eyes and the softening smile.

"What does that mean?"

"That was how Carly and I used to refer to him. *Just Ford*. I forgot about that. When we would lie in bed at night and go over our days . . . whenever one of the other boys would act out or get in trouble, she used to say, *why can't they be more like or just like Ford?* We laughed and said that wasn't fair to the others . . . but it stuck between the two of us, and eventually was shortened to *Just Ford*." He chuckles. "God, that feels like forever ago."

"Just Ford," the interviewer says.

"Yep. Ford is . . . the peacekeeper of our family. The even keel in our sometimes-stormy life. He's . . . *just Ford*."

The recording cuts off, but I keep staring at the black screen, hearing his words and seeing his smile.

Just Ford.

It meant so much more to him than the indifference I first read it as.

Tears are on my cheeks. I don't even know when they fell, and I don't fucking care. It's just my brothers and Ellery here. The three people in my life who matter the most.

Ledger squeezes the back of my neck and shakes me back and forth as Callahan pats my back with his palm.

I look up to find Ellery across the room. Her cheeks are stained with silent tears, but the smile she grants me is everything.

She knew all along there was more to the story.

Just as my brothers did. Just as they set out to prove to me.

The three people in the world who matter the most to me know the truth. Know the meaning behind *Just Ford*. My mom was right. Those are the only people whose opinions about me matter.

Just Ford.

It has a nice ring to it and one I'll gladly take.

EPILOGUE

Ellery

"YOU KNOW YOU COULD HAVE PICKED ANYWHERE IN THE world to do this."

"I know," I murmur against his lips. He pulls me into him and just holds on to me in the one place I've never felt safer. "But this is where I wanted to be. The place that started it all for us."

The late-afternoon sun makes the sand look whiter and the color of the flowers more vibrant. The beach beyond the Azure has been transformed into a paradise that even I couldn't believe when I saw it earlier today.

Fairy lights strewn about. In the trees. On the tables. A dance floor in the sand. A small gathering of those who we love the most . . . and my brothers. We're still a work in progress, but at least the word *progress* is in there. At least there's that.

"I couldn't agree more." Ford looks at me, love reflecting in every facet of his expression. "I still can't believe it." He brushes his lips against mine.

"Me either."

"You ready, Mrs. Sharpe?"

That name.

It's mine now.

Or rather, it's been mine now for a total of four hours and three minutes, and if it feels this good already, I can't wait to see what a lifetime of being Mrs. Sharpe feels like.

I'm married.

Married to Fordham Sharpe no less.

The woman who feared love, who pushed it away, can't imagine not having this love for this man.

And now he's my forever, and we're about to start our journey together.

I peek out the curtains to take in our guests lining each side of the walkway that leads to our awaiting limousine. Fordham takes my hand and smiles as he opens the door.

The rush of noise hits us. Laughter and cheers and whoops as we step outside.

How did we get here?

"Let's do this," Ford says with a squeeze of my hand, and we take the first steps toward our forever.

The rain and wind virtually knock me off my feet as I push into the inn. Chandler rambles in my ear about a project he's working on as if I'm not braving a tropical storm and trying to avoid being a lightning rod.

"Hello? Did you hear me?" I repeat for what feels like the tenth time. He's not listening to me, so wrapped up in his own self. "Closed. We're stuck."

"Brilliant observation. There's a reason we're all sitting in here, and it's not because of the ambiance," the man mutters to the left of me, as I drop my bag into a heap on the floor beside the only open barstool in this godforsaken place.

"I don't believe I was speaking to you," I snap. Mind your own business, buddy.

"Good. Great. Wait. They closed the roads?"

It's then that I look over and meet the eyes of the moody asshole giving me his two cents when I didn't ask for it. Chandler blathers on in my ear, but I don't hear a word he says because I'm too busy being knocked on my ass by the pair of stunning amber eyes.

By the man sitting before me who makes my pulse jump.

We pass Callahan and Sutton. Their two girls, Maxine and Carly, are dressed in frilly white dresses with flower crowns in their curly hair. Sutton reaches out and squeezes my hand, her smile reassuring and welcoming, while Callahan high-fives his brother and says something that makes them both laugh.

"C'mon, Celery Ellery. Take a chance on me. Take a chance with me." He holds his hand out—the hand he withheld from my brother's handshake. "Deal, partner?"

"I can't believe I'm agreeing to this," I groan as a thrill of excitement shoots through me.

"Is that a yes?"

I meet his eyes, take in his smile, and reach out to shake his hand. What the hell am I doing? "Yes."

Ledger and Asher are next. They're standing with grins on their faces. Asher is holding their two-month-old son, Oliver, in her arms. He's sound asleep as Ledger wraps his arm around her and pulls her into him.

"Have fun!" Asher whisper-shouts as she throws a handful of something in the air that falls all around us.

"Celery Ellery."

"Fordham the University," I say back to him with a straight face—since he seems so damn serious—before I start laughing.

He jumps onto the bed and tackle-hugs me, tickling me until I'm breathless and pushing him off me.

His lips meet mine in the tenderest of kisses. "I had all kinds of plans for this. Elaborate ones. They were put in motion and have been on standby for weeks. For the right time. But . . . it's burning a hole in my pocket, and I don't want to wait anymore."

"Ford." His name is a warning and a plea of hope.

He scrambles up and straddles me, his shy smile owning my heart. "I can give you the world in any capacity you wish. I could buy you anything you want, whisk you away to some far-off destination, or have fireworks write it in the sky. I could take out an ad in Times Square or devise some elaborate scavenger hunt for you . . . but I don't think any of that would matter to you. Pomp and circumstance aren't your thing . . . because from day one for you, it's always been about us. You see the real me. You saw it and still let me in. Marry me, Ellery. Marry me, and let's write that epilogue together and then live it out."

I smile through the tears. I knew this was coming at some point. We've talked about it and joked about it, and I knew it was inevitable. But even knowing about it didn't prepare me for the rush of emotion hearing his words and looking into his eyes is causing.

He reaches over and slides a ring box out from under his pillow. When he opens it up, a gorgeous oval-shaped solitaire sits nestled in the blue velvet case.

But he's right. I don't care about the pomp and circumstance or the spar-kle before me. All I see is him. All I want is him.

"Your silence is killing me here, Ellery."

"I think I had an answer that first night we met. It might have taken me a while to acknowledge it, but—"

"But thank fuck you did. So?"

"Yes. Of course, it's yes. How could it be anything different?"

Garland gives me the slightest of nods as I pass, and I reach out to squeeze his hand. My mom's sapphire ring that he had held on to and gave to me as my something blue reflects in the soft light.

We high-five a few other friends, past the cardboard cutout of a life-size Chris Hemsworth that Ford thought was an important throwback to the first night we met, before stopping at the end of the walkway.

Funny how you can meet someone in the oddest of times to find out they give you the advice, the hope, and the will to change something that you haven't had the strength to change before.

It's then and only then that I realize what's being thrown at us. It's not the traditional rice, it's Chex Mix *sans pretzels.*

I pluck one off Ford's lapel and throw my head back and laugh. He picks me up and spins me around. "Only the best for you, Celery Ellery."

When we stop, I slide down his front as he lowers me to the ground, our lips meeting again.

"You once told me to show you a man who knows love and romance isn't always about grand gestures and you'd marry him." He pops a piece of Chex Mix between my lips and then motions to everyone here to cele-brate us. "Lucky for me, you're a woman of your word."

"Always. Forever. Only you, Ford. Only us."

He meets my eyes. Tears glisten in them as our driver pulls open the car door. Ford motions to the open door. "Our epilogue begins right now."

Did you enjoy Ellery and Fordham's romance and happily ever after? Are you intrigued by both Callahan and Ledger and want to find out more about them? There are two other books in the **S.I.N. series.** (The books can be read in any order). You can find them here:

Last Resort
On One Condition

Were you intrigued about the sex scenes and the books that Ford reads to Ellery in **Chapter 40?** _Those are all scenes from other K. Bromberg books. You can read about those characters here:_

-The scene with Lilly is from my darker novella, **UnRaveled**

-The scene with Lennox is from my enemies to lovers, sports romance, **_Hard to Hold_**

-The scene with Sidney is from my single dad, first responder, small town romance, **Cockpit**

ABOUT THE AUTHOR

New York Times Bestselling author K. Bromberg writes contemporary romance novels that contain a mixture of sweet, emotional, a whole lot of sexy, and a little bit of real. She likes to write strong heroines and damaged heroes, who we love to hate but can't help to love.

A mom of three, she plots her novels in between school runs, sports practices, and figuring out how to navigate parenting teenagers (*send more wine!*). More often than not, she does all of this with her laptop in tow, and her mind daydreaming of the current hero she is writing.

Since publishing her first book on a whim in 2013, Kristy has sold over two million copies of her books across twenty different countries and has landed on the *New York Times, USA Today*, and *Wall Street Journal* Bestsellers lists over thirty times. Her Driven trilogy (Driven, Fueled, and Crashed) has been adapted for film and is available on the streaming platform Passionflix, Amazon, and other streaming platforms.

You can find out more about Kristy, her books, or just chat with her on any of her social media accounts. The easiest way to stay up to date on new releases and upcoming novels is to sign up for her newsletter or follow her on Bookbub.

Made in United States
Orlando, FL
31 October 2022

24086551R00193